RECLAIMED

BY

DIANE ALBERTS

&

Decadent Publishing Company
www.decadentpublishing.com

Reclaimed
Copyright 2012 by Diane Alberts
ISBN: 978-1-61333-234-4
Cover design by LFD and Cribley Designs

Published by Decadent Publishing Company
www.decadentpublishing.com

Printed in the United States of America

~DEDICATION~

To Greg, for believing in me. To my family, for supporting me.
To my publisher, for taking a chance on me.
And to Rie and Meredith, for making my baby shine and helping me
become a better writer. I love you both!

Chapter One

Sabrina Hodges never backed down from a challenge, no matter how daunting the task. When a bully named Mandy Warbuck grabbed her pigtails and demanded her lunch money in the cafeteria, she let loose a well-aimed kick. Sandy steered clear of her for the rest of their childhood years. In high school, the same type of kick, though admittedly in a different target area, saved her from a prom date who couldn't understand the meaning of *no*. Even so, the choice to move to a foreign country hours away from all her family and friends surprised her as much as them. Her late grandparents were British, but she was all-American.

Well, she had been.

She pulled her shiny red Smart Car up to the top of her newly acquired driveway, and shut off the engine. She exited the car and followed the flower-lined gray stone walkway. The flowers, which looked like carnations, were pleasing shades of pink and white. The spring-like colors seemed to make the crisp autumn air feel warmer. The beautiful blooms lined both sides of the walkway to the front door, and Sabrina's heartbeat accelerated in excitement as she followed their path in a trance-like state.

She studied the gray and white stones that made up the front of the house, which showed signs of a fresh washing beneath the vines that climbed past the doors and windows to hang tenaciously from the roof.

A twig snapped in the murky forest behind her, and she jumped. She rubbed the goose bumps rising over her arms and glanced into the forest. Did a shadow just move behind the tree across the driveway?

Or are you just afraid of the shadows?

She thought of the next afternoon, when the security company would arrive to install an electronic system and new locks on all the doors. Though she loved her new place, her mama hadn't raised an idiot. She had no desire for any late-night visitors. Well, not *uninvited* late-night visitors, she snickered.

Wandering around to the back, she admired the immaculate landscaped backyard with its vivid green grass and vibrant red, pink, and purple mums arranged in mulched flowerbeds. Roses, tulips, and pansies surrounded her, and she smiled and constrained a squeal of delight. She swore she heard the waves crashing against the cliffs.

Well, are you going to go inside, or stay outside all day, Sabrina?

Heading to the front, she unlocked the brick-red door—no, *her* front door—just as her phone rang. She placed her fatty, greasy, one-whole-day's-worth-of-calories cheeseburger and fries from the local fast food joint on the floor, threw her keys on the stairs, and scrambled through her purse to look for her Blackberry.

Lipstick, wallet, passport, mirror...phone.

Ignoring the endless pocket of junk inside her purse, she glanced at the caller ID.

"Hello, Marie." She clumsily shrugged her coat off while she walked further into the house. Since she hadn't bought a coat rack yet, she dropped it in a careless heap on the gleaming hardwood floor behind her.

"Did everything go okay?"

"Yup, I just walked into my new home," she replied.

"Woohoo. I must admit I'm confused why you'd prefer to be alone in a drafty old house in a country that never sees the sun. I would *think* you'd rather be in sunny California with me."

Sabrina rolled her eyes at the statement. She'd heard it at least a million times by now. She couldn't blame Marie's confusion, though, since she didn't understand her sudden obsession, either.

Sabrina didn't exactly enjoy being left to her own company, to say the least. Sometimes—okay, a *lot* of times—she'd get so lonely she'd leave her apartment to walk around Target to listen to snippets of hushed conversations as people passed her by. An argument between an old married couple about who should take out the trash, the excited murmurs of newlyweds planning the arrival of their first baby…she needed to hear life. To have company. Yet here she stood, in a new country with no friends and no family in a deserted, drafty, house—and perfectly, peculiarly content.

"I already told you, it's for me. It's mine." In the background she heard Samantha, Marie's two-year-old daughter, giggling.

Samantha won't even remember me as she grows up. What have I done?

"Well, congrats again. I have to get Samantha ready for a bath. Just wanted to make sure you got everything worked out. Love ya!"

"Love you, too." Sabrina sighed and pressed the end button. Loneliness crept over her for a brief moment, before she stomped it down in irritation. Time to stop reminiscing about her family thousands of miles away. Peeking into the kitchen, she got wooed once again, impressed at the way the modern conveniences mixed with the old-fashioned architecture surrounding her. It was next to impossible to tell that the house had once been a barn.

She inhaled the scent of the freshly stained mahogany wood cabinets topped with gleaming amber granite. She skimmed her fingertips over the cool stainless steel appliances, and caressed the double stove she had chosen. Images of cooking filet mignon and steaming mashed potatoes for her and her faceless husband, while the pitter-patter of little feet running through the house flashed in her mind. They—a boy and a girl—maybe twins; would race around the island in the kitchen and into the formal dining room, their giggles filling the silence that currently resided within. She had always wanted a pair; why go through labor *twice?*

She sighed and went into the foyer to retrieve her dinner and hunched over that same kitchen island for an early meal of greasy take-out dinner. She scrunched her nose in disgust at the bland taste of the hamburger and stalked across the kitchen to throw away the remains. First thing in the morning, she needed to go shopping for cooking items—and food. A yawn forced her to claim defeat from jet lag, not to mention her move from America to England, and she climbed the stairs to her makeshift bed in her empty room.

℠

Sabrina stood in the woods, staring up at the moon that cast an eerie purple hue through the leaves overhead. Goose bumps rose on her skin, and her heart quickened as a lone wolf howled in the distance. A twig snapped behind her, and she spun on her left heel. Expecting to see the wolf she had just heard, she found herself taken aback at what met her eyes instead. A man stared at her in silence. Never before had she seen a man like him—he was simply unbelievable. At about six and a half feet tall, he easily towered over her, and his body screamed of pure muscular power.

The exquisite perfection of his face looked like it belonged on an ancient Greek god's statue. Even more so in the purple moonlight. His thick, black hair curled around his head in flawless order—as if it would not dare to disobey his command. Even his casual gray T-shirt clung to his body, seeming to fear invoking the retribution of its owner. She read about men who looked like him before—she had even written about them in her novels, but never believed they were in existence. His bright blue gaze locked upon her in intense scrutiny. His stare hypnotized her—at once startling and somehow familiar.

He rushed toward her, and she flinched when he pulled her into his embrace. She battled the urge to break free of his hold and fought to get a breath of air. His grip was so snug that she suspected that she fought against iron chains instead of arms. His grip on her loosened a bit, and she wondered if he had realized how tight he held her.

"God, how I've missed you. I've hoped you'd return to me. Yet even so, I didn't believe it could happen. But you're here, in my arms, once more." He shook his head, and his eyes seemed to devour every detail of her face.

Did she know him? She didn't think so. Come on, if she was going to remember anyone, it would be this exquisite man.

His arms tightened around her once more, and an overwhelming

8

desperation to be away from him came over her. Her lungs burned for air, and she struggled to get out of his hold. She sensed freedom lurking in her mind; she just needed to fight a little bit harder.

"Let go of me!" She kicked his shin, and he didn't even so much as flinch.

"I love you, Amelia," he whispered in her ear.

His breath caused her to shiver. She continued to struggle in his arms, but he smiled seductively down at her, seeming not to notice she didn't clutch his neck but instead fought him. "Please, don't leave me. You don't really want to, do you?"

Confusion rolled over her even as she fought to free herself. Why would he call her Amelia? Jeez, even in her dreams men were jerks who called her by the wrong name.

ॐ

When Sabrina awoke the next morning, the dream remained fresh in her head. She almost sensed his presence next to her as she moved listlessly throughout the day. She couldn't seem to shove him out of her mind. Those eyes, that body….

She accidentally rammed her foot against the island, and pain shot up her foot at the collision. She hopped on one foot and squeezed the offending toe as she glared at the cabinet.

Stop mooning over some dream man. He doesn't exist, and never will. You're more likely to see a freaking vampire or werewolf, for God's sakes.

After a hurried breakfast, she drove into town to shop for furniture. She exited the car and stretched her sore muscles with a grimace. Last night had done nothing for her posture, to say the least. She longed for a hot shower—or better yet, a long soak in the huge tub that she now owned—and soft Egyptian cotton sheets and feather pillows. She stalked into the furniture store determined to take care of the latter.

Hours later, she emerged from the same doors with a sense of accomplishment. Tomorrow, she'd be sleeping in luxury and comfort—something she'd taken for granted until last night. Her stomach growled, and a glance at her watch revealed it was already one forty-five in the afternoon. The tea and croissant she'd indulged in that morning no longer held the gnawing hunger at bay. She stood in indecision as she debated whether or not she had enough time to grab a bite to eat before the security company arrived.

A tavern stood just up the road, and she approached it cautiously, given its ramshackle appearance. The exterior boasted of red brick, and the sign that hung over the door appeared to be hand-painted, lending it a quaint touch that lured Sabrina to give the place a try. Outside the faded green door, where paint peeled off in more places than it remained, a homeless man had an empty jar in front of him as he dozed in the mid-afternoon sun.

Deciding to take a chance, she withdrew a few Euros, dropped it in the man's jar—got rewarded with a snore as he jerked awake—and entered. Seated immediately in a dark wood booth topped by a mustard-yellow tabletop, she surveyed her surroundings. The single light hanging from the ceiling flickered in the middle of the small room, casting a gloomy tone upon the whole interior.

"Hello, ma'am. Welcome to McGuiness. May I take your order?" asked the waitress.

Her faded nametag had Patti imprinted on it...though the P had long ago been rubbed away to look like an F. She laughed inwardly at the image. *Fatti*...uh...Patti glanced up from her pad and her jaw dropped.

Sabrina studied her menu, uncomfortable under the weight of the waitress's stare. She'd been told she was gorgeous often enough, but the scrutiny always made her uneasy. Petite, she stood at only five-foot-two, but voluptuous curves graced her in her hips and bust, leaving her resembling anything but a waif-like model. She also knew her green eyes were a unique moss color that sparkled, but in her opinion her hair ruined all of these attributes. Though it was a beautiful shade of brown with red highlights streaked throughout the curls, it tended to be a frizzy mess most of the time. Less Shakira, and more Chia Pet, to be precise.

"I'll have the chicken cordon bleu and a baked potato and corn, please. Oh, and could I also have a cup of tea, no cream or sugar?" She lifted her gaze from the menu, pleased to see Patti had regained her composure.

"Sure, doll. Are you visiting the area? I noticed your accent. American?"

"Yes, American. But no, I'm not visiting. I moved here. Just yesterday."

"Oh. Well, welcome. You live in town?"

"No, on Wear Bay Road by the cliffs." She smiled politely.

"Oh, how nice. Well, I'll go get your tea and bring your salad. House dressing?"

"Sure."

Patti scurried away to the kitchen, and Sabrina shifted in her seat. Silence surrounded her, no one else in sight. Only the sound of clanging of pots and the low laughter escaping the kitchen as the door swung on its hinge met her ears. She tapped her fingers on the table, and her foot moved in perfect harmony. The sound of bells ringing disrupted her one-woman band, and she glanced in relief at the door.

Who would it be? An old man? A honeymooning couple? Instead of smiling as she had intended to do, her mouth dropped open, and she forgot to breathe.

The man of her dreams had just entered the same room as her.

Literally—the man from her dreams last night was *here*.

He strode into the room confidently before coming to an abrupt halt. His gaze focused on her as his eyes widened and he paled. She knew with certainty her face mirrored his stunned expression.

She took a gulping breath, and the air burned her aching lungs. In her shock, she'd forgotten the small necessity of breathing. Confusion came over her as the blood returned to her brain. Wait, why did *he* stare at *her* like he'd just seen a ghost?

Sabrina bit her lip as he lifted his foot to take a step toward her, but he froze. His brow furrowed, and his eyes remained locked on her face. Patti breezed by him, delivering the promised tea and salad before turning to greet the man. Sabrina watched as he tore his gaze from hers to converse with Patti. She strained to catch the muted undertones of their conversation—and failed. The man looked once more toward Sabrina before exiting.

She fought down her irritation at the nameless man, angry he'd stopped himself from approaching her side earlier. And even more so that he had left without coming to speak to her.

He obviously wanted to, so what made him stop?

When Patti returned, Sabrina warred with herself over whether to question the waitress about him. In the end, her curiosity won out over the years of etiquette drilled into her by her parents and teachers.

"So, dear, how is your tea?" Patti asked.

"Excellent, thanks." She cocked her head to the side and studied Patti. "Is the man who came in here earlier your friend? He looked kinda familiar to me."

"He's a regular customer, a local bloke. He wanted to talk to his friend who works here." She gave a sharp nod of her head. "I told him Connor had off today, but he'd be in tomorrow afternoon. So he'll probably come back."

"I see," she murmured. Patti bustled into the kitchen and returned a few minutes later carrying Sabrina's meal. For once, Sabrina hadn't noticed how alone she had been, or become antsy. She was too lost in thoughts of her dream man. She finished her meal, paid, and left a generous tip. Upon exiting, she spotted a liquor store nearby and darted in for Chablis. After the interesting turn of events—events that made her wonder if she were going insane—Sabrina needed a drink.

Or five.

Halfway back to her car, the hair rose on the back of her neck. She halted mid-step. Somebody watched her. She spun on a heel and gasped when she saw the man from her dreams in the alleyway a few feet behind her. He stood cloaked in shadow, but his face couldn't be mistaken for anyone else's. His image had been haunting her relentlessly all day.

She took a step toward him, but no sooner had she taken a step toward him, he disappeared. Where the hell could he have gone?

She took off at a run, needing to see if she could follow him. Men didn't just walk out of your dreams every day, did they?

No, they don't, you idiot. And now you are running into an alleyway looking for a man who, by all logic and reason, shouldn't exist.

She skidded to a halt in the entrance to the alleyway, one hand on her keychain…which no longer had any mace.

Crap.

She'd had to turn it in when she'd moved to England, and had yet to find a suitable replacement. No matter, for he wasn't there—nothing but trash and the overwhelming stench of urine awaited her. She cursed and kicked a crate that rested in disarray against the wall. Something dark and ugly scurried out of it at the resounding noise she'd made. She glowered after it, and cynically shook her head.

How could she think that a man could haunt her dreams and come to her in the light of day? Not possible. She couldn't have predicted this man would enter her life. No way for her to have known him when he walked into the room.

And yet he *had*. And she did.

There just had to be a logical explanation behind this. Maybe she had seen him somewhere yesterday, but not *noticed* him, and he'd appeared in her dream.

Not *noticed* him?

Yeah, right. And maybe the homeless guy a few feet away was really Prince William, too.

Maybe, just maybe, she should have stayed in California.

Chapter Two

She glanced behind her and forced her protesting legs to move faster. His footsteps grew closer each passing second. Hair whipped her in the eyes, forcing them to water in protest, which made it even harder to see where she ran in the purple moonlight, but she pressed herself to speed up even more. He'd gotten even closer. His steady breathing sounded in her ears above her own desperate gulps of air, somehow mocking her for her weakness, her vulnerability.

Her aching chest and weak legs forced her to stumble to the ground at a stream, bringing her frenzied flight to a halt. Her eyes focused on a blur of motion as a shape leapt overhead and easily landed on the other side of the wide stream rushing over the rocks. He emerged from the concealing shadows of the trees, and the moonlight illuminated the perfection of his face.

She wasn't shocked to see him. She'd known all along what, or who, she ran from. The hard glint of a predator in his eyes, however, did freak her out. He was clearly the hunter...and she the prey. And as quickly as he had leapt across the stream, his eyes softened, smoothing the harsh lines of the huntsman into that of a different chase—a seducer.

She couldn't shake the feeling that though he no longer chased her, she remained the prey. A shiver ran up her spine at the thought, and she watched him warily as her heart raced.

He flashed a grin at her, and she groaned as dimples appeared on both cheeks. As if the man were not hot enough, God had given him dimples.

Come on, man.

"Hello, Amelia," he murmured. The name rolled off his tongue like silk. "I've been waiting here for you to return."

"My name isn't Amelia." The hairs on the back of her neck rose, and she shuddered. "It's Sabrina."

"Sabrina? That's a pretty name, too. It suits you." He stalked toward her, and she shot to her feet and retreated. "But to me, you will always be my Amelia. Don't run," he said soothingly, his arm held out, palm up, to her. "Don't be afraid. I've been waiting for you a long time. I'll not hurt you. I promise to keep you safe."

Though her every instinct shouted at her to run screaming through the forest, she stood rooted to the ground watching him as he nimbly jumped over the water and landed in front of her. She watched his eyes move as he studied her face before enfolding her in his arms tenderly. For a brief moment she felt...cherished.

Until he threaded his hands through her hair and crushed her lips beneath his. Breathing quickly became forgotten as his lips plundered hers, and she clutched his shoulders, desperate to hold onto reality. Her ability to think fled, as all her senses and thoughts were consumed by the man holding her.

But was he a man?

Men didn't come to you in dreams before you ever met them in real life.

The thought sobered her as being doused with a bucket of cold water would have, and she jerked away from his kiss. His hands tightened painfully in her hair, and she whimpered in protest.

"Who are you? What are you?"

His gaze hardened. The hunter look returned to his face, and a shiver crept over her spine. Her mind shrieked at her, warning her of danger.

"You are mine, remember it always," he whispered. He tore his gaze from hers and looked behind her head and cursed under his breath. He kissed her hard—rushed—and turned from her and ran.

Only the sound of her speeding heart and the eerie purple moon kept her company.

વ્ય

The next week was filled with writing her current romance novel and decorating, and she didn't leave her house. Until today, anyway. It was Friday, and she'd decided to take a trip into town for some shopping. Checking off the last item on her list, she groaned when her stomach growled. Time for a dinner break.

She, of course, knew where to go.

She parked in front of the tavern where she'd seen him in the flesh and hopped out of the car with bated breath. Would he be there? She absentmindedly threw a bill into the jar in front of the homeless man— sleeping, again—and entered the dimly lit room. She searched, but only the flickering light hanging over the middle of the room met her eyes. Disappointment crept over her even as she searched the room once more. As if he'd appear from behind the door and yell, "Boo!" To make it worse, no dreams had come all week, and she yearned to see him, to see if he actually existed. This was ridiculous in itself, because of course he didn't.

Duh.

When lingering over her dinner didn't make him magically appear, she left the tavern heavy-hearted. Each footstep she took seemed harder than the last. She paused and considered the alleyway he'd appeared in the other day.

Could he be in there?

"Looking for him, miss?"

She jumped at the gravelly voice behind her, whirling to see who spoke. It was the homeless man—aware for once. Awake, he positively terrified her. Intelligence swam in his eyes, and that was all she could make out of him. The rest of his face was buried under hair and dirt.

She hesitated. "I'm sorry? Looking for who?"

"The tall bloke who came here last time you were, miss."

"I thought you were sleeping." Nonchalantly, she rested her hand on the mace hanging off her keychain—and found it missing…again.

His eyes followed her small movement. "I just see things, I do. And I saw him leave, and he watched *you* leave."

"So he was there," she said. "I *thought* I saw him in the alley!"

"Yes, miss. But right as soon as he saw you, he scattered like the rats that live there—always trying to steal my food, they are." He shook his head and grumbled something too quietly for Sabrina to make out.

"Are you always here?" she asked.

"I live here, ma'am. Keep an eye on the place to make sure the wrong sort doesn't get in." His chest puffed out in pride. She refrained from pointing out most establishments deemed *him* the wrong sort. She knew he'd take offense at the remark and had no desire to hurt his feelings.

"Well, obviously you do an excellent job. Have you seen the man here again, recently?"

"Oh yes, he came here today. Looked real out-of-sorts, he did. Hiding in the shadows, searching for something. Methinks he seeks *you*." His tone of voice held a sly tone to it, as if he were in on a secret she wasn't.

She shivered and glanced toward the alley. "Is he here, now?" She searched the shadows, but sensed no movement.

"No, he left a few hours ago. You're safe with old Zeke here."

She fought down the apprehension creeping up her spine and smiled at Zeke. "Well, I'm going home. Keep an eye out for troublemakers, okay?"

"Yes, ma'am. That's my job. Thanks for the money." He tipped his battered hat at her. His hair stuck out in several threadbare spots where the fabric had worn away. "You are the perfect woman. Looks and a warm heart."

She blushed, embarrassed by the praise. "Don't mention it, Zeke." She waved and got into the car to drive home, feeling curiously empty despite the full meal she'd ingested. She'd obviously gone insane. Why did this man haunt her so? Sure, he was ungodly hot—but did he have to consume her both night and day? *Ugh, time for some good TV.*

An hour later, she sat absorbed in the gripping drama of a team of police searching for a killer before they lost one of their own. A thud outside her door caused her to lurch to her feet and gasp.

Holding a shaky hand to her pounding heart, she tiptoed toward the door, without consciously having made the decision to go there. She peered through the tiny peephole, and her breath caught in her throat when she saw a shadow in the trees. The shadow, eerily enough, seemed to *creep* toward her.

Anything that moved in the night like that couldn't be a good thing. It crept far too stealthy, as if it were used to hunting things in the dark night. She watched the threat as it snuck closer to her house, afraid to make as much as a breath of a sound.

The shadow flew through the air and out of sight. It travelled so fast she questioned the validity of it. Nothing, human *or* animal, could move so majestically.

Except...no, it couldn't be possible. In the dream the man might have done it, but in real life he was simply a man. He didn't leap over buildings in real life. Unless...she'd fallen asleep. She pinched her bicep as hard as she could and winced as pain shot up her arm.

Nope, definitely not a dream.

She rubbed her aching arm as a sound came from above her. Frozen in fear, she glanced at the ceiling. The shuffling noises pulled her from her panic, and she scrambled for the phone on the coffee table.

A soft, menacing chuckle met her ears, and the phone crashed to the floor loudly, followed by an unmistakable rolling sound. She dropped to her knees to search frantically for the missing batteries.

"Shit, shit, shit!" she exclaimed.

Oddly enough, the feeling of terror that had come upon Sabrina left. Somehow, she *knew* whoever, or *whatever*, had caused her fear had left. This made no sense at all.

But hell, what *had* made sense lately?

Nothing, absolutely nothing.

෨

Sabrina sat by the stream in the purple moonlight once again. It seemed like she'd been watching the water move over the rocks for hours before she sensed him behind her. He walked to her side and held out his hand. She took it and rose slowly to her feet. His cool palm caused her to tremble, partly because his hand felt so cold against hers, and partly because of the sensations that shot up her arm at his touch.

"Hello, Sabrina. Did you miss me?"

"Why am I even dreaming of you? This makes no sense. I only saw you once, and yet I can't get you out of my mind." She met his intense blue gaze. "This is crazy. I'm asking questions of a person in my dream. And to top it off, I'm now imagining things jumping on my roof while awake. I have gone insane," she muttered under her breath.

"Something came to your house?" he asked. His grip tightened on her arms, and his eyes flashed possessively. "What was it?"

"I have no idea! But it jumped on the roof. It reminded me of you, except for one minor detail: you're not real. You're a figment of my imagination."

"Don't doubt me, Sabrina. I'm real. I'm here. I'm always here for you." He captured her hand and kissed it. "Go to McGuiness's Tavern tomorrow morning. I'll be there. You'll see I'm real, and not some silly dream." He caressed her cheek, and she trembled.

"But who are you?" she whispered. She licked her dry lips and clutched her hands into fists. His gaze followed the movement of her tongue, and he grabbed her and lifted her so her feet dangled in the air. Despite the roughness of the movement, fear didn't consume her. Hunger for his kiss overwhelmed her—made her tremble in his arms.

Instead, he seized her hair and jerked her head backward. Her neck exposed, he lowered his head to the sensitive spot where neck and shoulder met. She heard him inhale deeply, and she shuddered in his arms. His breath felt cool on her skin, and she trembled in an odd mixture of fear and desire. When his lips met her skin, it seemed as though a bolt of lightning jolted through her body, making her jerk in his arms.

Instant lust.

"I'm yours, Sabrina. And you'll get your questions answered. All you need to know right now is you're mine. I'll see you tomorrow."

"No, wait. Tell me now," she demanded. But she spoke to air, for as quietly as he'd come, he had left. Once again, she stood alone in the dark night. She looked up at the moon and shivered.

"Son of a bitch," she mumbled. Only the silence of the forest *surrounding her answered.*

ଚ

Sabrina had lost it, simply lost it. They might as well slap on the straightjacket now and strap her to the bed.

Padded walls, here I come.

Things were getting out of her control. She obviously struggled to separate dreams from reality, and night from day. While awake, she saw shadows jump onto her roof and heard evil chuckles echoing in the night. Yet, when sleeping, she would dream of a man tempting her to fall in love. Everything had become backwards.

It made no sense.

Yet, even knowing she hovered only a couple of steps away from being committed didn't stop her from taking extra care arranging her hair and applying her makeup before rushing out of the house.

She had no errands to run, nowhere she needed to be.

One thing remained certain, however: she was going to the McGuiness's Tavern for every meal necessary. Hell, she'd even *sleep* there next to Zeke. Desperation to see if her dream became reality, or if she was going insane, ruled her.

And yet, she feared the answer.

ଚ

Upon arriving at the tavern, Sabrina discovered, much to her disappointment, they didn't open until lunchtime. Even Zeke, ever present, hadn't shown up yet. His empty jar still sat there, but he was nowhere in sight. Lunchtime wouldn't arrive for two more hours, so she hovered outside the door. She could go shopping until lunch, or go home and come back later. Or she could, more sensibly, return home and forget this whole idea. The very suggestion a man in a dream could tell her she would meet him in the reality of daylight rang of ludicrousness, so why had she even come?

She cursed and decided to head home.

Absorbed in contemplating her stupidity, she spun and crashed into a rock-solid wall. She broke free from her thoughts and raised her gaze to see she hadn't run into a wall at all. She'd collided with a man. A very tall man, considering the fact her nose throbbed from slamming into his chest. She stumbled backward and embarrassed herself further when she tripped over her own feet. Arms reached out to steady her, and she blushed in mortification.

"Oh, I'm so sorry, I wasn't watching where I—" She broke off. Finally finding her feet steady on the ground, she lifted her gaze to his face.

Mistake.

Huge freaking mistake.

It was *him*. She stared, stunned into speechlessness. He'd come. He'd actually showed up. And, perhaps even more shocking, he looked even more attractive when she rested in his arms. A small tingle raced up her spine, and her heart quickened.

"It's okay. Please, don't worry." He cocked his head to the side with a small smile and inquired, "Do you come here often? I think I've seen you here before. Oh, that sounded like a horrible pick-up line, didn't it?"

She laughed—with a hysterical undertone, to be honest—and mentally flinched at the forced quality that rang through it. "No, I do come here quite a bit. I'm new to the area, and this has become a common place for me. Um, my name is Sabrina. Sabrina Hodges, nice to meet you." She stepped back to offer him her hand. A covert glance at her outstretched fingers revealed they weren't shaking like the rest of her body. But it went to hell when his fingers closed over hers. Pure electric energy shot up her arm, settling into unadulterated lust.

Dear God.

"I'm Isaac Sterling. Nice to, uh, run into you, Sabrina." He smiled fully and her eyes widened. It was not fair to unleash such a devastating creature upon women. It became obvious to her, here and now: God was a man.

Unfair.

"If you were looking for breakfast, it isn't open yet, but I might be able to take care of you. My friend Connor is the cook here, and we had a meeting planned inside. Why don't you come in? He'll make you an omelet you'll never forget."

"Oh no, I couldn't. I just wanted to grab a bite to eat. It's nothing that can't wait." She protested and shook her head. "Really, I'll be fine."

"Ach, now, you wouldn't be turning me down, would you? Talk about breaking a man's heart on the first meeting...." He held his left hand dramatically over his heart.

She couldn't help but return his smile. She watched his eyes widen and then darken, and she beamed even wider at seeing the evidence of her effect on him. "Well, I'd hate to break such a kind man's heart." She leaned in and whispered, "You did forgive me for running you over."

"Indeed. I saved you from falling, too," he said. He chuckled and gave her an exaggerated wink.

"A gentleman wouldn't have reminded me, you know."

"Who told you I'm a gentleman?" he teased. His crooked grin caused her heart to do odd little flip-flops in her chest.

"I just can't interfere in your meeting, though. It wouldn't feel right."

"Okay, I've got a solution, if you're sure I can't convince you to join me. Why don't you give me your number, and maybe you can make your recklessness up to me at dinner? We'd be able to call it even, I'd say."

"Hmmm...maybe." She glanced up at him through her eyelashes and hoped her cheeks weren't blushing from the excited racing of her heart. "Do you have paper to write it down on, or a phone to put it in?"

He smiled and pulled his cell phone out while responding, "How about I give you my number now, and you can call me on your phone—presuming you have one—and we'll have one another's phone numbers right away?"

She agreed and called the number he gave her. His ringer went off, and she couldn't help but notice he had chosen an old-fashioned phone ringing noise for his ringtone. No fancy ringtones for this hunk of a man.

"Ah, the pleasures of the twenty-first century, huh? Now I don't have to worry you brushed me off by giving me a fake number," he said.

"And now I have your number so I can call and harass you if you don't call me. It works both ways, buddy," she replied. She couldn't believe that she could smile and joke. In her dreams, tenseness usually revolved around them, and the air always filled with a hint of danger.

"Yes, true. I have to ask. Are you American?"

"Guilty as charged." She raised an eyebrow and inquired, "Is that a problem?"

"Certainly not. I love Americans," he assured her.

Too quickly, she snickered.

"And are you British, or Scottish? I'm having hard time placing your accent. I'm usually so good at that, too."

"You're not to blame for the confusion. I'm a mutt."

"From?" she asked. Curiosity made her want to know everything about him, right here, right now.

And tell me, how do you come to my dreams?

Yeah, because that would make a good impression, Sabrina. Run from the crazy lady, Isaac.

He shrugged. "I'm a local, but I've moved around a lot. Well, my American friend Sabrina, have no doubt you'll be hearing from me about our date." Gallantly bowing over her hand, he brushed his lips across her knuckles so lightly she thought maybe she'd imagined it. When he withdrew, however, she swore she could feel the fire where his lips had been moments before.

She barely resisted the urge to place her lips in the same spot on her hand, like a teenager kissing a Robert Pattinson poster.

Get a grip, Sabrina. He kissed your hand. It's not like he threw you to the ground and had his way with you.

I bet you would like him to, wouldn't you?

Plastering a smile on her face, she said, "Yes, I'm looking forward to it." She smiled one last time in what she hoped seemed a demure fashion—but more than likely took her another step closer to a padded room—and attempted to walk gracefully to her car. She wondered how graceful she could appear, though, when her heart felt like it would race right out of her chest.

Great, just great.

She reached the car and couldn't decide whether to be terrified her dream had come true, or excited she had met him, and better yet, had a tentative date planned.

Some way, somehow, her dream had come true. But to even think this man, this Isaac, could invade her subconscious and tell her he would to meet her at a tavern reeked of stupidity. Men didn't come to you in dreams and claim you as their own, and they certainly didn't meet you in real life at the places they named in said dreams.

Things like that just didn't happen.

The man from her dream and the one she met today didn't even seem like they could be the same man. They were identical in appearance, yet the man in her dreams seemed harsh, rough, and dangerous as opposed to the subtle magnificence of the man at the tavern.

Concluding it an odd coincidence, she shoved any lingering doubts aside. She had gotten a tentative date with an incredibly attractive man.

She didn't have time to sit around worrying. She had a date to plan.

Chapter Three

She'd somehow gotten back in the woods, though not alone. He already stood beside her, and he seemed angry. His eyes accused her as if she had done something to betray him.

"What's wrong, Isaac?"

He tensed and hissed at the sound of her voice. His eyes looked hard, bitter. "You went to the tavern today?"

After a slight hesitation, she nodded. "Yes, you were there."

Looking up into the sky, he muttered something under his breath. She followed his gaze and noticed the stars twinkled merrily above in the purple moonlight, completely at odds with the tension swirling around them both.

"I see." He jerked her into his arms and pressed against her. "You're mine, you remember that." He threaded his hand through her curls roughly, making her scalp sting painfully. She bit back a gasp, narrowing her eyes at him.

"You're hurting me," she said.

He released his tight grip upon her curls instantly, and his eyes darkened in remorse. "I'm sorry. I didn't mean to hurt you," he whispered. He gently rubbed her scalp to soothe away the pain.

"You're much nicer in person, I'll have you know. Maybe I need to stop having these dreams," she muttered.

His face turned red, and he glowered at her. "Never say that again," he ordered.

"Or, what? I'll never see you again? This is all fake. As a matter of fact, I am leaving. Now."

Thunder boomed overhead, causing her to jump and look at the sky. Grimacing at the clouds hovering above, she started walking faster, Isaac forgotten in the face of the coming storm. Dream or no, she despised storms.

She got caught off guard when he swept her off her feet and into his arms. She hadn't even heard him behind her. He scowled down at her, his eyes practically shooting fire balls at her. Why would he be mad at her?

No. Not mad—furious.

Absolutely irate.

"Put me down," she growled. She shoved his shoulders with both hands.

"No. You need to be home, but you walk too slowly."

She realized he prepared to run and instinctively closed her eyes to avoid the dizzying speeds she knew he would achieve. She'd seen him run before. It was mesmerizing, yet terrifying.

When he halted, she opened her eyes and realized they were on her doorstep. She met his gaze, surprised to see that instead of his usual arrogance, he looked down at her desperately, his eyes beseeching hers.

"May I come in?"

She opened her mouth to reply, but before she could, Isaac got thrown violently to the side. He crashed into a tree, and she tried to run toward him, but couldn't move.

Her legs wouldn't move. She was…

Frozen.

ॐ

She awoke terrified of something—or someone. But she couldn't remember…. Oh God, her dream. Isaac had been hurt.

No, no. It had been a dream. Not reality.

He was okay. She felt fine, too. All remained good in her world. *Right?*

She checked the clock, groaning in dismay when she saw it was only two o'clock in the morning. She punched her pillow and tried to relax and seek more sleep.

Eventually she found it, in the form of dreamless slumber.

༂

Sabrina attempted to keep busy by writing her latest book. Even so, it seemed the past two days had been more along the lines of two weeks, since they'd passed unbearably slowly. She couldn't stop thinking about Isaac. Even now, one word sat alone on her computer screen.

Isaac.

The reason she couldn't stop thinking of him? Simple. They had a date tonight. And she couldn't seem to think about anything else, no matter how hard she tried to focus.

Marie had called yesterday, and she'd filled her sister in on her new love interest. Perhaps she had been too enthusiastic in her descriptions, while trying to be, at the same time, cryptic in how much information she revealed. She had been forced, as well, to repeat the whole conversation that had occurred over the phone between her and Isaac verbatim to her sister. She smiled, remembering.

Her phone had rung, and she immediately knew it would be him, even before she had looked at the caller ID.

"Hello, Sabrina. It's the man you ran over yesterday. Isaac, in case there's more than one of us." His unique chuckle had washed over her to whisper of pleasures to be had at his hands. "I've called to cash in on that date we spoke of."

"Hmmm. Sabrina? Nope, I think you have the wrong number," she said.

"Mm. Nice try. I'd recognize your American accent anywhere."

"Betrayed by my heritage, huh?"

"Yup," Isaac replied. The amusement in his voice made her smile. "So, you run me over, promise me a date, and then try to get rid of me. You Americans *are* ruthless. It's not just a rumor, is it?"

"No, it's definitely true. We're a rough, merciless lot. You'd better

29

remember it in the future," she replied. Giddiness came over her and she realized she felt like a teenager again. Heck, she hadn't even been this excited when the school football captain had asked her to prom. "So, now that you found me, what are you going to demand from me for recompense?"

"Oh, you think you're so tough. You haven't met a wronged Brit. You've got no idea what it is we're capable of anymore."

"Uh oh. I'm quaking in my, uh, slippers."

"Slippers, huh? Are they fuzzy bunny ones?"

She laughed out loud before glancing down at her slippers, which were, indeed, fuzzy. "That's none of your business, sir. There are numbers you can call if you want to know what I'm wearing."

"Ouch. You're cruel, you truly are. You certainly have a talent for crushing a man's ego, don't you?"

"And running over them, as well. We can't forget."

"Okay, you've put me in my place. Now, we must move onto the punishment, as you call it." He paused, and she tapped the fingers of her right hand on the table as she waited for him to continue. "I'm thinking dinner. Also some wine, maybe conversation, and soft candlelight? Does it sound too horrible to you, lass?"

"Oh, well, now that does sound pretty horrible. Horribly wonderful. I love it."

"Great. How's Monday night for you? Are you free? Not working, I hope?"

"Oh, no. I'm free. I usually have a flexible schedule." She rushed to assure him while frowning at the blank page in front of her. The cursor blinking rapidly taunted her and she flinched. Maybe she sounded *too* eager.

"Sounds good to me. If you give me your address, I'll pick you up at eight."

After providing him her address, they'd hung up and time had proceeded to stand absolutely still. She gave up trying to work on her current manuscript and closed her laptop.

Her characters were giving her a hard time. Her hero wanted to leave her heroine, and she couldn't allow that. But they were fighting her...and winning.

Her writing wasn't going nearly as smoothly as she would like. Kind of like her life.

હ

Isaac glanced in the mirror one last time when his phone rang. He pulled it out of his pocket as he sighed and answered without bothering to look at the caller ID. Only his friends had the number to his cell, so he knew the call would not be a professional one.

"Hello?"

"Hey, remember the problem we discussed on Saturday?" Connor asked. His voice came through urgent, yet hushed, as if he were afraid of being overheard. The clanging of pots in the background confirmed Isaac's suspicions. Connor called him from work.

"Mmm-hmm," he murmured.

"Tonight, at one in the morning."

He glanced at his watch, noting he needed to leave in five minutes to pick up Sabrina. "Okay, I'll be there." He hung up his phone and paced. He kicked the couch and cursed at having not acted fast enough. This could have been avoided if he had been more proactive. But instead, they were embroiled in a tangled mess, disturbingly familiar, and he didn't like it one bit.

Isaac ran his hands through his hair and finished his preparations for the evening before leaving for Sabrina's house on time, despite the addition to his post-date plans. It wouldn't do at all to be late since he couldn't afford to get off on the wrong foot. It remained imperative he'd get as close to her as possible.

હ

At eight o'clock sharp, Isaac knocked on Sabrina's door. It swung open a few seconds later, and he drew in a breath he hadn't even realized he'd been holding in.

She looked gorgeous. Too bloody gorgeous.

"Hello, Isaac." She answered the door smiling, dressed in a black T-shirt and tight jeans that clung to her hips like a second skin.

God, he'd pay anything get into those jeans. Hell, to *be* her jeans.

"Hello, Sabrina. You look wonderful."

His hand had been behind his back, but he brought it forward to hold out a bouquet of lavender roses for her. Something crossed in her eyes that looked like apprehension, but it melted away as she smiled.

"These pale in comparison to you, but I thought you'd like them regardless." He grinned as she took them from his hand and brought them to her nose to inhale their fragrant scent.

"Thank you, so much. I love them, truly."

She headed to the kitchen, and he remained in the doorway, feeling uncertain. Should he follow her, or stay in the doorway? She paused and blinked rapidly while she tilted her head to the side and stared at him.

"Please, come in. I'm going to put these in some water." She made a sweeping gesture to invite him inside.

He grinned as he stepped inside and closed the door behind him. He followed her into the kitchen and remarked, "This is a beautiful house you have. So quiet and charming."

"Thank you. Truth be told, I fell in love at first sight. It seemed to call to me. It's lovely."

While Sabrina fussed over the flowers, Isaac studied his surroundings. Despite his words, a chill ran up his spine at the sight of her home. Sure, she had a security system, but it needed more protection. The kind only he could provide. He'd have to fix that immediately.

And the location? That was a whole other story.

Isaac watched as she flowed through the kitchen and forced himself to take a calming breath. He felt as if an eternity had passed since he had seen her, last watched her smile. It took every ounce of his control to not sweep her into his arms and carry her up the stairs. Though he wanted to do just that—*God*, did he want to—he knew he couldn't. He had to act normal.

He couldn't afford to push her away; they were running out of time. He pulled himself out of his thoughts, only to curse silently at the sight of her pursed lips.

Shit.

How long had he been standing there, brooding?

He flashed what he hoped was a bright smile. "Well, should we head out?"

"Sure, I'm ready," she assured him. She collected her purse, shut off the lights, and followed him outside.

He watched as she locked her doors and set the alarm code. When she finished, he grabbed her arm and led her to his car.

ბი

The restaurant Isaac chose radiated elegancy. After he worked some sort of magic on the manager, they were seated at a secluded table in the back, behind deep red curtains. A single candle burned in a crystal votive on the table. After they ordered their dinner, filet mignon for both of them, hers medium-well, his rare, they sipped red wine as he began a subtle interrogation.

"So what do you do, Sabrina?"

"I write." She took a leisurely sip of wine.

"Oh? Anything I would know?"

"I write a series called *Darkness*. It's a love story between two vampires. Each book progresses through time, and I've started the final book in the present day. The tale started in the seventeenth century." She fiddled with her wine glass and shifted in her seat. She hated when people asked her what she wrote about. She used to stutter while trying to sum up in two sentences what her entire book was about, until she forced herself to come up with a generic reply to the question.

It made life a heck of a lot easier.

"I've heard of it. Charlotte Hannigan, right? That's your pen name?"

"Yes, it is," she replied. "I like to keep my identity a secret. Keeps any overzealous fans at bay. What about you, Isaac?"

"I'm in real estate. I acquire and sell a variety of land and structures spread throughout the world. I either sell the properties after extensive remodeling, or I rent them out. Quite boring, compared to your occupation."

"No, it sounds interesting," she assured.

"No, it really isn't." Isaac laughed, and she joined in. "Any siblings?"

"Yes, one. Her name is Marie. She's married, and has a daughter named Samantha. Her husband's a lawyer, and they're expecting a boy in February. They live in San Clemente, California." A pang of homesickness came over her as she thought of Marie. She missed her laugh and her smile.

"Are you from there?"

She tore herself from her inner thoughts and responded, "Yes. And you? Siblings?"

Isaac tensed, and his eyes hardened almost undiscernibly. Why did the mere mention of siblings cause him to close up in such a visible way? Maybe there was a rift between them?

He hesitated before answering. "Yes, a brother. We're not close, though." He gave a sharp wave of his hand, as if to wave away the awkwardness of the current thread of conversation. He *obviously* didn't want to talk about his estranged brother.

"No? I'm sorry," she said. She couldn't imagine her life without Marie.

"It's okay. Do your parents also live in California?" Isaac asked.

"No, they died. I only have Marie. Yours?"

"With yours."

"I'm sorry for your loss."

"And I yours," he returned.

Dinner arrived and interrupted their conversation. When she caught sight of Isaac's entree, she got immediately taken aback at how bloody he'd ordered his steak.

"Wow. It looks like that should still be mooing. Is it done enough for you?" she babbled. Sabrina checked her steak to see if it appeared done enough. It did.

She returned her gaze to his and saw him regarding her with amusement.

"Yes, this is how I like it. I know, it's not healthy, but it is so worth the risk. Just try a bite, you'll see." She watched with a marked lack of enthusiasm as he cut a bite off of his steak, holding it out to her. He unleashed both dimples upon her before pleading. "Please? For me?"

Next thing she knew, she chewed it, and she struggled to remember having agreed to try a bite.

Unfair.

Surprisingly enough, he spoke true. She closed her eyes and chewed on the tender meat, groaning in pure culinary delight.

"Oh my God, you're right! I would never have thought it could be so good. It's moist, and tender, and, and, and…delectable." She gazed from her steak to his and fought down disappointment. What had once appeared perfect now seemed overcooked and bland.

Isaac laughed and casually flicked his wrist. Immediately, the waiter arrived by his side. "Please, I must have made an error. Can we have another steak, done rare as well? The lady will eat mine, as we wait." He handed off her previous order before she had a chance to object and placed his plate in front of her. "Now, please do enjoy."

"Oh, no. I can't. You just gave me your dinner, the least I can do is wait. You didn't have to do that!" she exclaimed. Her face heated as she realized what she'd just done. She'd just stolen his dinner.

Good first-date move, Sabrina.

Yet even as she protested, she stole a peek out of the corner of her eye at the plate before her. It looked irresistible. She fleetingly wondered if they'd drugged it. The waiter returned inexplicably fast, holding another plate.

"Here you are, sir. Sorry about the wait." He observed Isaac for approval before refilling their wine glasses and leaving.

"Here, give me yours," Isaac murmured as he reached across the table. He snatched up her plate before she could as much as blink in surprise, switching them yet again.

"Isaac, please." She moaned. "You're killing me here." She dropped her head to her hands in embarrassment.

"Hey, don't do that," he soothed. "It's okay. I want your dinner to be perfect. How else will I get you to agree to see me again?"

She met his teasing eyes, and a grin tugged at her lips despite her hot cheeks.

"Why would you want to see me again? Are you on a diet?"

His mouth quirked until he threw his head back and burst into laughter. Sabrina saw several people—women, to be exact—glance over at his laugh. "My, God, you're delightful."

She grinned and leaned toward him to whisper. "I think you're just trying to make me feel better for stealing your dinner."

"The fact that I let you do it shows how very much I like you, my dear. I don't share well." He smiled crookedly.

"Neither do I. So back off my plate before I stab you with my fork," she warned, while raising the silver in a threatening manner. They both laughed, and the awkwardness of her stealing his meal— *twice*—disappeared.

Thank God.

ଞ

A strange stillness sat in the air outside Sabrina's house. No trees swayed in the breeze, no animals scampered in the forest, as if the world itself had come to a halt.

Uneasiness rolled over her, and she studied Isaac out of the corner of her eye. Surprisingly, he seemed to be as tense as her. His grip on her arm was tighter than necessary, and his lips were pressed together as well. She could *feel* the tension pulsating off his body, and she got taken back into her dreams. For the first time in real life, he made her shiver in apprehension. As if sensing her fear, he shot her a quick grin.

"Well, I had a lovely evening." He spoke over his shoulder as he practically dragged her to the door. She stumbled in an attempt to keep up with his pace. At the door he pointedly stared at her, causing her to realize he waited for her to open it. She fumbled through the mess she called a purse to find the key. She turned to him and smiled as she studied him through the cover of her eyelashes.

"Would you like to come in for a nightcap? I have wine...or coffee...or tea, or...." She stuttered to a stop, unsure of what to say.

God, she sounded like such an idiot.

Nightcap?

Who the heck said *nightcap* anymore?

"While I'd love to take you up on that offer, I have something I have to take care of tonight. Could I get a rain check? For say, tomorrow night? We could do a movie and wine? Or is tomorrow too soon in the dating world?"

"No, not too soon at all. I'd love to see you tomorrow." She tried to hide her disappointment behind a bright smile. "You can call me, and we'll firm up a time. Good night."

She turned to go inside and got caught off-guard when he grabbed her elbow and spun her to face him. It happened so quickly she leaned back against the door in confusion; one hand on the doorknob and the other braced against the cool steel of the door. He moved his body closer to hers and placed his hand at her head. His other hand cupped her cheek while his thumb stroked her jaw line. All thought fled as his body pressed against hers, and a small swoosh of air escaped her lips at his touch.

"I didn't think it even possible for you to grow more beautiful, but you have proven me wrong." When his lips met hers, she lost all thought, all ability to move. She'd somehow been tied to this spot—this *man.*

She needed to be like this. To have his arms around her, his lips on hers. The emotions washing over her were so powerful that if he hadn't supported her with his weight, she'd have fallen to a heap on the ground.

When he ended the kiss, it took all of her control to stand upright. She fought the urge to fling herself at him and knock him to the ground in her haste to seduce him.

To have him inside her.

He stroked her cheek one last time and ran his thumb across her lower lip, pleasantly swollen from his kiss. It tingled at his gentle touch, and she quaked.

"Good night, Sabrina."

"Good night."

He reached around her trembling body to push open the door she still rested against for support, and Sabrina half-expected him to follow her inside despite his earlier words, but the door clicked shut. She sagged against it and closed her eyes as she remembered his gentle touch, his lips burning against hers.

"Lock up," he said through the door. She jerked guiltily, almost scared he could read her thoughts, and did as he asked. His car engine revved to life, and she listened as he sped away.

She stumbled to the couch and collapsed into the cushions before she pressed shaking fingers to her lips. She longed to feel his lips against hers again. Preferably, right now.

Ugh, she had to get control of herself, or she'd be like one of those crazy people planning their wedding after the first date. Though she had always wanted a June wedding....

She thrust away visions of herself walking down the aisle in a stunning, strapless white gown and forced a deep, calming breath. She didn't want to scare him away by being overly excited, or too clingy.

She needed him too badly.

ಬ

Isaac's hands gripped the wheel so tight he wondered if he might snap it in half. When the cool leather wheel started to bend under the pressure, he forced himself to loosen his hold. Leaving Sabrina hadn't been as easy as he might have hoped. But he had a job to do. A job that, unfortunately, required he'd leave her.

He shouldn't have kissed her goodbye, he acknowledged grudgingly. His control hung by a mere thread, ready to snap at a moment's notice. Her soft lips under his had almost done him in, and still haunted him.

Cursing loudly, he slammed his foot on the brake. While fantasizing, he had almost run through the red light shining above. Bloody hell, he hated cars. He couldn't exactly blame the car, but he did despise them.

No, it was his fault, and his alone. He needed to stop obsessing and start paying attention. Too many mistakes had already been made. He'd set the plan in motion, and he would stick to it, by God.

This time, he would win.

Arriving at his destination, he shut off the engine and sighed in relief as he exited the sports car he called his. He set off toward the forest and forced himself to concentrate on the matter at hand.

Someone lurked in the woods.

છ

"*Sabrina, Sabrina, what should I do with you? How will I keep you safe, my love?*" *He caressed her chin in feather-light strokes, and her heartbeat quickened as she trembled at his soft touch.*

"*I don't know what you mean. I'm safe. I'm with you.*"

"*Yes, of course, Sabrina. But you have to trust me and come with me.*" *He smiled at her and held her gaze, and she caught her breath.*

"*Where?*"

"*Trust me,*" *he whispered.* "*Let me in.*"

"*Let you in? We're in the middle of a forest.*" *She made a sweeping gesture with her hand.*

"*We'll go to your house, and you can let me in. Let's go.*"

He held his hand out, and she studied it before putting her hand in his. He seemed to be in a good mood tonight, at least. Something that must have been triumph entered his eyes, and he swept her into his arms. Knowing what came next, she closed her eyes and grabbed his neck.

When he twisted her in his arms so she stood behind his back, instead of running as she'd expected, she looked around in confusion. She hadn't even seen him move her. She yelped at the unexpected action and clutched his shirt in fear. Isaac shoved her to the forest ground to hunker down in front her.

A feral snarl broke the silence of the night, and she sought out the beast that made the terrifying sound. She blanched when she realized no beast made the noise—Isaac had.

Isaac? No, that couldn't be right....

In front of them, a dark form landed in a crouch, causing Isaac to growl louder. She stumbled away when the shadow straightened, and she saw Isaac.

No, it couldn't be Isaac. Isaac stood right in front of her. Yet he looked identical to the man she gripped in fear. What the hell was going on?

"*Stay away from her,*" *growled the new Isaac.*

"*I will not.*"

"*She is* mine. *I will* fight *you for her.*"

"Go ahead and try, baby brother."

Brother? Well, at least it explained the resemblance—but it still freaked her out. Even for a dream. Hoping they were distracted arguing, she crept backward. Her legs shook as she stealthily separated herself from the scene in front of her. Though she knew she dreamed, the fear coursing through her felt very, very real. Every instinct in her screamed to get away.

Now.

"Sabrina!"

She groaned at the shout and broke into a full run. She didn't need to worry about being quiet anymore—but she needed to run as fast as her little legs could manage.

Stinking short legs.

She glanced over her shoulder nervously and caught a glimpse of the fighting brothers. Not daring to watch, she turned back to her flight, only to tumble to the ground. Her foot had gotten stuck in a grasping root, and it twisted painfully from her fall. Her hands burned where rocks had scraped into the tender skin, and her ankle throbbed.

When her stubby legs weren't slowing her down, her damn clumsiness did the trick.

Knowing she couldn't waste time nursing her wounds, she yanked, pulled, and cursed at her foot, but could not get loose.

Come on...couldn't she catch a break?

A thud sounded beside her, and Isaac reached for her foot. She screamed and pulled free, falling backward from the power. Isaac hovered over her, his face bathed in concern, and she shoved him away using all her force. His widening eyes and mouth falling open comically as he tumbled flat on his back were the last things she saw.

She jumped to her feet and ran away from him as fast as her short, annoyingly clumsy legs could take her, and didn't look back.

❧

Sabrina sat upright in her bed, panting for breath. A glance at the clock told her it was a few minutes past one. Her body still trembled from the adrenalin rush she'd experienced in her sleep, and her legs ached from her desperate escape earlier.

Wait, *why* did her legs hurt? It's not like she'd actually been running. It had been a dream. She brushed her hair out of her face in confusion and flinched at the stinging pain in her palms.

Her hands shook as she reached for the light beside her bed. The first try, her hand slipped off the switch, the second she knocked over the cup next to her bed, the third she plain old missed, and the fourth, she finally succeeded in turning on the stupid light. She blinked rapidly as she waited for her eyes to adjust to the blinding light. Once she could see again, she raised her hands in front of her face with dawning dread. Blood and dirt streaked her palms. She bolted out of bed and screeched when she noticed the dirt and leaves scattered across the sheets.

She clutched the edge of the bed for support as dark spots swam before her vision. Dismayed, she realized that for the first time in her life, she was going to faint.

Chapter Four

Sabrina noticed three things upon awakening. First, she wasn't on the floor. Second, morning had come. And last, she didn't have dirt all over her any longer. Her hair seemed damp to the touch, yet she couldn't remember having showered. She hopped out of bed and ripped the covers back.

Spotless.

A glance at her hands revealed they were a little red, though they no longer stung or had blood on them. She sank onto the edge of the bed and dangled her feet. What *exactly* had happened last night? Had she dreamed she had woken up, when in reality she had still been sleeping?

It had happened before, many times. She was a writer, for God's sake. Overactive imagination kind of came with the trade.

But why were her hands sore? And why couldn't she remember showering?

It *sounded* feasible she had been distracted yesterday by thoughts of Isaac and walked around in a daze, preparing for bed and not paying attention. It made much more sense than believing she dreamt about being in the forest while two Isaacs fought over her, only to awaken dirty and hurt.

Now *that* would be impractical.

ꕤ

Frustration coursed through Isaac's tense muscles as he thought of Sabrina. He'd had his second-in-command, Connor, watching Sabrina, and discovered his fears had come true. His bloody brother came to her in her dreams. Isaac had been dream-stealing—so to speak—and he'd seen Elijah come to her. He'd managed to scare Elijah away while not being seen all the other dreams, until tonight. Tonight, he'd lost his cool. It only made sense when, upon first seeing her in the tavern, she'd look at *him* as if she'd seen a ghost. No one looked at someone in something akin to horror and excitement unless they had a damn good reason to do so.

He knew why he gaped at her, of course, but she had no excuse.

He wondered how long his brother had been appearing to her, and if she thought Elijah was actually Isaac, appearing to her in her sleep.

That left just one question running through his mind: could any of that be used to his advantage, rather than his disadvantage?

He wished he could hear what she had going through her head this morning, and that he kept her company in her bed so he could question her. Tactfully, of course, so she wouldn't run away, screaming for help.

He knew with a certainty he couldn't explain, or describe, as he sat thinking of her, she surely attempted to make sense of her "dreams." She'd probably insist to herself they were just dreams—nothing more. She probably sat in her normal little world, analyzing her normal little life, and tried to make all the latest occurrences fit into a pretty little box.

Unfortunately, in his world, and now hers, it wouldn't be bloody possible.

ꕤ

Damn it, Elijah really *hated* Isaac sometimes.

He'd been the one to find Sabrina first…not Isaac. He'd been the one courting her since she first came to England…not Isaac. And yet, once again, his brother swooped in to win the girl. It enraged him.

He had, of course, known that Isaac contacted Sabrina. Though

Isaac might hate him passionately, Elijah didn't despise Isaac. Well…not *most* of the time.

Sabrina, as expected, was falling for Isaac. And now he'd gotten stuck coming to her in her dreams, because Isaac would never leave the blasted place unguarded. If only she would let him inside, he could get closer to her. Instead, his brother once more stole his place by her side. Somehow, Isaac had discovered of his plan to meet Sabrina during the day at the ridiculous tavern she seemed to love, and appeared in his place. And in one simple step, he snatched away any chances of gaining entry to Sabrina's life. And house.

He'd tried to go about "wooing" her slowly. Cautiously. But when had that ever worked well for him? After all, his style of seduction— and warfare, for that matter—tended to be more of a "shoot now, take no prisoners alive" type of style. The time had come to start acting like it. He would make her love *him*, not his brother. He'd make her realize he, not the real-world Isaac, had to be the one she needed. His twin wasn't right for her, and never had been. Isaac couldn't love her like he could.

He remained far too strict in his ways. He'd never be able to let go of his so-called "duties" to be able to spend a lifetime with her. Only Elijah could give her life.

His little brother would only sit by to watch her die.

They'd been down this road before, the three of them. She might not remember it, but he and Isaac did. This time, it would end differently, much differently. They were destined to be together, written in the stars.

He needed only to prove it to Sabrina.

❧

Sabrina busied herself writing throughout the next day. As the pages piled up, she came to the conclusion that nightmares, and no sleep, were great for creativity. For once, she was ahead of schedule— and liking it.

The ringing of the phone broke the silence, causing her to yelp. Holding a trembling hand to her heart, she answered breathlessly.

"Hello?"

"Hello, Sabrina. Did you sleep well last night?" Isaac asked.

Fighting the unease his words stirred, she forced a cheerful tone. "Like a baby. It was a great night." The hollowness in her voice made her cringe and clear her throat. "How about you?"

"Well, it was a late night. I had a few, well, problems to see to. I'm sure you know how that can be." He sighed. "But, tired or not, I'm all ready for the rain check you promised me. You've been on my mind quite a bit. I had a wonderful time."

"I did, too, very much." She relaxed against the chair and rubbed her forehead. "What time would you like to come over?"

"How's eight sound? I don't have any other commitments tonight, so we can indulge in some coffee like you mentioned before. It might help me stay awake so I don't end up snoring next to you halfway through the movie."

His light chuckle brought forth a resounding giggle from her as she pictured him drooling beside her on the couch.

Did he drool?

"Well, you could always bring your fuzzy bunny slippers, just in case." She laughed, cringing as she realized it sounded as if she asked him to spend the night.

Desperate much?

"Oh, I wish I could take your words as an invitation to stay the night. But, if I know you as I think I do, you're biting your tongue right now."

She winced and asked with no small amount of suspicion, "Hey, where's your spy camera?"

"A man can't give away all his secrets on the first date, lass."

"But, it's our second date," she pointed out.

"Ach, well, maybe I'll show you my secret hiding spots."

"Isn't 'ach' a Scottish thing? Not British?"

Silence met her ears through the phone, and she pursed her lips. *Interesting.*

He laughed. "Why, yes, yes it is. But, it's always been a favorite phrase of mine. Must be more Scottish than I thought, or admitted to."

She chuckled. "Okay, then. Never thought to hear *those* words from a Brit."

"I'm not a normal Brit," he joked.

"Why doesn't that surprise me?"

"Well, shall we continue this conversation later?"

"I look forward to it. I'll go buy some black spray paint so I can go around and cover all the cameras."

Isaac chuckled. "I'm going to scare you away before I even get inside," he bemoaned.

"I don't scare easy."

"Yeah, I kind of gathered as much about you." His voice grew serious, making her sober instantly. The joking mirth seemed to have left his tone. She couldn't shake the feeling he was trying to tell her something she didn't want to hear.

She got enough weird things in her sleep, damn it, couldn't her life be a little bit normal in the daytime?

Please?

Fighting the apprehension creeping up on her, she gave an uneasy giggle. "Well, eight it is. Coffee a must. Fuzzy slippers optional."

"Right. See you then, Sabrina."

"Bye."

She hung up the phone and bit her lip. Had she imagined the serious undertones in his voice, like she'd imagined everything else lately? Or was he trying to tell her something, something even she couldn't conjure up?

No, she sounded like an idiot. His asking about her night had nothing to do with her dreams. He simply made small talk.

She rolled her eyes and shut the computer down for the day. Now she'd never be able to concentrate on her book.

She couldn't wait for tonight.

෨

A few hours later, she glanced at the clock as a knock sounded at the door, and Sabrina saw Isaac was on time once again. She opened the door and studied him hungrily, though she tried to tamp the feelings down. He may have mentioned being exhausted on the phone, but he looked amazing in person. No bags were visible under his bright blue eyes, and he stole her breath away with his raw masculinity. A DVD and a bottle of wine occupied his hands, and she smiled in pleasure. Lust caused her stomach to twist when his gaze darkened with desire.

"I figured I could help contribute to the evening's festivities." He held out the DVD, the latest *Harry Potter* movie, and she procured it as he locked the door. His eyes met hers, and her pulse raced at his expression. "Wow, you look gorgeous. You'll have to forgive me, but I just can't help myself."

He grabbed her by the nape of her neck and yanked her toward him to conquer her lips. Passion overwhelmed her at his arduous kiss. He gave no quarter and took all she could give. Her hands clung to his shirt as his tongue moved against hers like liquid fire. He deepened the kiss, and she melded her body to his. Her heart raced, and she pressed against him urgently.

She needed him; she needed more.

She needed…everything.

His fingers skimmed up her back before diving into her hair. She moaned when he tugged gently, exposing her neck to his tender onslaught. He trailed hot kisses down her throat and just when she suspected she might to die from the pleasure, he jerked away abruptly. He sighed and kissed her nose. Thunder boomed in the distance, causing her to jump in surprise.

Where had the storm come from? The sky had been crystal clear moments before.

Still wrapped in his arms, she stared at him as he examined every inch of her face, almost as if memorizing every last detail. Desire blazed in his eyes. An answering need burned in her, and she moved restlessly. Why had he stopped? She hadn't objected to his embrace.

It's the second date, you slut. Have some control.

"I wouldn't have thought it possible you could grow more beautiful. Somehow, you've managed to accomplish the impossible." His voice was husky, and it showed her more than words ever could. Longing still burned through him…as well as the need to have her.

Touch her.

It was a heady thought.

"Funny, you just took those words out of my mouth," she replied.

He cocked his head to the side and grinned. "Is that what I just did?" She laughed at his joke, and he chuckled in return. "I love to hear your laugh, Sabrina. It is the most beautiful sound in the world."

She blushed and changed the subject. "So, would you like to come into the kitchen and open the bottle of wine up?"

She stepped out of his arms and fought down the wave of emptiness hitting her. The DVD he'd handed to her lay on the ground, and she stooped to pick it up.

"Good thing you didn't give me the wine," she joked. Looking at him from under her eyelashes, she jutted her hip out suggestively and crooked a finger at him before heading into the kitchen. Surely he'd follow her playful invitation.

When she didn't hear him behind her, she whirled to retrieve him.

Sometimes men were *so* dense....

Instead, she yelped to discover him behind her. Clasping a hand to her chest, she exclaimed, "You scared me. How did you move so quietly? I didn't even hear you walking behind me."

He shifted on his feet and gave an odd twist of his lips. "Sorry, I've always been light on my feet. I used to scare my mother all the time by sneaking up on her. Even as a little child, she would tell me I could sneak into the kitchen, steal a whole jar of cookies, and she'd never even know it." He smiled at her, and an answering smile lit her face at the thought of Isaac as a boy.

He must have been absolutely adorable and irresistible.

Just as he is now.

"Well, I'll have to get used to it, I guess."

"Please, do," he murmured.

She retrieved two wine glasses as he opened the wine. They worked together in a companionable silence. She led him to the living room to watch *Harry Potter*. She loved this series. How did he seem to know the right things to get her? He'd even gotten her favorite wine.

He was a genius. One could only hope he had as much talent in bed as he did out of it.

Cradled in the crook of his arm, they started the movie while sipping their wine.

"I like that," he murmured in her ear.

"Like what? The car?" She gestured toward the TV and looked at him.

"No, I hate cars. I love hearing you say you have to get used to my oddities. It speaks of...a possible future. Though, now you'll probably run away from me. Men aren't supposed to worry about the future, are they? Or plan further than when to get their next drink." He shrugged his left shoulder. "I don't know. It just slipped out. You make it hard for me to think straight at times."

She wracked her mind to recall what he spoke of and remembered her words in the kitchen. Pleasure filled her when she realized he was still thinking about their conversation—and possibly their earlier embrace, as well.

"Well, maybe men aren't supposed to, but I like that you are. And I like that you're different," she assured him. "Actually, I like you."

"I like you, too," he whispered.

He kissed her nose and pressed downward to capture her lips. They both moaned in unison at the instantaneous flame of desire and strained to get closer to one another. But suddenly, Isaac tensed and jumped to his feet. She was left to flop to the couch in the empty spot he had occupied seconds before.

How in the heck did he move so fast?

"What's wrong?" she asked in alarm. Every instinct poised for some unseen fight to be had.

"I heard a noise...I think there's something outside. Give me a second, please." Racing to the door with inhuman speed, he spun back to her as a fierce determination took over his features. "Lock the door behind me. No matter what you do, don't open it until I come back and say it's me, and I want to watch *Harry Potter*. Got it?" he growled at her.

"Um...yes...got it..." she stuttered. She sprinted to the door and obeyed his command.

What the hell had just happened?

An inhuman, and non-animalistic, snarl broke through the silence of the house, echoing loudly in her ears. She blanched at the somehow familiar sound. Where had she heard it before?

Good God, it sounded just like in her dreams. She jumped back in alarm and began searching for a weapon. She had to help Isaac.

No matter how much it sounded like her dream, it was real, and in real life, growls like those were generally caused by large animals looking for meals. She grabbed the biggest butcher knife she had and sped back to the door.

She threw it open and crashed, then bounced off of Isaac's hard chest. His arm, which had been raised to knock, shot behind her to steady her, and she hastily checked her knife hand.

Thank God, she hadn't stabbed the poor guy.

Relief swelled over her at seeing him whole and uninjured. But relief was overcome by confusion at his fuming glare. He let go of her and closed the door.

"You didn't listen to me," he snapped. "I told you not to open the door until I said, 'Sabrina, it's Isaac, I'm ready to watch *Harry Potter*'. Instead, you grab a knife and try to kill me?" He rubbed his jaw and paced in short, irritated strides.

An answering anger rose in her, and she responded, "I was trying to help, you ass. If I wanted to stab you, I can assure you, you wouldn't be standing here arguing now."

They glowered at each other in silence until he sighed and ran his fingers through his hair. "I'm sorry. I guess I got carried away. I shouldn't have yelled. Forgive me?" He smiled crookedly, and her irritation dissolved a bit.

"I'm sorry, too. I should have been more careful. You're right. But once I saw you, I relaxed. I knew I would be safe with you. Unless you have a twin running around?" She didn't know what had made her say those words, but she instantly regretted it. Reality and fiction were getting blurred together, and she didn't like it.

Her heart dropped when his smile melted away, to be replaced by the face of a cold, hard stranger. "Yes, actually, I do. My brother we spoke about is my twin. We no longer talk. He's a dangerous person. Reckless. As of now, I don't even know where he lives," he snapped.

This man, standing before her, resembled the man in her dreams. His eyes glittered, and a hard mask came over his face as he glowered at her. She shuddered at his expression. He seemed so...unforgiving.

His words suddenly clicked in her head, and a whoosh of air left her lungs, and none returned. He had a twin, an *identical* twin. Blackness swam in front of her eyes, and she reached a hand out to the wall to steady herself.

Air. Air is important.

She took a deep breath and focused on Isaac once more. He leaned in toward her, his face no longer icy and cold. Instead, concern clouded over his eyes, and he fumbled for her.

"Are you okay?"

She nodded. She didn't think she could put two syllables together right now, let alone a whole sentence. This changed everything. This brought her dreams into day—and it blurred every line she had drawn.

"Sabrina, please. Talk to me, tell me what's wrong," he pleaded in her ear.

"I'm...I'm okay," she stammered. "I'm sorry. I think all the...excitement got to me." She finished on a whisper. She did her best to look suitably weak and probably failed miserably. Weak damsels in distress weren't her style.

How exactly did one feign feebleness anyway?

Maybe she should have fanned herself with feminine flourish as they did in movies so well? Eh, probably not. He already studied her far too close. As if he yearned to say something to her—demand something of her—but held back. Though his reasons for doing so were unknown, she remained grateful he did.

What a mess her life was rapidly becoming. As if her dreams weren't odd enough, now she came to find out he indeed had a twin brother. One he hated?

What the *hell* was going on?

"Are you sure?"

"Yes, I'm sorry. I'm okay. And, I'm sorry about your brother. That must be...uh...well...tough," she stuttered. *Man, she sounded like a veritable font of eloquence tonight.*

The cold mask returned, and she took a step away from him. "I know you're dying to know what happened, so I'll tell you. There was a woman. Amelia. She was everything good in the world. Beautiful, kind, charming. We were in love, and due to be married. Elijah, my brother, had been promised to another woman, but he loved my Amelia. There were some problems, and Amelia...died." His voice faded away on the last word.

It appeared obvious to her from the tightened fists at his side and the hard set of his mouth as he pressed his lips together, the hurt plagued him still.

"Oh, my God, I'm so sorry. How horrible. I don't know what to say."

"Yes, well, it happened a long time ago. Time moves on, people heal. But I have no interest in speaking to him, or even knowing where he is. The whole situation was his fault. If he hadn't—" He bit his lip and looked away. She wondered what he had been about to say. The cold mask he seemed to put over his face when he no longer wished to speak on a subject came back, though, so she dared not ask. "Well, now that I've ruined the evening, maybe we should call it a night, hmm?"

"You could stay here. On the couch, I mean. If you want. I'm kinda freaked out," she said. He stared at her, and she shifted on her feet at his scrutiny. Maybe it had been a mistake to invite him to stay. Something was going on here, something bizarre. And he was smack dab in the middle of it. And yet, she'd invited him to spend the night?

A loud bang sounded outside the window, and she jerked at the noise. She raised her hand still gripping the knife and started toward the window in determination. She'd had enough of this shit, already. Isaac stretched out to stop her and chuckled.

"Sheath the knife. It's just the wind. It must have kicked up some debris." He reached forward prudently to extract it from her rigid grip.

Over his shoulder, she saw a shadow move in the darkness. "I just saw someone out there. Whoever you chased away is back! I'm calling the cops." She whirled on her heel and grabbed the knife back from him in one smooth gesture. She sprinted to the kitchen, knife in hand.

"First of all, let's take this before someone gets hurt." He snatched the weapon back from her once more.

"Hey," she protested. She held her hand out with an impatient wave, and put the other on her hip. "Give me back my knife."

"Absolutely not." He ignored her furious intake of breath. "Second, please put down the phone. There's no one out there anymore," he declared.

"But, I saw—"

His finger pressed against her lips silenced her.

"Trust me, okay? You're safe tonight. I'll spend the night here, on the couch, if it will make you feel better. I'll hear if someone comes. It's almost a sixth sense of mine." He grinned and pulled her into his arms and kissed her nose before he buried his face in her hair and inhaled.

"You smell so delicious." He breathed into her ear.

Oh *please*, if he thought she was easily distracted, he had another think coming.

"Nice try, but I still say we should call the—"

"And you taste even better." He groaned as he nibbled on her ear. Her head fell back against his arm, and he kissed a path across her neck and to her lips. His lips latched onto hers with a desperation that called to her very soul. Right here, right now; he needed her. And, *God*, she needed him.

He leaned her against the wall, and his hands roamed from her hair, down her back, to cup her buttocks before he pressed against her and moaned deep in his throat. She rubbed against him, and she heard his swift intake of breath before he pulled away. His eyes burned in need, and it took all her willpower not to yank him back into her arms.

"It's been a long evening. Perhaps we should say goodnight." He looked obviously reluctant to let go of her. His hands and lips hovered over her for another few seconds as he seemed to fight an inward battle.

Lightning flashed beside him, silhouetting half of his face in absolute perfection, and leaving the other half in shadows. The desire burning inside him appeared painfully obvious to her eyes. But, he spoke true. Damn it, she *knew* he was right. She'd never climb into bed with a guy she'd met two days ago. But…this guy felt so *perfect.*

Numerous times, she'd written about people being so caught up in passion that nothing else mattered to them—not their families, their jobs, even their lives. It had always been fiction for her, up until today. Now, she knew it existed.

And she had to be grateful to him for being such a gentleman to realize she didn't remain sensible in his arms, to realize her weaknesses and manage not to take advantage of it. And, damn it, it made her want him even *more*.

"But what about the noises outside?" she insisted. Though he'd distracted her, she hadn't forgotten.

He groaned and rubbed his temples. "I swear there's nothing out there anymore. I know it sounds weird, but you just have to trust me, okay?"

She snorted. "Yeah, sure. I'll just believe that simply because you say so?"

"Yes, it would be spectacular." He grinned.

"Yeah, not gonna happen." She scoffed. "Besides, if there isn't anything out there, there's no harm in me looking, right?"

He sighed, grabbed her hand, and pulled her to the door. She followed him until he opened the door. Skidding her feet against the floor, she called out, "Wait!"

She ran to the table, grabbed the knife, and nodded to show her readiness. She ignored the slow shaking of his head and the look he threw upward, as if praying for assistance from above, and glared at him.

They walked outside, and she stepped closer to him as she sought out any signs of danger. Nothing lurked in the bushes, or in the forest beyond the house. Nothing hovered in shadows, or rushed toward them at their entrance outside. She hesitated on the stoop, unsure of her next step.

Nothing moved; no huge beast loomed over her.

"Satisfied? Or do you want to walk around the back, too?" he questioned in her ear.

She turned to him and studied his face. No signs of anger or sarcasm. "I'm satisfied now, I guess. Still want to sleep on my couch?"

"If you still want me to," he answered as they walked inside. She nodded and climbed the stairs. She returned carrying pillows and a blanket to find him sitting on the couch. His shoes were placed side by side in front of it, and he'd unbuttoned his shirt. His chest taunted her to touch it, to sink her fingers into the coarse hair dusted there. To feel the hard muscles flexing beneath. She wanted to trail her fingers down his abs, to caress his....

She tore her gaze from where it currently rested, at his belt. Afraid to be caught gawking at him like a pervert, she blurted out, "Thank you, Isaac. You must think I'm a complete idiot."

"On the contrary, I find you brave, beautiful, caring—"

She laughed and rolled her eyes, and he seemed to sense her discomfort at the compliments, for he broke off and smiled ruefully. He grabbed her hand and kissed her knuckles.

"Good night."

"Good night," she whispered. She cast one last longing look in his direction and climbed the stairs to her empty bed.

Being good sucks.

୧୦

God, he'd been a complete fool. How had he not sensed Isaac inside? Now Isaac knew he'd tried to get in during the day, and he'd guard her house even more. He had botched his chance to get inside without fight.

Blasted fool.

He'd just wanted to see her. He often came here when she was home, enjoying her beauty. Granted, this time he hadn't been planning on just looking. He'd been planning to pretend to be Isaac.

Low? Hell, yes. But, damn, he heard the desperate clicking of the clock in his head, taunting him with his inadequateness.

He hadn't even *sensed* Isaac. He couldn't afford such a colossal mistake again.

Fleeing in surprise had been a mistake as well. He didn't fear Isaac. Please, Isaac had never been able keep up to him, even as a child. And besides, he had every right to see Sabrina.

As much, if not more, than Isaac.

Amelia had picked *him.*

In the meadow long ago, he remembered her choice....

The sun had warmed his face as the gentle breeze kept him from baking alive over a roaring fire. It had seemed like a perfect day to spend outside with his love. And since Isaac had left on their father's business, he had leave to do so. He didn't have to seek her out. He knew she knelt by the stream, a bouquet of flowers clutched in her hand. It had been easy to convince her to join him, since she loved being outdoors on days like these.

Hell, so did he.

Especially when she sat by his side.

Her soft curls escaped her coiffure to blow in the breeze as she headed toward him, and he returned her bright smile. Her cap-sleeved lilac dress spoke of the latest fashions, and the bonnet she wore to protect her milky skin matched it to perfection. He'd never tire of seeing her perfect face.

Sometimes, he wished he'd never fallen in love with her. Indeed, she loved his brother. He knew it. But sometimes, just sometimes, he swore he saw something more. A brief glimpse in her eyes maybe. Or maybe he just imagined it. God knows he was desperate enough to wish it were so.

He pushed his thoughts aside and sighed. Even if she did somehow love him in return, she'd been promised to Isaac. And he, well he'd been betrothed to the rich Lady Louisa Harding. It had been arranged for years, before even Isaac and Amelia. It was his duty, damn it. He'd been named the heir, and so he had to marry whom his father wished.

Louisa appeared beautiful, with long, flowing red hair, gorgeous eyes, and a flawless body to match. She spoke of perfection in every way. Except for one small, tiny problem. She wasn't Amelia.

Amelia sat next to him and laid her head on his shoulder. He rested his cheek on her hair and inhaled her lavender-and-sunshine scent so hungrily it gnawed at him like a monster.

"Oh, my Lord, isn't it just gloriously wonderful out?"

"Yes, my lady, it is. You make it even more so. Were I to be in the company of any other, it would be dull and dreary, to be sure." He teased, but the truth in his words rang in the air. They always did.

Pathetic.

She laughed and looked into his eyes. It must have been something about the way she observed him, the way her eyes sparkled. He had no idea what caused it, but he snapped. The hold on his control broke, and he moaned in pure agony. When she reached a trembling hand out and cupped his cheek, he stopped fighting it.

"Elijah..." she said so quietly he might have imagined it.

She made the slightest of movements toward him, and Elijah thought of all the reasons why he shouldn't—couldn't—kiss her. Nonetheless, he let out a sharp cry and yanked her into his arms. Maybe just one time, he could taste heaven. No harm, no foul.

Correct?

Urgently, he crushed his lips against hers, and her arms wrapped around him. His fingers trailed over her back to bury his hands in her hair. Her soft moan made his desire rise to a frenzy, and he positioned her on the ground, before moving his body to cover hers. Cradled against the heat of her core, he surged against her readily.

At the startling need coursing over him, he pulled back hesitantly. He met her gaze and drew in a deep breath at the love and desire burning in hers. He'd waited so long to see that exact expression cross her eyes, and now she was his. By God, once would never, ever, be enough. But he no longer gave a damn.

Crushing his lips to hers once more, he vowed to make her his.

Elijah pulled himself out of his memories and into the present. He could recall with perfect clarity how sweet her lips tasted, how soft her body had been curled into his. And, damn it, it had felt the same with Sabrina. For years he'd been tormented by his small glimpse of heaven, before hell had descended. And hell he had been in for too long to count. Deep down, he'd always hoped she would somehow return and pull him out of the darkness consuming him.

And here she stood, by Isaac's side once more.

He kicked a tree, watching in satisfaction as it cracked beneath the force.

Through her window, he spotted her sleeping form. Her brow furrowed, as it always did when something troubled her. He knew he'd caused her stress, and he could fix it. It would not be as simple as before, due to the guards, but he could do it.

He needed to see her.

Now.

∞

The wind whipped her hair into her face, obscuring her vision. She didn't feel afraid, merely irritated she couldn't see. She sensed him lurking somewhere nearby in the purple moonlight. She could sense him by her side just before he gripped her arm in an urgent manner.

"Sabrina, please. We must talk."

Returning his stare, she knew with certainty who stood before her. The pieces fit together with a clarity as undeniable as it was unbelievable.

"Elijah?"

He paled, staring at her in shock. "Yes, how did you—?"

"Isaac. He told me about you. I still have no idea how I've been dreaming of you. This all just seems to be out of a novel. A story I would write. It can't be real. It isn't possible." She shook her head, reeling from shock.

"Feel me." He brought her hand to his face and kissed the inside of her wrist. The combination of the smoothness of his cheek and the coolness of his lips caused her to shiver. "Touch me. Do I feel real?" he whispered roughly.

"Yes. But this is a dream." She ran her thumb over his soft lip and caught her breath. "I just had a weird sense of déjà vu. As if I've done this before. Why?"

"Because you have. I can't explain it right now. You have to trust me. I'll be over tomorrow, once Isaac leaves. Let me in, and I will tell you everything I can. Please?"

Not giving her a chance to protest, he kissed her aggressively. Her body came to life, and she clung to his arms. She'd surely burst into flames, and he was her refreshing bucket of water. Lifting her weight into his arms, he pressed every inch of her body to his, in all the right places. He fit her like a glove, a glove meant just for her.

A small voice whispered in her head, told her though he might look like Isaac, but it wasn't him. This man who kissed her had killed Isaac's fiancée. She betrayed Isaac in the worst way possible. She ripped herself free from her passion-filled daze, pulling away from his grasp to covered her mouth in dismay.

What had she done?

"Sabrina, what's—" He stopped mid-sentence and growled as his eyes scanned the forest behind her.

Sabrina recoiled and jumped out of his arms. She knew what the sound meant. Danger skulked near.

She yelped when a woman landed in front of them. Her beauty made Sabrina feel dowdy in comparison. Though certain she'd never seen her before, she looked somehow familiar. The hair rose on the back of her neck in recognition. Of fear, or of the woman, Sabrina had no clue.

But this woman was bad news.

"Again, dear? You seem to be a bit dim-witted, don't you?" she taunted. Meeting Sabrina's wide eyes, the woman bared sharp, tiny teeth in a mockery of a smile.

Elijah growled, seeming to read the woman's intentions. They leapt into action, colliding in mid-air. The crash produced an ear-shattering bang, echoing through the night ten times louder than the boom of thunder on a dark, stormy night. She covered her ears in pain and watched the pair in a mixture of horror and astonishment.

Elijah ended up on top of the woman, but that didn't stop her from snapping her sharp teeth at him before flinging him through the air. He connected with the same resounding boom, and Sabrina, horrified, watched the tree crash to the ground, Elijah under it. He leapt to his feet. He met her eyes, almost apologetically, and she wondered what he planned to do next.

She didn't wonder long, though. For in a split second, he picked up the tree he had knocked down and threw it at the stranger, who was sprinting toward Sabrina at the same speed Elijah possessed.

Sabrina stumbled backward, both at the gesture and from the advancing woman who glowered at her as hatred curled her lip and filled her eyes. She didn't get far, because she was scooped into Elijah's arms as he sped away from the crazy woman. Elijah slid to a halt when a figure appeared before them. Sabrina screamed in terror and clung even tighter to his strong arms.

Chapter Five

"Sabrina. Sabrina! Wake up, please wake up *now!*" Isaac shook Sabrina in panic, terrified he wouldn't be able to pull her out of her dream. Damn Elijah and his sick hold on her. He'd taken Sabrina from her own body, and now he very well might kill her. Removing humans from their bodies was *never* a good idea. Sometimes, unable to return, they were forever stuck in a dream-like state.

Otherwise known as a coma.

A rarity, but still a risk he could not allow.

Couldn't he see the harm he caused her? The danger he put her in? Elijah could never be with Sabrina. Surely even he could see it?

Sabrina jerked in his arms, and he watched in horror as her eyes rolled to the back of her head.

Shit.

He shook her and hoarsely called her name. "Sabrina, please. Wake up! I *need* you to wake up. *Please.*" The last word came out as no more than whisper. He froze when he saw her stare transfixed on him. She gulped for air, her eyes wide and her face ghostly pale, as she struggled to breathe. He sat her up in his arms and pounded her back in an attempt to help.

When her arms flew out to the side in shock, he realized he had maybe pounded a little *too* hard. But…she was breathing. He could hear her gasping breath, see her shoulders heaving at the effort. Pulling her back into his arms, he hugged her to his chest.

Dude, don't suffocate her now that she's breathing.

Dumbass.

He forced himself to loosen his grip and whispered soft words into her hair. He had no idea what he even said, but they seemed to help. In no time at all, she lay limp in his arms, curled into his body.

Where she damn well belonged, thank you.

"Isaac?" she asked.

Anger swelled over him when he realized she asked if he was Elijah or Isaac. God, he hated his brother. He should make it clear to her, right here and now, that her soul mate held her in his arms. Life by Elijah's side would *never* be possible.

But if he came on too strong, too fast, he might scare her away. By now she had to know something unearthly surrounded her. But she didn't know *what*. And he suspected she couldn't handle the truth tonight. She'd been through too much already.

Hoping she would confide in him, he forced himself to take a calm breath before pasting a smile on his face. He schooled his features into an easygoing appearance, determined to look as non-threatening as possible.

Act clueless.

"Yes, who else?" He raised an eyebrow in question. With bated breath, he awaited her answer. Maybe, just *maybe* she would trust him. If she showed just a small sign of being ready, he would tell her all about his life. And all about Elijah—and why he posed such danger to her. He was a vampire, for the love of God. They tore pretty little girls like her apart—literally.

Those hopes were dashed when she waved a dismissive hand in front of her face.

"Sorry, Isaac. I think my brain is a little confused. I had a nightmare. It's all very humiliating."

She blushed, avoiding his eyes. He knew why she would look away. She lied through her teeth, but why the hell would she *blush*?

"Um, just out of curiosity, how did you know I had a nightmare? I hope I didn't scream and wake you." She bit her lip and studied her clenched hands, and he tensed as he realized she felt mortified to have been frightened.

Embarrassed.

Jesus, she should be bloody scared.

He smiled tensely and forced a chuckle as he fought the anger washing over him. "I'd like to be a gentleman and say no. But how would I explain my presence in your bedroom? Voyeurism? Sorry, lass, but yes, you screamed. What did you dream about?"

"Oh, nothing. A shadow chased me in the woods. Someone called my name, and I tried to escape them, but it kept getting closer. Then, you woke me up. Thanks for pulling me out of it."

He closed his eyes in an attempt to conceal the fury coursing over him.

One, two, three.

He sighed and opened his eyes to focus on her once more.

"You must think I'm such a wimp. Terrified of shadows."

"On the contrary, I don't think you are enough of a wimp, as you call it," he countered. He held her gaze intently, silently pleading for her trust. For her love. Her eyes widened, showing she saw all the emotion he wished her to see, and more. She bit her lip, and he watched the movement curiously. What was she thinking? *Feeling?*

Damn it all, if he couldn't get her to trust him, he'd damn well make her need him. He growled and pressed his lips to hers, offering the things he felt not aloud, but in action. Passion, love, need: they were all there. And not just on his side.

No, it was just pure imagining on his part. Obviously, he loved her. He'd be an idiot to deny it. He always had, and always would. He'd loved her since the first time he met her in the countryside by their houses, and he'd loved her when he was still a human. Love like that didn't just go away.

But for her to love him so soon? When she didn't remember those moments? Not bloody likely.

A loud bang of thunder shook the house, and she shrieked. Isaac pushed her away in frustration to glare out the window at the storm raging outside. Bloody storms. Already, the absence of her arms around him left him cold. He wanted her to writhe against him, to hear her breathy moans fill his ears.

Instead, he had, well, *emptiness*. Where there had been fire, there was now cool air.

He might as well have left.

Out of the corner of his eye, he saw her reach out to him, her face showing her pain at his rejection. Yet she stopped halfway, her hand hovering in the air. She chewed on her lower lip and laid back against the pillow, her scrutiny focused on his back.

He ignored her scrutiny and indecision. He needed to get outside, before he made a fool of himself even more. He rose to his feet and murmured a hasty good night, before striding from the room. He hoped it looked more like an exit than a panicked retreat. If he stayed even one more second, she'd either be flat on her back, or he'd be shaking her in frustration.

Maybe both.

He headed outside in search of Connor, the man he'd assigned to protect Sabrina. Apparently, he'd failed. It appeared Elijah had grown stronger than Isaac suspected.

Connor normally kept unwanted guests away adeptly; it was one of his talents. His gifts, so to speak. In this life, they all had gifts. And there were the creatures like Isaac. The Enforcers. Enforcers were capable of becoming *any* of the monsters in order to defeat them. They used their powers for good—to save humans from the monsters roaming the world. Monsters like Elijah.

Damn it.

Connor's gift consisted of being able to block *guests* from trying to enter any property he protected with his mind. And if they came in person, he handled them as well. His record remained—or had been, anyway—undefeated. No one could get around him; he was infallible.

The key word being *was*.

Isaac had a very powerful gift as well. He could, in essence, control the weather. A sunny day could turn into a turbulent tornado at the blink of an eye. When he got too emotional, or out of control, the weather matched. The first few years of this life had been quite disastrous. Many villages had been destroyed by his anger. It took years for him to manage it, but he had gotten to the point where he could easily stay under control.

Or he had been, until Sabrina walked into his life a few weeks ago. Now, nothing felt under his control.

The ground shook from the force of the thunder overhead as he contemplated Elijah's growing power. His brother's gift had always been his speed and strength. But…now he disguised himself as well.

So he was not only up against an unarguably superior opponent in speed and strength, but also one immune to his defenses?

Shit, shit, shit.

Kicking a tree, he stalked into the dark woods. Sabrina's screams from her nightmare echoed in his head, no matter how far he walked.

Come on, man.

"Connor? Get over here." His voice came out so soft a human would not hear it.

Sensing Connor's presence, he swung to face him and scowled. Connor smiled sheepishly.

"Sorry about earlier. I ran into the side of the house. I thought I had more room, but obviously calculated wrong. Did she see me?"

"Yes, but it's okay. I took care of it." He snapped as he waved his hands. "What I *really* want to know is how Elijah managed to get to Sabrina. Didn't you sense him? Try to block him? What happened?"

Isaac *knew* he sounded like an ass. He didn't care.

"Wait, what? Elijah has been nowhere near here, I'm sure of it. I would have known." Isaac watched as anger, disbelief, and finally shock crossed his friend's face. "No. No way he came here. Even now I can't sense his presence. You've gotta be wrong. It's not possible," he whispered.

It was as bad as he'd feared. Connor couldn't even sense Elijah had been here, yet alone whether or not he *remained* here? The world would go to hell in a freaking hand basket.

Lovely.

Lightning and thunder crashed overhead.

∞

The next day, Sabrina yawned for the fifth time in one minute before giving up and heading into the kitchen. Time for another cup of coffee.

A damn storm had killed any chance she had of getting any sleep last night. Where the hell had it come from, anyway? As she inhaled the hazelnut aroma steaming from her mug, she contemplated her dilemma. Isaac had left this morning after an admonishment to be careful, which she knew translated to *do not let Elijah in*.

A knock sounded at the door. Weird, she hadn't been expecting anyone. She grabbed the knife off the island, just in case, and went to open the door. She gripped the doorknob and froze. She didn't need to wonder who stood on the other side. Elijah.

She could *sense* him.

Why could she sense Elijah, without even seeing him, but Isaac could walk up behind her and grab her, and she'd be none the wiser?

Why would she sense his soul, his essence, calling to her from the other side of the door?

And why did it feel like such a betrayal?

Oh, right. Because it *was*.

She should be attached to Isaac, the man from her real life. Not the one that haunted her dreams. Yet, even knowing she should avoid him at all costs, some invisible pull led her to wrench the door open.

She studied him by the light of day for the first time. Though his eyes and features were identical to Isaac's to the casual observer, Elijah was distinctly different. His face seemed harder, more cynical. Like he had seen and done it all already—and life no longer held any fun for him. His mouth also appeared to be set tighter than Isaac's, and his body held more tensely. She wondered if he always looked so harsh.

So *dangerous*.

Realizing she gaped at him, she burst out, "Why are you here?"

"Please, you've let him talk to you. Why not give me a chance?"

"Because I don't trust you," she stated flatly.

Anger crossed his eyes. He shifted his weight from one foot to the other and ran his fingers through his hair as he clenched his teeth. "Sabrina, it's not without danger that I have come to you. For once, can you listen to me, and *let me in*?"

"Why can't we talk like this?" She motioned her hand to show what she meant: him outside, and her safely inside.

"I can't stay out here in plain sight."

She stared at him as she chewed on her lower lip. He made sense. If she listened to Isaac and let him in her house...why not Elijah as well? What harm could it do to hear both sides of the story, so to speak? Any intelligent woman would seek out both sides. Wouldn't they?

Damn right they would. Making up her mind, she nodded. "Elijah, please, come inside."

He smiled at her, causing her to catch her breath in apprehension. Had she just made a horrible mistake?

"Thank you for allowing me in your home, Sabrina. I promise you, I am not here to hurt you. I would never want to hurt you." His stare beseeched hers as he held her gaze and did not let go. He leaned closer to her, and she softened.

"I believe you."

Walking into the living room, she knew he followed despite the fact that his footsteps were as quiet as his brother's. She started in surprise when she saw him sitting on the couch before she even neared it, however. Taking care to place the knife obviously in arm's reach, she perched on the edge of the couch, resting her hands uneasily in her lap. "This is all very, um, new for me. I'm sure you understand my confusion."

"Yes, of course. I will try to tell you what is happening, but I'm scared to tell you too much. You might get frightened away. Some of it is not...normal." Tilting his head to the side with a somber expression, his gaze bore into hers so intensely she flinched and looked away. "Also, I am unaware of what Isaac has already told you."

"How about if I ask the questions, and you answer them? No lying, though, or I kick you out and never let you in again," she demanded. She waited for his nod of agreement, crossing her arms across her chest. "How old are you?"

He relaxed, an amused expression crossing his face. As he grinned, she saw a dimple flash her way. "Twenty-seven."

"Hmm...and what year were you born? I'm bad at math," she lied.

The amusement vanished and coldness took over his features again. "You really want to ask that one?" He spoke between clenched teeth. "I don't think you do."

"Actually, I do," she insisted. "I certainly didn't invite you here to discuss the weather."

"Oh, and how *has* the weather been, Sabrina?"

"Stormy." Her voice rose at his odd question. Who the hell *cared* what the weather had been like?

"I'll bet," he scoffed.

She studied him curiously. It sounded almost as if he had some hidden meaning behind his words, one she wasn't privy to. She pushed aside her confusion at his derision and looked at him, making a great show of dragging her eyes from him to the door. "Now that we've discussed the *weather*, answer my question."

"Sabrina," he ground out. "I already did. Twenty-seven."

"Did you come here to lie to me? To play games? Time for you to leave. Now." She rose to her feet and glared at him. She was done. This whole situation seemed ridiculous. When he didn't leave, she put her hands on her hips and leaned closer to him. "I said *get out*."

He mumbled something, and she leaned in closer. "What did you say?

"I was born in eighteen-fifty-four!" he yelled. "Is that clear enough for you, my lady?"

Shock filled her at his answer, and she collapsed back onto the couch. She'd been expecting something like this, but to hear it out loud still struck her like a blow. Things like this didn't happen. Well, maybe it did in movies and novels, but not in real life.

Man up, Sabrina. No time for shock.

"What are you?"

"I won't—*can't*—say. It's not possible. So, you might as well move onto the next question. You can threaten all you want, but I *can't* answer you."

She stared at him, trying to make sense of his words. He hadn't said he wouldn't tell her, but he couldn't. Why? An order, a covenant, or did he just not know?

Interesting....

"Okay. Give me a second here...." She rested her head on her left hand, rubbing her temple as she racked her brain for her next question. She tried really hard not to dwell upon the one question he couldn't answer. She had been sure what his answer would be, yet even in fiction she had never heard of a vampire not being able to admit his secret. Could she be wrong?

Was he something else?

Stop wasting time and get your answers.

"Why couldn't you come inside until I invited you in? And why come into my dreams, instead of talking to me the normal way?"

"I can't come in until you let me."

"And once invited, can I kick you out?"

"No, once you invite me in, you can't rescind it." His smirk did nothing to hide his satisfaction at sharing the small detail with her.

"Well, that would have been some useful information. Don't you think?"

"Useful for whom? Not me." He smirked, and she itched to wipe it off his face. "And I never came to you in the daytime, because Isaac had already wormed his way into your life. If it weren't for him, none of this would be happening."

"So you blame Isaac for everything, huh?" she asked curiously. "Interesting. I had the impression things went down the other way."

"Meaning, of course, I'm a horrible monster, and he's an angel? Of course, gentle Isaac could never do any wrong." He rolled his eyes. "Well, you're wrong. Dead wrong. You placed your trust in the wrong man, my dear."

"Hmm, I'm not so sure about that." Hesitantly, she continued. "You and Isaac both cared for Amelia. Right?"

He nodded. "Yes, of course."

"You fought. He seems to blame you for her death. Did you…kill her?"

Anger, pain, and finally resignation crossed his eyes before he whispered, "Yes."

She choked on a breath and coughed in an attempt to inhale. She'd been so sure he had to be good, that he couldn't possibly be the evil monster Isaac seemed to believe him to be. But if he was guilty of *murder*, she had just invited a murderer in her home.

Oh God, what have I done?

Remembering to breathe, she leaned imperceptibly away from him.

He tensed at her action, but she didn't care. She needed to get out. Smiling, she said, "I'll be right back. I need some coffee."

She rose from the couch, making sure she moved in a non-run-for-your-life-manner. Hearing him curse behind her, Sabrina reached for the knife in blind panic. Her hand barely brushed the handle before she got thrown through the air and buried beneath him on the couch. She managed to throw one solid punch to his ear, and he grunted in pain as he pinned her arms above her head.

"Jesus, knock it off! That bloody well *hurt*," he exclaimed.

"Let go of me," she snarled. "Or you'll hurt even more." She threatened him, trying to free her knee from between his. He cursed and pinned it down under his leg as he looked at her in something akin to horror. No matter, she had all day to kick his ass.

"No, wait, please don't be scared. Let me explain. You can't leave. I can't let you. I'm sorry." Though his voice pleaded with her, his face looked like it had been set in granite.

In fact, he felt as heavy as stone as well.

And just as unmovable.

"I'm not scared, you ass. I'm pissed. Let me up, now!" She squirmed beneath him, fighting for freedom, until she froze and her eyes widened in shock. That, she knew, was *not* stone. It was an erection, pure and simple.

She drew a deep breath, prepared to scream at the top of her lungs. He must have sensed her intentions, because he cursed and swallowed her cries into his mouth. His lips moved over hers, stealing her breath away. Panic overwhelmed her, and she thought with certainty that she would soon die. She would die because, like an idiot, she'd ignored Isaac's warning.

Anger ripped through Sabrina like a knife, and she lay still, afraid to move. It seemed useless to fight his strength in this way. She'd seen him yank a tree out of the ground; he could handle a mere woman. But she'd be *damned* if she would respond to his assault, either in fear or desire. Elijah pulled away from her lips and rested his forehead against hers.

He seemed oblivious to her anger as he held her closer to him and kissed her forehead tenderly. It melted her heart...just a little. Not enough for her to stop wanting to kill him, though.

"Are you going to stop and listen to me?" he inquired.

She refused to speak and give him the satisfaction of winning. She didn't lose well. She settled for a glare that would have frozen him on the spot—if he weren't already made of stone.

"You don't understand a damn thing," he argued.

"I understand you killed your brother's fiancée," she returned.

"There were things that happened you would never, *ever* understand. Not in a million years. And you should thank God for it."

"Let me go, Elijah. Now."

He glared and opened his mouth to respond. Whatever he'd planned on saying, she would never know. For instead of replying, he hissed and ran to the door, threw it open, and slammed it shut behind him as he left.

She was left alone, quivering from the fear consuming her.

What had she done?

ဢ

Blaringly aware of the fact he'd scared Sabrina away because of his honesty, Elijah ran with a desolation he'd not felt in a long, long time. He could have made her understand, made her see why he had done what he did. But *Louisa* had showed up.

Louisa, the bane of his existence.

There had been no choice but to flee after the deranged bitch, since she had no business being so close to Sabrina. But in protecting her, he had managed to alienate Sabrina for good. To top it all off, Louisa had gotten away.

But not for long.

His legs quickened each stride he took, and the wind brushed his skin like a caress. Even if he passed a human, they would feel nothing but a slight chill. Invisibility suited his mood today.

He was in no shape to be seen.

Chapter Six

*T*he sound of the phone ringing echoed in the silent room, but Sabrina refused to answer. Her encounter with Elijah had left her shaken, and for one night, she didn't want to have any of the craziness that now defined her life. She needed a freaking break.

Unfortunately, she really needed some sleep—but *he* might come to her. And she didn't want to see him. What a position to be in.

She'd toyed with the idea of inviting Isaac over and sleeping in the shelter of his arms, but she fought it. It would be a cop-out, and she didn't fit the mold of a weak damsel in distress, damn it. But she'd take a knife to bed. As she headed toward the kitchen, she checked the door one last time.

No, Sabrina, it didn't unlock itself in the last five minutes.

Besides, a locked door wouldn't keep him out, anyway. He'd just get her in her sleep. Like Freddy Krueger, but hotter.

The phone rang again, and she jumped in alarm. God, when did she become such a wimp? Time to answer it so she didn't get a heart attack every five seconds.

"Hello?"

"Hi. How are you?"

"I'm okay, Isaac. You?"

"Eh, today passed slow and boring." He chuckled.

She opted to lie. "Yeah, I hear you there."

"Any more strange occurrences?"

"No, it's been very quiet. Too quiet."

"Hmm. Would you like some company?"

God, yes. Come hold me and keep me safe.

"I think I'm gonna go to bed. A storm kept me up last night, and I'm beat."

"I'm sorry," he apologized.

"Why would you be sorry? It's not like you caused it." She laughed and rolled her shoulders as she sighed. He apologized for the weirdest things sometimes. Especially storms.

Odd.

"Can I come over tomorrow, instead? I need to talk to you."

She choked on a breath, certain he would soon fill her in on some of his mysterious past. The writer in her wanted to hear his side—to understand.

"I changed my mind. You can come over, if you want."

"No," he insisted, "get some sleep. I'll see you tomorrow. Good night."

"Good night." She sighed in dejection. She headed upstairs to attempt some sleep, though she alleged she'd get none. But hopefully, she'd be blessed by some quiet, empty, dreamless sleep.

Please.

ଊ

Isaac spent all the next day tracking Elijah, to no avail. Anger coursed through him at his brother's ability to escape him, but with considerable effort, he tamped it down. Eight o'clock had finally rolled around, and he pulled his car to a stop in Sabrina's driveway. Had Elijah visited her dreams last night?

Had she moaned beneath his body, welcoming him into her open arms? Did she show him the same eagerness she always showed him? He exited the car and slammed the door behind him, before leaning against it.

Get a grip, man.

She wasn't Amelia. He could trust her. Right?

Not if the past repeated itself….

ᔥ

"This way, Lady Harding. I am certain they are out here." Isaac glanced at her out of the corner of his eye as they crested the hill. Did he imagine things, or did she seem even more silent than usual? He desperately hoped Amelia and Elijah were here. He couldn't stand another moment of her stone-cold beauty.

Arriving at the meadow, he stopped as pain grabbed hold of his heart and squeezed. They were here, indeed, but not awaiting their betrotheds. No, they were quite content to be alone. His loving brother and fiancée were making love.

The pocket watch his father had given him for his eighteenth birthday fell out of his hand as he studied the pair in horror.

When the hell had this happened? How long had it been going on? Son of a bitch.

A growl broke him away from the horror before his eyes, and he swung toward Lady Harding in surprise. The sound seemed too feral to come from such a small slip of a girl. She crouched on the ground, her silk dress getting dirty from the mud at their feet, and snarled as she bared her teeth.

Bloody hell, she couldn't be human. Not if she had those teeth. He ripped his gaze away from her face and ran toward the lovers embraced across the meadow. They had to get out—now. As enraged as he felt, he didn't want to see them eaten alive by this monster. Whatever she—or it—was.

He got maybe two steps before being thrown to the ground, Lady Harding straddling him in a mockery of an embrace with her long skirt hiked up to her hips. She slammed his head into hard stone, and his vision blurred. She jerked his head to the side, and he heard a bone snap.

Damn, that hurt.

Unfortunately for him, it only symbolized the beginning of his pain. His blurry vision caught sight of shining teeth headed toward his neck before the agonizing pain ripped through his body.

She must be a bloody demon of some sort.

Who even knew they were real? He tried to break free. To scream his agony to the world, but he'd been paralyzed. He couldn't even fight.

And worse yet, when Lady Harding twisted his head to the side, she faced him toward the traitorous pair across the meadow. He didn't know which hurt more: the pain wracking his body as she sucked the life out of him, or watching Amelia and Elijah make love. The anguish of their betrayal echoed deep inside of him, and he closed his eyes to the sight of their writhing bodies.

It didn't work. He saw them as vividly as if he were standing above them, cheering them on.

Son of a bitch.

Tears escaped his eye, rolling down his face to land in the grass below, like raindrops falling from the sky.

Mercifully, the world faded to black.

ꟷ

Sabrina slowly opened the door and peeked around the side of it to examine her visitor. She studied his eyes most carefully before she sagged in relief. It was Isaac. She motioned him in and locked the door behind him.

Thank God he'd come.

Unsure of how to act, she hovered by the door. How did one greet a non-human guest? Her indecision got miraculously taken away when he opened his arms to her. She lunged into their welcoming warmth, and the fear that had been a constant companion all day rolled off her shoulders.

He put his finger under her chin and lifted her face to his. Just before their lips touched, he froze and seemed to wait for some form of approval from her. Instinctively knowing he sought her compliance, she pulled his head the rest of the way down so their lips met. It was all the reassurance he needed before entwining one hand in her hair, while the other crept down to cup her buttocks firmly. Lifting her, he pressed his hard erection against her, causing them to groan in unison.

This was too much, too fast.

Gasping for air, she tore her mouth from his and rested against the wall for support. Desire burned throughout her body as she fought the primal urge to fling herself back into his arms.

Before his arrival, she had lectured herself to keep her distance. Get her answers. Yet not two seconds in the door, and already she clung to him like a dog in heat.

Have a shred of control, woman.

He cursed and reached for her, his intent written clear as day on his face. She shook her head and put a defensive hand in front of her. "Please, no. I can't think straight when you kiss me." Taking a shaky breath, she met his eyes, only to see pure male satisfaction glowing on his face. Why, the smug son of a…. "You do it on purpose, don't you?" she demanded. His dimples flashed at her as he smiled charmingly, and she forgot why she felt angry. In fact, she forgot why she'd stopped kissing him at all.

Maybe she should remedy that.

"If you're accusing me of kissing you until you lose all thought or purpose, I'm guilty as charged." He cocked his head to the side before continuing. "But if it makes you feel better, you have the same effect on me."

"Yes, I do believe it does." She chuckled softly and shook her head. Mesmerized by his brilliant blue eyes, she carelessly stated, "Your eyes are just so beautiful. Every time I see you, I'm amazed at the shade of blue. So like Elijah's, but much softer." Anger crossed over his features, squashing the sparkle she loved. Gasping in horror, she put her shaky hand over her mouth and took an unsteady step away from the angry man advancing upon her.

Did I say that aloud?

What a freaking idiot.

"Elijah?" he muttered. His jaw clenched, as did his fists.

"W-wait, let me explain. He came into my dreams, and only the dreams. Well, until yesterday, anyway—"

"Until *yesterday*? He came here, inside this house? When?" His voice rose with each word, until he ended on a shout. She flinched at the volume. "I thought he'd only been in your dreams. But it's gone past that, hasn't it? You let him inside, *knowing* he could hurt you.

Knowing what he has *done!*" His fist slammed on the foyer table, and she jumped as it echoed throughout the house. It seemed like a miracle the wood didn't shatter at the force. She swore the windows shook at the blow. Or had it been from his shout?

"Isaac, please, calm down. You're scaring me." She backed away from him and covertly searched for her knife. She didn't have it close by. She'd never dreamed she'd feel the need for it with Isaac. "Yes, he came here, but just once, and I haven't seen him since." She watched his body tremble. She had never seen anyone this mad. Ever.

Holy crap.

A loud bang of thunder shook the house, and she yelped. A glance out the window revealed torrential downpour accompanied by flashing lightning, gusty winds, and deafening thunder. Even though she feared storms, she gauged the storm less of an imminent threat than Isaac, so she turned her attention back to him.

"What did he do? You invited him in, after what I told you? How could you? I'll kill him. I swear I will. He won't do this again. This changes *everything*." With one last angry scowl, he spun on his heel, opened the door, and left. The door swung in the fury of the storm, banging against the wall so hard it knocked down the picture hanging next to it. She gaped at the door before rushing to close it against the tempest outside.

She stumbled to the couch in a daze and sat on the edge as she dropped her head in her hands. Her stomach lurched and tears welled in her eyes. How had she become such a freaking idiot? To announce how much prettier his eyes were than Elijah's?

In her defense, whenever he held her she turned into a babbling idiot. He was a devastating force who stole her senses with one smile, every time. So could she *really* be blamed for what she blurted out?

Yes.

She collapsed onto the soft cushions of the couch and leaned back, only to notice the storm had ended as fast as it had begun. What the hell was up with the weather lately, anyway?

A shadow moved over her, and she shrieked in terror. It took a split second for her to realize Isaac crouched in front of her, but it took long enough, thank you very much.

"Jesus Christ, you've *got* to stop doing that!" She wailed as she clenched her fists in anger.

"I'm sorry. I lost my temper. You don't know how dangerous he is. How much he could hurt you. I shouldn't have yelled, but I'm terrified of seeing you get hurt. I'll tell you anything you want to know about him, and me, if you will *listen*." His eyes were pleading, and she knew she would forgive him. Hell, she forgave him already. They were both stressed out and tightly wound. It was natural they would snap. And she'd been the idiot who had said Elijah's name

"Should I leave?"

"No," she stammered. "I think it's time you told me what's going on. *Everything*." He hesitated, and she nudged her foot against his. "I mean it, I want to know. No lies, no excuses. I think I deserve that much." Her chin jutted out, and she folded her arms across her chest. She wasn't moving till he bared all.

He could start by removing his pants....

No, wait, he could start by telling her how he had become—well, not *human*.

Whatever that meant.

He sighed and settled on the couch beside her. "Well, I'll start at the history and work my way up. I'm sure you have realized by now—" He hesitated over the name and grimaced. "Elijah and I aren't what you'd call...normal. Human. We were born in the year eighteen fifty-four." He paused, clearly expecting a reaction from her. Receiving a simple, serene nod, he gritted his teeth and continued. "Elijah was born ten minutes before me. As the heir, he was always so tense. So wound up. In what was probably a way to rebel against his responsibilities, he became a rake and *loved* taking risks. The only time I ever saw him relax was in Amelia's company. He'd been betrothed to a woman, a young lady of quality, a few years before Amelia died. He'd have gained a lot of land with the match. Her name was Louisa. Back then, though, she went by Lady Harding.

"Amelia grew up by us, but when we reached an appropriate age, it became more than friendship. We got betrothed six months before she died, and life was never better for me. Stolen kisses in the barn. Long walks in the meadow. She had the most gorgeous curly hair." He rubbed

Sabrina's hair between his fingers of his left hand. "And absolutely glorious green eyes." He ran his fingers over her brow with his right hand. "Like I had never seen...until now."

"Wait, a second. I didn't want to interrupt, but are you telling me she looked like me? *That's* what this is all about? I *resemble* her?"

"Yes. She looked as much like you as I do like Elijah. When I first saw you, in the tavern, you took my breath away. I knew, as surely as I was seeing you, Elijah would, too."

Bewildered, she took a deep, calming breath. She was the spitting image of Amelia—their long-lost, cheating love? Whom they both wanted back?

Jeez, it sure sounded like a healthy start to a new relationship. *Not.*

"Well, I dreamt about Elijah before I saw you."

His cold mask was back, and he inquired, "You did? I had no idea."

"Yes. It's why I stared at you like you were a ghost. I thought I was going insane."

"I was too busy thinking *you* were a ghost to notice you staring at *me*." He snickered and grinned. The ice-man was gone, thank God.

"Understandable, I suppose," she murmured.

"But I digress. One day, Elijah and Amelia were alone in the meadow and we walked upon Amelia and Elijah, entwined in the grass." His eyes held a haunted look, and she knew he was replaying the scene in his head. Reaching out, she put a comforting hand on his knee. He covered her hand with his and smiled lopsidedly. "Louisa walked beside me, but I picked up something odd from her. She *scared* me. I scoffed at myself even though I quickened my stride to match hers.

"I heard her hiss, and she was crouched on the ground. I tried to run. To warn them." He chuckled. "I never stood a chance. She was on me before I took more than three steps. She slammed me to the ground, and I knew I was going to die...and so were they. The last thing I saw before her teeth ripped into my neck was Elijah and Amelia, kissing and whispering words of love. They looked so *happy*." His words drifted off as he stared into space. His eyes focused on hers once more, and they held a sad and angry tone to them she'd not before seen him have. She realized he looked more like Elijah than ever before.

"I have no idea what happened after, but I heard the screams. I knew she'd gotten them. She killed Amelia, but me and Elijah, she…bit. I guess she thought it would be funny if he had to live eternally with a brother who despised him." He smiled in a mocking manner, and she squeezed his hand in an attempt to reassure him.

"So, you're a…vampire?" she whispered.

"Nope, I'm not. Elijah is. I am an even weirder freak of nature. There are very few of my kind. We were chosen to be a group of the elite. The elite monsters, what a joke." He chuckled coarsely. "We're called Enforcers. Believe it or not, all the mythical creatures you've heard of do exist: werewolves, vampires, shifters.

"Well, we are the top of the food chain, so to speak. We attempt to protect humans by eliminating the dredge of all immortals. If I need to fight a vampire, I get those powers. The same goes for the other creatures. I'm all of these monsters, in one neat package. But, Sabrina, Elijah *is* a vampire. He could kill, crush, or bite you, and you couldn't do a thing to stop him. I got taken down by a tiny woman. Picture that. Imagine how strong they must be. You can't trust him, not even for one measly second," he pleaded.

She ignored his pleas for a more pressing question on her mind. "How? How do you get chosen to be an Enforcer?"

"They look at the time you died. Were you pure of heart? Or doing things that don't match their values? Are you willing to put your life at risk to save others, or do you care only for your own wants and desires? Since I died trying to save Elijah and Amelia—even in the face of such a betrayal—the Council deemed my moral qualities upstanding. Therefore, I am an Enforcer.

"Whereas people like Elijah, who died betraying his brother, are deemed beneath their notice, and therefore become whatever monster they are doomed to be. In Elijah's case, a vampire."

"So, if you die while helping someone, you are automatically an Enforcer?" she questioned in confusion. "If so, there should be a lot of you around."

"Not as many as one might think. They don't just look at the moment of your death. They look at your whole life. From the time you were a child to the time you die. It's not a split-second decision. It isn't even up to the Enforcers. It is up to the Council."

"The council?" she squeaked.

"Yes. There's a judge's panel, of sorts, although no one's ever seen them. Or will. But, we all answer to them. And by us, I mean the Enforcers. They decide who's worthy, and who isn't, and we're sent by their orders to 'collect' them."

"Is the order sent by carrier pigeon?" She fought back the urge to burst into hysterical laughter. Un-freaking believable.

"Don't be silly." He grinned. "They're too unreliable. By owl, of course."

"Seriously?"

"Seriously," he assured her.

"Holy crap." She breathed deeply. "How in the world do they figure it out so fast whether you are worthy or not? I assume they don't have warning you're going to die?"

He raised an eyebrow. "Out of all the stuff I told you, you question *timing*, and only timing?"

"Well, it seems a bit of a rushed decision," she argued as she blushed. "But I see your point. If all this other crap is possible, why question the how, huh?"

"Right." He chuckled. "Anyway, my job is to kill all the monsters walking alongside humans like you. Monsters like Elijah," he emphasized.

"Oh, my God. So if you see him, you have to kill him? That's *horrible*." He was duty-bound to kill his brother? This didn't seem fair at all. No matter what he had done, Elijah was still his brother. He couldn't desire his twin's death *that* much.

Right?

"Yes, if ever I see him, I'd be duty-bound to kill him. Or to try, at least. He's very fast and strong. Even with my powers, it's not an easy fight. And even worse, if Elijah knows you're here, inevitably Louisa will know as well. I've been hunting her throughout this life and have yet to catch her. She's cunning. Dangerous. She'd think nothing of killing you again. Trust me."

Stillness came over her as his words clicked in her head. A beautiful woman who would want to kill her....

Her horror must have been written on her face, for he grabbed her hand and squeezed it gently to get her attention.

"What? What is it, Sabrina? Have you *seen* her?"

"Yeah, in my dream," she whispered. "She had long red hair, and brown eyes. Elijah fought her off by throwing a tree at her. It was the dream I had the night you were here. She kept trying to get to me, but Elijah wouldn't let her. Now I know why." She shuddered as she remembered the woman—Louisa—trying to get to her, desperate to kill her again. Great, so now she had a jealous vampire who wanted her dead, too?

So to sum it up, she was dating an Enforcer, who was required to kill his brother—who *happened* to want her—and had a jealous fiancée who wanted nothing more than to see her dead?

How had this become her life?

"Shit. I'd worried this would happen. I've been watching, but haven't seen her. At least Elijah protected you."

This time.

"So you believe, both of you, I'm Amelia"—she put a hand to her chest "—reincarnated or something? Or I bear a striking resemblance to her? Is it even possible, to be the same person, reborn?" The condescension in her tone rang clear even to her ears, but she couldn't help it.

"I believe anything to be possible. I've seen it *all*. And yes, I think you are she. I'm sure Elijah feels the same."

Her mind reeled, but she had too many questions to linger. Shock would have to wait until later. Way later.

"Can you be hurt by these creatures? What do you eat? Are you immortal?"

He stopped her by pressing a finger to her lips. "Slow down, honey." He laughed. "Yes, I can be killed. When I change into one of them, whichever I'm fighting, I'm as susceptible to death as they are. But it's not an easy task to kill my kind. There are different ways to kill different species. Vampires, for example, need to be decapitated and thrown into salt water. It eats away their skin. If you don't do both those steps, they come back to life. Werewolves go down when shot by silver bullets and burned in fire. But, when I'm in front of you, like this, as a human, I'm one in every way.

"The only way I differ from you is you can't kill me. In human form, if I got hit by a train, I'd get up and walk away after a short break to recover. Run over? I'd heal almost immediately. Shot? My body absorbs it. The only way to kill me is if I am one of them. Then, I'm vulnerable.

"As far as food—well, you already know I eat normal food. When I phase, however, I take on the tendencies of the creature I become. If I'm a vampire, I thirst for blood. As a werewolf, I hunger for meat. I become that creature, and act as such." He paused to await any questions she might have about his last statements.

"All those things are *real?*" she asked incredulously. It made sense that if Elijah and Isaac were real, the rest would be, too. But come on, man. All the things kids were terrified of, the things that went bump in the night, really did exist?

"Yes, everything you've heard of, and some you haven't."

"What do you mean 'some I haven't'?"

"Shines, mongrels, fourwers—"

"Okay, enough. *Way* too much information. I don't even know what the heck those are." She held a hand up when his mouth opened. "And don't need to know right now. Maybe I'll never need to know." She shuddered. "Let's get back on track. Why not stay an Enforcer to battle these…creatures? If you are, as you say, immortal as an Enforcer?"

"When I've changed into one of them, I'm faster, stronger. My reflexes are improved greatly. It makes it possible for me to beat them. As an Enforcer, while unable to die, I'm not as strong, nor as quick. I'm also susceptible to human weaknesses, such as being knocked unconscious. Not a good thing in a battle."

Okay, that, at least, made sense. "Have you ever, as a vampire—?" She stuttered to a halt, scared of his answer.

"No, I've not bitten anyone. If I do, there's a hefty price to pay. If I succumb to my beastly desires, I'm cursed to remain that creature for all my days, and in turn will be hunted down and killed. So, you see, I can't afford to be weak."

"Elijah, as a vampire, does he…act like one? I mean, kill people?" She shivered as she pictured Elijah jumping out at an unsuspecting old woman walking down the road.

The now familiar ice-mask he wore when he no longer liked the subject at hand reappeared when she mentioned Elijah's name, and she cringed. Her inquisitive writer's mind had to be getting the best of her. Perhaps she shouldn't ask about Elijah.

Gee, do you think?

But she needed to know every detail about his amazing life. It felt so new and incredible.

"Yes, he *acts* as a vampire and drinks blood, though he tends to stay away from people. He has, on occasion, weakened and succumbed to his desires. But he mostly feeds off of wildlife and blood banks. He doesn't change into a bat or anything, and sunlight doesn't bother him, either. Elijah does, however, hate garlic. It will keep him away from your blood."

"Crucifixes?" she asked.

"Hates them, especially gold ones. Gold burns vampires."

"Gold? I thought silver hurt them."

"A myth they put about to make everyone steer away from gold," he stated as he shook his head. "It worked, too."

"Son-of-a-bitch," she grumbled. "I need to get a gold crucifix."

"It won't stop Elijah, or Louisa. It's merely an annoyance for ones who are as strong as they are. They'd rip them off and heal right away. They're most effective on newborns."

"Well, there goes my grand plan. At least he hates garlic, since I happen to love it."

"That doesn't, I repeat, doesn't make him safe or *trustworthy*. Sometimes, no matter how much a vampire tries to be good, he just can't resist the lure of human blood—garlic or no garlic. I'll be honest and say there are ones who succeed in resisting their animalistic nature. Elijah is one of them, and as such, he's not high on our list of targets. But if I were to come across him, it would be different."

She nodded, accepting the warning for what it truly meant: *stay away from Elijah, or I may run across him and have to kill him.* She didn't want to put *any* of them in that position. Isaac had been trying to protect her, and in some twisted way his brother, all along. Her suspicions at his secrets faded away.

He hadn't spoken to her about it before because he'd feared to turn her away. Plain and simple.

"If you came across him and let him go, what would happen?"

"Theoretically, if no one knew, nothing would happen. But if I were caught doing such a thing, I'd be tracked down and killed, like any other target of ours."

His eyes glittered like ice, and she could almost hear his teeth gnashing together. "Did you find him earlier?"

"No, he'd already left and I didn't follow his trail. I wanted to come here to explain this whole mess to you."

"Can I ask another question, about Elijah?" She hated making him mad, but she had *one* last question. At his nod, she continued. "When I talked to him, he told me he couldn't tell me what he is. Not wouldn't, but couldn't. Why? Did I misunderstand his words?"

"No, you understood. Just as my kind have their sets of rules, so do his. He's not allowed to tell anyone of his existence, unless it's a person he's about to change. Or a person about to become his dinner, neither of which you are. Or *ever* will be."

It would be impossible to miss the proprietary tone in his voice, or the warning he gave. She belonged to him and him alone. That didn't sound too bad, even if he were some kind of freak of nature.

She'd never been normal anyway.

"Oh. I-I see."

Staring off into space, she wondered what had happened in the meadow after Isaac had lost consciousness. Elijah had said he had killed Amelia, but had he really? Or did he blame himself for his weakness?

Isaac believed her to be Amelia reincarnated. It could be possible, she supposed. She'd been drawn to this area, and God knew she'd become obsessed with Isaac. And, to be honest, to some extent she felt drawn to Elijah as well. They were like two incredibly hot magnets, pulling her in opposite directions.

But she couldn't deny it any longer; Isaac's pull was stronger. And would win, hands-down.

"You've been quiet for a while now. Are you okay? Got any more questions for me?" He smiled playfully at her.

"Um, yeah. Tons. So many I can't even sort them out to make sense." She massaged her temples and flinched at the headache rapidly gaining strength. "You said you change into the creatures you fight. Do you have to become a werewolf to fight a werewolf, or can you fight a werewolf as a vampire?"

"I can become whatever I feel I need to be to win the fight. More often than not, I morph into the same species. It makes sense." He shrugged his right shoulder, and then rubbed his head. It left his hair sticking up in places, looking delightfully mussed. Sabrina yearned to run her fingers through it. She reached out to touch his soft waves and jumped when a pounding on the door broke into their conversation. Before she could even hop to her feet, Isaac stood at the door, swinging it open.

Would she *ever* get used to how fast he moved?

Probably not.

All thought left her as she caught sight of their visitor. The man was huge, at least six-and-a-half feet tall. He had to be a bodybuilder or something, judging by the bulging muscles straining underneath the black skin on his biceps. It didn't even look like he could *fit* through the door.

Yikes.

"I smell a mongrel." He scrunched his nose as if disgusted. "I'd say it's close by, no more than a mile. It must be looking for—" He threw a meaningful glance in her direction, and finished, "dinner."

Isaac tensed, looking torn. She could tell he couldn't decide whether to stay here, or to go after the mongrel. "Please, Isaac, I'll be okay. Go. I'll stay inside. I promise." She met his eyes, eager to show him she told the truth.

After all, she didn't have a death wish, and she could do without seeing this 'mongrel', thank you very much.

He rushed to her side and grabbed her arms. "I'll get him. Connor will stay here to watch the house. He won't let anything by."

She had no trouble believing *that*.

"Be careful, Isaac." Even knowing his strength, her heart dropped to her stomach at the thought of him chasing a dangerous...*whatever* it had been called. He grabbed her face and kissed her, leaving her clinging to him in need. But unfortunately, the kiss was brief. He had a mongrel to kill.

She staggered when he released her, and she didn't miss the smug smile on his face as he vowed, "I'll return soon."

You better.

She bolted to the window to watch him jog away. Wait, why could she still see him? She knew for a fact he could move faster than the human eye could see. His pants hit the ground, and she caught a glimpse of bare buttocks before he disappeared in a cloud of smoke.

Well, duh, mongrels didn't run around in clothes. Whatever the hell a mongrel was.

A mongrel turned out to be a huge freaking beast that stood eight-feet tall and had long, black fur. The fur didn't look shaggy or coarse, surprisingly: in fact, it looked silky. He stood on his hind legs, sniffing the air. Catching the scent of his prey? She shivered at the sight. These beasts were out there, and humans were none the wiser.

It horrified her.

Isaac took off into the woods, and she rested a hand on the window pane, silently wishing him luck. Studying the empty spot he had left, she headed to the door to collect the clothes scattered about the lawn. A form stepped into her path, and she shrieked in surprise. Holding a hand to her racing heart, she gaped at the face looming over her.

Oh, right. The giant man Isaac had left behind to guard her. How had she forgotten about *him*?

What had Isaac called him? Connor?

"I'm sorry. I forgot you were there...." She let her voice trail off, seeking his name.

He smiled. "Connor."

"Connor. Right. I'm Sabrina. Nice to meet you." She held out a hand to him, and he shook it. Oh God, her hand disappeared inside his—like a newborn baby and its father.

Yikes.

"I know who you are. I've been here the past few days, keeping an eye on things."

"Oh...really? I had no idea." Though it felt a bit unnerving to have a strange man lurking about, it also comforted her. He sure looked like one heck of a man.

"Don't be frightened. Isaac sent me to help keep you safe, not guard you. You're not a prisoner, or anything."

"Well, thanks for keeping an eye on things. I'm gonna go outside and grab his clothes." She gestured at the door and moved toward it. She paused when he blocked her way a second time. She stepped to the side and tried to pass him, but he blocked her way once more. She raised an eyebrow in question.

"I don't think it's a good idea, Sabrina. I'm going outside to keep watch, so I'll gather them for him. You stay inside, okay?"

Well, if that wasn't a contradiction, she didn't know what would be. Not a prisoner, but not allowed outside?

Okay.

"Wait!" she exclaimed. "Can I ask you a question?"

He paused mid-stride, turning to her with a raised brow. "Sure thing, ask away."

"You're like Isaac, right? An Enforcer?"

"Yes, I am." His chest puffed out as he straightened to his full height. How the *hell* did he fit in the house?

"So, why did you come tell Isaac about the problem? Why not run and take care of it yourself? I'm not upset or anything," she hurried to assure him. "Just curious."

"Oh, well as the Ruler, Isaac gets told of all incidents, no matter how minor. Also, he has more powers than any Enforcer. He's faster, stronger, and more capable than all of us combined. So it makes sense he would choose to go, since the mongrel—" Again his nose scrunched in disgust. "Came so close to you."

"The *Ruler*?" Her mind raced as she tried to figure out what that meant. It sounded as if he insinuated Isaac was a leader of some sort. And Isaac certainly hadn't mentioned being in charge of anything. Or anyone.

Connor stiffened imperceptibly at her question and cursed under his breath. "I'm sorry, but I have to go outside. If you have questions, please ask Isaac." The door slammed shut behind him, leaving her accompanied only by the unanswered questions filling her mind.

Chapter Seven

*L*ouisa lurked close-by. Elijah smelled her stench. Well, she didn't *actually* smell bad, but to him, it reeked of evil. Since scaring off Sabrina, he'd been following Louisa across the country, in a game of cat and mouse, one he didn't like to play. She, however, loved having his undivided attention.

Sick bitch.

He'd been trying to kill her for years. No matter how fast he ran, she always escaped due to her gift, her ability to see the future. Not the distant future, but she saw the world five seconds ahead of the rest of them, in her own unique time zone.

In battles, it proved to be an invaluable tool to have. She'd be dead by now—by his hand—if she hadn't been blessed with such a gift. Instead, she lived to watch him suffer in the hell she'd put him in. She laughed as he resisted blood and mocked him in his feeble attempts to remain more human than monster.

And Isaac being an Enforcer thrilled her to no end. She never missed an opportunity to gloat over it. He skidded to a halt when her trail disappeared.

Where the heck did she go?

"Hello, Elijah. Lovely to see you. What brings you to see me on this glorious day?"

Following her voice, he located her on the highest branch of the tree overhead. She always hung around in trees. He wondered fleetingly if she had been a cat in her previous life. *Hah, more like a lion.* Her eyes glittered in the sunlight, and she smiled in the face of his frustration.

He growled in return before replying. "You know why I'm here, Louisa. Leave her alone. She's done nothing to you. Take your anger out on me. *She* is innocent."

Louisa dropped to the ground in front of him and tossed him through the air. He slammed into a nearby tree and slid to the ground. He leapt to his feet, ready to defend himself.

"Take your anger out on me," she mocked. "Amusing, I know I've heard similar words before. The memory escapes me, though. Oh, where have I heard it? Hmm…." She tapped her finger against her chin as if she strained to remember. Her eyes focused on him, and he glared in return. "Oh, silly me. It was from you as I broke your little harlot into pieces in front of your very eyes. Such a delightful day, too." She cackled.

Anger consumed him, causing him to rip a nearby tree out of the ground and throw it at her. Futile effort at best, but that didn't stop him.

He *despised* her.

She sidestepped it before continuing. "Now, now Elijah. Don't be a poor sport. You'll ruin my fun. And I'm so looking forward to breaking her apart again."

He roared and lunged for her. His arms sought for purchase, but met thin air. He crashed to the ground and rolled to his feet. Though he lacked the ability to outthink her, he didn't lack the ability to *outrun* her. He effortlessly caught up to her and knocked her face first on the ground. She snarled while she fought to free herself, and he howled in satisfaction as he grasped her head in one hand and her neck in the other. Just before he had the chance to rip her head off, she managed to free herself by kicking him in the balls.

Vampire or not, *that* still hurt like hell.

Son of a bitch.

Not allowing the pain to rule him, he leapt to his feet, only to have them swept out from under him. He landed on the ground, and his head slammed on a tree root.

This time, the pain ripped through him intensely enough to cause him to lie motionless for a split second, allowing her to disappear into the woods.

He didn't give chase.

છ

Isaac studied the mongrel as it followed Sabrina's scent. Thunder crashed above even though the sun beat down on his thick fur. Sabrina adored being outdoors, much like Amelia had, and could easily stumble upon this monstrosity and become its meal. She'd stand no chance against the thing as it jumped on her, gnawing her limbs from her body.

He leapt on the unsuspecting beast in sheer fury. How *dare* he hunt Sabrina?

He wasted no time dismembering the creature, devouring the chunks whole. He swallowed a paw before pausing to break the leg bones using his massive teeth. Once only the torso remained, he slowed his pace.

The tender muscle always tasted the best, and he savored the flavor of his enemy. To kill a mongrel, one must eat every last piece, or else they'd simply regenerate. Afterward, he lounged in the sunlight. Shifting too soon after a meal would give him a hell of a stomachache, so he forced himself to enjoy the feel of the breeze ruffling his fur.

When he had become an Enforcer, his stomach and mind had rebelled against the very nature of the mongrels, more so than any other monster. He had to *eat* the creatures, bones and all. But during his first battle, he'd discovered he thought like a mongrel when in their form, and therefore could enjoy the task. In human form, however, he tried to not dwell upon his dining habits in his alternate forms.

Hopefully, it would be something he'd never be forced to tell Sabrina, either. It would be enough to send any sensible girl running for the nearest airport. Although Sabrina, he snorted, had proved less than sensible so far. She'd be far too brave to be scared by a beast.

She liked *him*.

Nonetheless, he'd rather keep this part of his job hidden from her.

93

Just like he wouldn't tell her that he was technically a king. Telling her of his position might scare her off as no monster could. Loving him would take a big commitment on her part. And she *would* love him.

Glancing at the disappearing sun, he lumbered to the nearby stream to bathe before returning to Sabrina's house.

Isaac dressed hurriedly, thankful Connor placed the garments in an easy-to-find spot. He preferred not to wander around the woods naked for *too* long. Appreciative he had worn a sweater today, he pulled it over his head and shivered.

God, it was cold.

He entered Sabrina's lawn, noticing the whole house had remained cloaked in darkness. Had she gone to bed already? If so, would the door be locked or open in anticipation of his return?

"Everything go okay, sir?" he inquired. Isaac had been so preoccupied worrying over his welcome, or lack thereof, he hadn't even heard his approach. Luckily, it was friend and not foe.

"Yes, the beast is dispatched. How did the night go?" he asked. Connor paled before looking away guiltily, and Isaac tensed. "What happened? Is Sabrina okay? Did Elijah come back? Tell me, now."

"If you'd stop asking questions, I *could*!" he exclaimed. His eyes widened when he realized he had yelled at his ruler, and he met Isaac's glare a bit more hesitantly than before. "I mean...yes, sir. Sabrina asked why you chased the mongrel, instead of me. I got caught off guard, so I told her it only made sense you would go yourself, seeing as you are the ruler." The last word drifted off into nothing as Connor stared at his feet.

Isaac's angry hiss made him snap to attention.

"I'm sorry, I thought she knew." He shrugged his shoulders and dug his hands into his pockets before rocking back sheepishly on his heels.

Isaac stared up at the moonless sky while attempting to rein in his frustration. Connor hadn't known what he'd already told Sabrina. He couldn't be too angry. Sabrina could make a man confess his every sin by batting her eyelashes over her emerald eyes. "It's okay. But it means there will be more questions to answer tonight. Ones I'd been hoping to avoid. Stay outside and watch for any disturbances. Let me know if anything happens."

Connor nodded, and Isaac went inside.

Testing the knob, pleasure rolled through him when he found it unlocked. Since the whole house lay bathed in darkness, he crept up the stairs to her room, eager to see her even if she'd fallen asleep. He could watch her sigh in her sleep, her face unguarded in deep slumber. Unless Elijah interrupted, anyway.

He halted as his heart lurched painfully in his chest and stopped beating altogether as he examined the empty bed. Maybe she huddled in the middle? He ripped the covers back and growled when he found the bed empty. The mattress felt cool to the touch, which meant she'd been gone for quite some time.

He sprinted down the stairs and went straight to the front door. Had Elijah taken her? Or even worse, Louisa? Had she broken her promise and left, leaving herself vulnerable to attack?

Or had she simply left him, out of disgust?

His hand on the doorknob, he stopped. If he were Sabrina, would he go to bed, or stubbornly try to stay awake to greet him, no matter how tired he might be?

He crept into the living room and peered at the couch. Sure enough, there she lay. A cold mug of coffee, filled to the top, rested on the table near her head. She seemed to have fallen asleep before she could drink it. It warmed his heart she'd tried to wait up for him, even though she'd been exhausted. But it also terrified him.

He collapsed into a nearby chair as a swell of emotions overcame him. He knew he loved her. For him, that much had been a given from their very first meeting.

But he hadn't realized the sheer power she held over him, nor how much he needed her. His eyes took in every precious detail about her. From the way she lay on her side with her legs curled up against her chest, to the gentle sweep of eyelashes against porcelain skin. He reached forward to brush her soft cheek and his fingers came away wet.

Had she cried herself to sleep? What other reason would her eyelashes be wet? Allergies?

And more importantly, if she indeed had cried...why? Because she worried about him, or because she couldn't stand being with someone like him?

His heart lurched at the thought. Cursing under his breath, he leaned in to kiss her forehead. Her lids slowly fluttered open, and her sleepy green gaze met his.

"I'm sorry, Sabrina," he whispered. Confusion crossed her features until he ran a finger over her cheek.

"No, don't be." She let out a big yawn and her eyes drifted shut.

He shook his head and leaned over her to scoop her into his arms and up the stairs. Though she stirred when he picked her up, she quickly relaxed once he assured her he was only carrying her to bed. She let out a soft snore, and he glanced down in surprise. He bit his lip to keep his laughter at bay, barely succeeding.

She'd just *love* to know she snored in front of him.

He laid her in bed and gently placed the covers over her body. He saw something black sticking out from under the pillow and reached underneath. He chuckled as he retrieved the huge butcher knife. She apparently slept armed now. He rolled his eyes and put it on the table next to her bed. Still within reach, but he didn't need to worry about her hurting herself in her sleep. After casting one last longing look at her, he spun on his heel and headed for the door.

He planned on spending the night. Downstairs, of course.

"Why are you always taking my knife?" she grumbled. He turned to see her leaning on her elbow, her long hair cascading to the mattress beneath her. Did she know how tempting she appeared? How much she tortured him by making him stay in the same room, when he couldn't do a damn thing to ease his hunger? Her face was softened by sleep, and her hair tousled as if he had been running his fingers through it.

"I didn't take it. I moved it somewhere safer. It's right next to you, still in arm's reach." He gestured to her table, and she followed his movement before pinning her gaze back on him. Her eyes glowed in the moonlight. He bit back a groan and shifted on his feet.

"Well, good night."

"Please, stay," she whispered. He made it to the doorway, only to stop at her words.

His heart lurched in his chest at the words she spoke, and the feeling behind them. To his ears, it seemed like she asked him to stay by her side *forever*.

No, only his foolish heart imagined hearing what it so longed to hear. Nothing more, nothing less.

Idiot.

He returned to the bed and cupped her face in his hands. "I am. I'll be on the couch. I'm not leaving."

She shook her head. "No, please stay here. In my bed."

Surprise racked over him at her words, followed by a jolt of lust so strong he thought he might double over from it. He wasted no time removing his shirt and smiled as he noted her swift intake of breath.

It seemed only fair she be as turned on by him as he was by her.

Climbing into bed, he saw the desire burning in her eyes and fought down the answering surge in him. He grew hard as she scooted back against him, her soft buttocks teasing his erection. She wouldn't turn him away if he persisted, but he knew now wouldn't be the right time for seduction. She'd been worn down by exhaustion. He couldn't take advantage of her.

No matter how much he longed to rip her clothes from her body and bury himself inside her welcoming warmth.

Bloody hell, it's going to be a long night.

She tilted her face to his and whispered, "Kiss me."

He swallowed past the lump that appeared in his throat and groaned at the answering twinge in his cock at her words. He'd love to kiss her.

Everywhere.

He almost denied her the affection out of self-preservation, but in the end, the temptation proved too much to bear. He crushed his lips to hers and plunged his tongue possessively into her mouth. He briefly enjoyed the sweet taste of her, scared to allow himself more. He tore away from her addictive mouth, closed his eyes, and counted to three before kissing her nose, and turning her away from him. He buried his face in her hair and smiled as her fragrance washed over him.

Mmm…he could spend at least the next fifty years in her hair. God willing, he would.

A little snore escaped her as he lay beside her, keeping watch.

Chapter Eight

The next morning, Sabrina awoke to see Isaac's blue eyes sparkling as he watched her. Blushing hotly, she smiled before burrowing into his open arms.

Now that was a sight every woman should wake up to.

"Why are you staring at me when I'm asleep?"

"Because I love watching you at any time of day."

"Oh, please. I'm sure I looked mesmerizing with my mouth hanging open." She snorted. "What really happened? Did I snore or something?"

"Of course not! You slept quite peacefully all night long." He was quick to assure her and even shook his head for extra measure.

Perhaps *too* quick. And too emphatic.

"Humph. How'd you sleep?" she asked against his bare chest. His chest hair tickled her nose, but she didn't care. It felt too good to move.

"Wonderful," he quickly said.

"Mmm…me, too. Thank you for staying."

"Anytime."

"I have a question." His groan at her words made her chuckle lightly. "Yesterday when you were gone, Connor mentioned something, and it confused me. He told me you went after the mongrel because as the 'Ruler' it was your right and duty. What did he mean?"

He mumbled something under his breath that sounded suspiciously like feeding Connor to mongrels.

"*Isaac.*"

"It means I am, in a way, a king of sorts. Not by choice, but I have some talents that have relegated me to such. The old ruler had grown corrupt—yes, it happens to Enforcers. We'd hunted him down to exterminate him—"

"You'd kill one of your own just because they were being greedy!"

"It's more than that. He lived the lifestyles of the beasts we hunt. Somehow, he found a Shine who could mask the treachery under a spell, so none would be the wiser. When the Shine got caught, we discovered the truth," he explained.

"What's a Shine? And what happened to it?"

"Picture a witch, but more powerful, and much prettier. They're extremely rare. They've been eliminated one by one. They're evil, cruel creatures. The old ruler should have disposed of her, but instead got lured by her beauty and promises. They became a team. His perfidy became clear when I caught her in his private quarters. We fought, and I won, at the cost of her life.

"Once the spells broke, I realized what had been happening all along, just in time to turn around to ward off his attempt to kill me. He attacked me from behind." His face scrunched up at the memory, and he glowered. "Cowardly move. We fought. I won, and got named ruler. Mostly because I discovered his dirty little secret, and also because I have a special skill. I'm one of the strongest and fastest of my kind, but I also have a gift, or curse, of…weather."

"Weather?" she croaked in disbelief.

"Yes, when I'm angry or upset I can cause storms…thunder, lightning, wind. It can be very dangerous. When I first changed into an Enforcer, I was a menace. Always angry and depressed over having lost Amelia. Tornadoes followed in my wake. Vicious storms took down buildings, and even villages. It devastated me." He put his head in his hands, and his shoulders slumped.

He could control the freaking *weather*? *Wow, just…wow.*

She thought of the fight they had gotten into yesterday, and the crazy storm that followed. The past few days had been unpredictable weather-wise, causing her and everyone else to scratch their heads in confusion.

And it had been him all along. And inadvertently, her.

"Wow," seemed to be all she could say. "Amazing."

He flinched.

"It can be a blessing at times, to be honest. I can make the wind blow a certain way to disguise my scent from the enemy. Or cause a storm in the middle of a fight to help beat my opponent. But at the same time, it's a curse. I can get out of control, if I become too emotional. If I don't keep a tight rein over my feelings, it gets ugly really fast. It can be dangerous to hang around me." He stopped and looked at her. "If you'd like me to leave…if the thought of my powers scare you…."

"No, it's amazing, truly! I don't want you to *leave* me." She threw herself into his arms, and he hugged her. She added silently in her head, *ever.*

"Well, then, just try to get rid of me," he joked.

She pulled away from him and bit back a grin. "Besides, this could totally work to my advantage."

He arched an eyebrow and asked, "Oh? How so?"

"When I'm not sure how you're feeling, all I need to do is look outside. No guessing involved."

He laughed, and she joined in.

"I'm so glad to help out."

"Hey, you men always complain women are moody and impossible to read. I disagree. It's men who are impossible. But this talent of yours can be my CliffsNotes. I won't have to ask if you had a bad day, all I need to do is look out the window," she finished.

He gazed at her so intensely, she asked, "What, what's wrong? Why are you staring at me?" She quickly smoothed her hair.

"Nothing's wrong. You're perfect. Absolutely perfect." He leaned in and kissed her lips before hopping out of bed and heading to the door. "And now, you need to feed me, or a storm might come. I get cranky when I'm hungry—"

"I *need* to feed you?" She scoffed. "Sounds a bit bossy, if you ask me."

He grimaced and nodded. "You're right. But it's proof I'm telling the truth. I'm cranky *already*. How about this? You come down," he offered, "and I'll cook *you* breakfast."

"Hmm...sounds better. And in the interest of being polite, I'll even help."

He beamed at her. "Perfect. A joint effort. I'll head down and get started. Wouldn't want a storm to come."

Eyes wide, she glanced outside, only to see the sun shining. "Humph," she muttered as she followed him hastily out of the bedroom.

ဢ

The next two weeks went by in a blur for Sabrina. Isaac often remained by her side, leaving only for work. Every night he'd return, and they lived a seemingly normal life—despite the fact Isaac couldn't be further from normal. They cooked dinner together every night in her kitchen and spent the evenings sharing their pasts. Though his sounded *much* more interesting, in her opinion. He had such intriguing stories about times she could only imagine. He told her tales of wars, the fights and triumphs of time. It never ceased to amaze her.

There were times when a natural storm came upon them, and she turned to him in her best wide-eyed innocent look, and exclaimed, "What did I do?"

He'd smile at her and say something along the lines of him not being responsible for every storm. Or, he'd teasingly tell her he'd gotten angry because she hadn't kissed him yet, or she buttered his toast wrong, or other such silliness. When nighttime approached, they went to bed and he pulled her into the safety of his arms, and she drifted off to sleep dreamlessly.

Every couple of days, he left to run after one creature or another, and it disturbed her that so many of the mythical creatures existed. Not all of them were nearby, however. Isaac confessed he ran faster than any car drove, and so he often traveled far distances on foot. Even so, he would sometimes delegate someone else to do the battles for him and remain by her side. She preferred the latter option by far, for she no longer liked being without him.

At all.

She'd met quite a few more of his kind over the past two weeks as well. They never ceased to amaze her. There was Derek, who had quite the impressive ability of being able to vanish into thin air. And Scott with similar talents to Derek, but more powerful. He could appear anywhere he wanted, at any time. If he was in France and decided to go to Sabrina's house, he could open his eyes and be there. Isaac later told her he was the second-most-powerful Enforcer.

And Sheila, the only female Enforcer she had yet to meet. Sabrina didn't know how many existed, but got the feeling it happened rarely. Sheila read minds. She focused on one person at a time, but could be very useful in battles. Connor and she often sat together, Sheila trying to read his thoughts as Connor attempted to block her out. They'd laugh at each other's efforts and restart trying to defeat the others talents. Sabrina thought they had something else going on between them, but Isaac laughed when she mentioned her suspicions.

"You women are always matchmaking," he'd joked.

&

Elijah watched Sabrina and Isaac cook dinner, and his jealousy felt so overwhelming he almost howled under the sheer force of it. All he'd been waiting for these endless years on his own was a chance at love. A chance to have Amelia in his arms once more.

Instead, he watched as Isaac laughed by her side. Kissed her. And though he hadn't seen it, he supposed Isaac made love to her every night as well. Sometimes he wished the legends about vampires turning into bats were true, for he could fly up to her window and perch there all night long. And Isaac wouldn't be able to do a damn thing about it, either.

It seemed only fair, since Elijah couldn't do anything to stop Isaac from screwing his long-lost love.

Argh…it's maddening!

If only he had gotten to Sabrina first. If Isaac had burned in Hell, instead of him. Or that he, Elijah, were not so broken.

He turned away from the torturous scene of domestic bliss in front of him and melted into the shadows. He didn't want Isaac to see him, or Isaac would come charging out into the night like a mama bear protecting her cubs.

And he didn't feel like a fight. Not tonight. His body felt worn down. Beat.

Yet his exhaustion did nothing to keep the memories at bay.

℞

Nothing warned him. He heard no one approach. One second he lounged happily in Amelia's arms, her skirts around her hips, and he inside her, and the next he flew through the air and crashed against an oak tree.

It swayed from the force of impact, and pain burst over him as his head collided against the rough bark.

What in the world had happened?

He opened an eye, expecting to see Isaac glaring at him. Instead, his fiancée crouched in front of him, taking in every inch of his features.

He groaned and rubbed his forehead. His head hurt like hell.

"Lady Harding? What happened?" He hesitated. How much had she seen?

"We found you and your harlot naked, my lord," she replied.

Bloody hell.

"Where's Isaac? I have to talk to him...."

"What about me? Do you not have to speak to me, as well?"

"Lady Harding, I am immensely sorry. You have to know I never meant for this to happen. We did not plan it—"

"Oh, it had to be an error of judgment, never to happen again?" She smiled slightly.

He did not have time to waste soothing her. He needed to find Amelia and Isaac. He'd tell her as quickly as possible, and find the ones he really cared about.

Surprised to see the anger cross her face before he spoke, he faltered and said, "No, my lady. We love each other, and she will be my wife. Surely, things might be tough for a while, but I am certain we can work out something to help soothe over the legalities of such a match."

He broke off when she snarled, and his heart stopped in his chest.

Bloody hell.

He stared at her in astonishment when she lifted him by the throat, his feet dangling in the air. He pulled at her hands using all his strength, frantically trying to breathe, but she didn't budge.

He kicked her in the chest, and she didn't flinch. He tried again—harder—in the stomach.

She bloody well laughed in his face.

"Wrong answer, Lord Stirling."

She threw him through the air, and he crashed into the ground, the thud filling his ears hurting him almost as much at the compact had.

This had to be a dream. A hallucination.

Maybe when he hit the tree earlier, he'd lost consciousness and this would all turn out to be a nightmare. Yes, that had to be the case. For none of this could be real.

He sat up cautiously, looking for any sign of Louisa. Instead, he saw something that caused his heart to stop beating, and painfully accelerate in his chest—all at the same time. Next to him lay Isaac, with his neck twisted at an unnatural angle, and unseeing eyes.

Crying aloud, he bolted to Isaac's side. "Isaac, blast it to all hell...Isaac. Answer me. You cannot be dead, oh God no. Please, no." A frantic sob escaped him, and Elijah hurried to check for a pulse.

Thank God, he felt a slight pulse against his fingers. Weak, but there. He needed to get Dr. Hamilton right away.

But what happened? Why did he lie there with open eyes and a beating heart?

His neck...it had looked strangely twisted, hadn't it?

He carefully probed the right side of Isaac's neck, and finding no injuries, moved onto the left. He gasped when blood gushed onto his fingers and leaned in to get a better look.

Bloody hell...there were two perfect puncture wounds on the side of his neck, oozing blood and foaming white pus.

What the hell could it be?

Louisa. Could she be some form of a demon? One that fed off men?

No, it couldn't be possible. Those things didn't exist.

He needed to escape her immediately.

"Isaac, I'm going to get you out of here. I will get you help, I promise." A thud sounded behind him, and he whirled. Louisa lounged

against a tree a few feet away, looking as if she had not a care in the world.

Heartless traitor.

"I apologize for our late arrival. We had a wee bit of difficulty rousing ourselves." She sent a pointed glance at his feet. Elijah followed her gaze, only to freeze in horror.

Amelia lay at his feet, struggling to breathe. A trickle of blood ran out of her mouth and down her cheek, and blood crept from her swollen nose.

"Help," she whispered.

ം

Sabrina walked Isaac to the door, her body tightening in anticipation for the kiss she knew would come. Expecting the usual sweet goodbye kiss, she got surprised when he gripped her and led her back against the wall in one smooth motion. He melded his body to hers and rubbed his erection against her. Hot desire pulsated through her, and she wrapped her legs around his hips, desperate for more contact. They groaned in unison at their heated embrace, and Sabrina tugged at his shoulders.

She wanted him inside her. Nothing felt more important to her at this moment than being filled by Isaac as he plunged into her.

His hands skimmed her legs, tracing a molten path to her buttocks, and he pulled her even tighter against his body. She moaned in pleasure as his hands followed an invisible path from her hips to her breasts. He cupped them and rolled his thumbs over her swollen nipples. She moved wantonly against him and threaded her fingers through his hair, seeking something to hold onto so she wouldn't dissolve from desperation.

A boom of thunder exploded overhead, and he tore his lips away from hers. He leaned his forehead against hers as they attempted to calm their raging bodies and catch their breath. She moaned huskily and moved again. Satisfaction coursed through her when he moaned and moved against her.

Maybe...just maybe...they didn't *have* to stop.

He seemed to think otherwise, though, for he put a firm hand on her hip to stop her tempting movements. "I better get control of myself before I attempt this again. I'd hate to have a tornado come and rip us apart while we were…um…busy."

She looked at him in surprise, and her mouth dropped open in shock.

"Has that happened before?" She immediately regretted her impulsive question. Did she *really* want to hear about his sexual exploits?

He flushed and refused to meet her eyes as he muttered, "I wouldn't know."

"What?" she whispered.

"There's been no one else since Amelia. No one else could tempt me, or even interest me. Believe me, I tried." Isaac gave a shrug of his shoulder and grimaced as he spoke. He studied the wall at some random spot over her shoulder. When she stared at him in silence, registering his words, he adjusted his tie, fixed his hair, and then hers. All in a ten-second span.

And he didn't look at her eyes once. He obviously didn't enjoy admitting his lack of sex life. Who could blame him?

Well, Sabrina, I haven't had sex in over a hundred years. No pressure, or anything.

And she thought it had been a long time for her. Yikes. She put a finger on his chin, lifting his face to hers. He studied her jawbone as if it held some secret code he alone could crack.

"Look at me." She commanded him when he did not remove his gaze from her jaw line. "You have nothing to be embarrassed about. Got it?" She kissed his nose, mimicking the gesture that never failed to melt her heart. "But until we figure this out, maybe you should put me down." She grinned playfully and leaned her head on his shoulder in a warm embrace. He rubbed her head and pulled her closer as he kissed her curls, and she fought the urge to wrap her arms around him even tighter in direct contradiction to her words.

He sighed and gave her one last kiss before he unwound her legs from his waist. She didn't realize she still clung to his neck until he removed her arms, and chuckled. "Need help standing?"

Her cheeks flushed, and she glowered at him even as she leaned against the wall. Her knees were so weak she worried that not even the wall would be enough to save her from an embarrassing fall. He laughed in delight at her lack of composure, and the glare she shot him *should* have made him collapse into a pile of ashes.

She must have overestimated the strength of said glare, because his smile widened even more.

"If you're done mocking me, you may go now."

"I'm sorry." He rushed out the door and shut the door firmly behind him. She didn't need his superhuman powers to hear him snickering on the other side as he walked away. She smiled in amusement at his laughter. On anyone else, it would have come across as cocky. On him, however, it seemed picture-perfect.

Damn him.

ৰী

A few hours and a lot of written pages later, Sabrina sipped her coffee. She'd been productive, sure, but her mind never seemed to stray from Isaac for long.

Well, that hardly counted as top news. He had been a constant in her life since the first dream. Her body quivered as she thought about the kiss they'd shared earlier, the pure intensity of the embrace. Things had never gotten so heated between them as they had today, and Sabrina knew the time had come to take the next step. Though he slept by her side every night, holding her close to his delicious body, they had yet to seal the deal.

But, God, she loved when he kissed her and held her. She loved when he smiled, she loved—*him.*

Sitting straight, she choked on her coffee. Her hand flew to her throat as she coughed and struggled to breathe, but even while not breathing, she knew it to be true. She'd fallen in love. It didn't surprise her a lot, really. He was the impeccable man, in almost every way. Hell, in every way. Who was she trying to fool, anyway?

She suspected, as well, that he loved her. And once she got over the shock of the realization, and the ensuing choking, really, it felt quite, well, *perfect.*

Now, she had only to tell him. Excitement coursed through her as she planned the evening in her head…strapless black dress, candles, red wine, and steak. Add in some red lingerie underneath and satiny-smooth skin would, hopefully, be too much for him to bear. And the *coup de grace*: telling him of her love.

It would be flawless.

A knock at the door pulled her from her fantasy, and she walked to the foyer in a daydream-filled daze. Isaac wouldn't knock, so it must be Connor. She yanked the door open, gasping in surprise.

Nope. *Definitely* not Connor.

Chapter Nine

The shock must have been clearly written on her face, because her sister asked, "Surprised?"

"Uh…yeah. Marie, why didn't you tell me you were coming? Not that I'm not thrilled or anything, but…*wow*. Are you alone?" She craned her head to look behind her sister, seeking signs of anyone else.

"Yup, it's my last getaway before this little guy comes." She rubbed her rounded stomach fondly as she grinned. Fascinated, Sabrina followed the movement and focused on her sister's familiar face once more.

"Aww. You look great. Come in," she invited, and made a sweeping gesture of her hand. Her mind spun in circles, amazed to see her sister in her house.

"I figured you'd be surprised. I just really wanted to see you, and this house of yours. I must admit, it is as gorgeous as you said. Stunning, even."

"Thanks. Yeah, I love it."

"It looks so isolated, but I saw a neighbor outside. Where are the other houses?"

Oh, don't worry, that's just Connor. He protects me from the evil vampire trying to kill me.

"What did he look like?"

"Black and gorgeous. And unbelievably tall."

"Sounds like Connor. He is…yeah…he's a neighbor." Marie shot her a curious look at the stutter, and Sabrina flinched mentally.

Step up the game, Sabrina. This is Marie, not some stranger who is fooled by a smile.

Deciding to try anyway—what the heck, right?—she smiled. It got her a skeptical look in return.

Crap.

She almost groaned out loud at the mess she'd found herself in. The other Enforcers, besides Connor, would need to stay hidden, and Isaac would have to stop spending the night. The loss of his arms around her would hurt. Heck, it already did.

"So, I assume you are staying here?"

"If you wouldn't mind…."

"I'd have it no other way. I have the *most* comfortable bed. You'll see. I, of course, will take the couch." She held up a hand at her sister's protest. "I insist. My pregnant sister won't be sleeping on the couch. End of discussion."

"We could share—"

"Heck no. Last time you pushed me out of bed!" she exclaimed.

"I was ten," Marie protested.

"Yeah, and you're a lot bigger," Sabrina gestured at Marie's protruding stomach, "and have an extra person inside you. You'll take the bed, I'll take the couch."

"Did you just call me fat?" Marie asked incredulously.

"No, I called you pregnant."

"I show up on your doorstep unannounced, and you give me your bed. I've missed you." She promptly burst into tears.

Ah, the joys of hormones and jet lag.

"Shh…don't cry. You'll ruin your makeup," Sabrina half-joked. If anything would upset Marie more than being called fat, it was smudging her makeup. She pulled Marie into her arms and reached around her sister's stomach to pat her on the back. "There, there now. Everything's fine."

"I'm sorry. I'm such a mess."

"It's okay. I'm sure you're exhausted. Why don't I show you the big, comfortable bed I told you about?" she asked soothingly.

"But I just got here. I haven't seen anything yet."

"Yeah, but if you go nap for an hour or two, you'll be more alert. You'll see so much more, I promise. Your baby needs a rest. Let's go."

"Well, maybe a little nap." Marie spoke through a yawn. She followed Sabrina silently to the bed. Sabrina bit back a gasp when she pulled back the sheets and saw Isaac's black shirt lying on the mattress. She tried to nonchalantly ball it up before Marie noticed the shirt, but failed. Her sister snickered and ripped the shirt from her hands.

"Sabrina Hodges, has a man been sleeping in this bed?"

She lunged for the shirt, but Marie moved it out of reach by holding it above her head. Marie stood five-foot-eight, easily towering over Sabrina. Anger washed over her at the childhood trick. She had hated it then, and hated it *now*.

"Marie, I am not above beating a pregnant woman, I swear," she threatened. Her sister lowered the shirt, smiling apologetically, but raised it before Sabrina could snatch it back. To her dismay, Marie repeated this action three times before she got it back. She glared at her sister as she clutched the shirt to her chest and fought the urge to bring it to her nose to inhale Isaac's scent.

"So, he sleeps here, or what? Don't tell me you're living together already. I know you're smarter than that," Marie stated.

Sabrina knew only one course to her sister's interrogation. Pure denial. "Of course not. He spent the night once, only once. It just so happened to be last night. You *barely* missed running into him."

Marie arched an eyebrow. "Part of the reason I came out here is because I've gotten a bad vibe from you lately. You're always so distracted. You never seem to be listening to me, like you are in your own little universe, or something. I'm worried about you."

Sabrina flushed. Perhaps she had been a bit preoccupied. But certainly it was normal to be distracted when you found out the man you loved was immortal, and loved you over a hundred years ago? *Right?*

She thought so, anyway.

"I'm sorry, Marie. My being unfocused isn't Isaac's fault, though. I've been busy writing, is all. Honestly. You know how distracted I can be when I'm sucked into my writing." *Liar.* "Now get some rest, we'll talk later, okay?"

"Okay, but I want to meet this paragon of a man, and soon," Marie grumbled while climbing into bed.

"Yeah, sure," she replied before closing the door and walking downstairs.

She couldn't help but feel she had just escaped torture as she sat on the couch cradling her head in her hands. She'd missed Marie. God, she had. But now didn't seem like a good time for a visit. Louisa lurked nearby. Close enough for the Enforcers to sense, but smart enough to evade capture.

And to top it off, Isaac would not be able to stay inside to protect them, so it left them even more vulnerable. She'd never hear the end of the tirade Marie would throw her way if she knew he had all but moved in. So, she needed to hide it.

And hide it good, darn it.

She ran to her phone to call Isaac.

"Hello?"

"Hi, Isaac, we have a bit of an issue."

"I'll be there in two minutes," he said in a rush and hung up. She sighed at his quick response and walked outside. She hadn't meant to pull him away from work, but if he'd come on foot—and he probably had—he was already halfway here.

She might as well tell him in person, and maybe get a kiss or two to hold her over. She paced across the walkway for a few steps before deciding to head into the woods for more privacy. She didn't want Marie to overhear them. And besides, Isaac could follow her scent.

She found a cozy clearing and sat on a stone to await Isaac. Not long after, she heard a twig snap behind her, and she jumped to her feet, eager to feel his arms close around her and hold her close. His lips were compressed, and his face shuttered. She stopped in mid-flight to his arms.

"It's okay, nothing's wrong. I just had some bad news."

He didn't seem to hear her, asking instead, "Why are you here, Sabrina?"

"Here? You mean in the woods? I wanted privacy. What's the problem?" she asked in confusion, before an idea dawned on her. "Oh,

God, is there another mongrel loose?"

"No, I'm sorry. I guess I'm a bit paranoid after your phone call. Why do you need privacy?" He quickly changed the subject as he ran his hand through his hair.

Well, he'd obviously been upset by something if he did *that*.

"My sister decided to surprise me with a visit. I have no doubt it's because she wants to meet you, and see what's going on between us. She already found your shirt in my room." Sabrina sighed.

He cringed. "Oh, well this does complicate things. I'm guessing she wouldn't like to see her sister spending every night with a man she just met?"

"No, she wouldn't. She's already given me the third degree about how much time we spend together, and why your shirt is here, etcetera."

"Shit."

"Yeah, shit."

He opened his arms, and she catapulted into their welcoming warmth.

Heaven.

"Do I get to meet this sister?"

"Yes, she already commanded she wants to meet you, and soon." She giggled.

He chuckled in return. "Tonight, or should we wait until tomorrow?"

"Hmm, maybe tomorrow would be better. Make it seem like we didn't already have plans. I'll give her my undivided attention tonight."

"Ugh, I don't like this. Can I at least sneak into your room at night?"

She laughed, and though he sounded like he joked, she knew he didn't. And, God, she wanted to say yes.

"You could try." She waited until his eyes lit up before continuing. "If you enjoy spooning a six-month pregnant woman who kicks."

He groaned dramatically. "The baby or the woman?"

"Both!" She responded.

"So, if she's in your bed, that means you'll be on the couch?"

"Yup. Don't worry, it's a comfortable couch."

"Yes, I remember." He winked. "I *much* prefer the bed, though. So how long will we be forced to be apart? Oh, I sounded mean, didn't I? Let me rephrase: how long will your sister be visiting?"

"I didn't get to ask her yet," she replied. "She was tired, and I wanted to let you know...."

"Ah, well hopefully it will go by fast. No offense or anything."

"But what about Louisa? What if she gets to my pregnant sister?"

"Connor will be nearby, like usual. He'll just have to practice being less visible, is all." He assured her as he gave her a light squeeze. "It's good for him to test his skills sometimes."

She breathed a sigh of relief and burrowed deeper into his muscular chest. "Let's go and get you inside. I'd rather you stayed indoors until we can hunt down Louisa. Maybe tonight I'll work on doing exactly that, since you won't be seeing me until tomorrow." He frowned as his eyes took in every inch of her face.

"I guess it would be a good thing to do. But please, for me, be careful."

He smiled and kissed her nose. "I will. I promise. Nothing will stop me from returning. I want to attempt another experiment when your sister leaves." He waggled his eyebrows, and she giggled.

He'd removed her worries over his safety for now. But she really hated it when he left her.

Really.

∞

Elijah jumped from the cover of the tall tree as Isaac and Sabrina headed back to her house, hand in hand. Watching their intimacy hurt more than he could imagine. Their closeness appeared more than physical. It seemed like they were in *love*.

He hadn't been gone that long, had he?

Isaac planned on leaving tonight. Elijah had heard him say so. He would chase Louisa—just as Elijah had been doing the past few weeks. Elijah wished him all the luck in the world. Lord knew he'd been chasing her shadow the past few days, to no avail.

And while he'd been chasing the bitch, Isaac had been lounging in

Sabrina's arms.

Bastard.

Now, the tables were reversing, and Isaac would be on the chase, leaving him to gather the spoils of war. He loved Sabrina, too. He even loved her enough to let her go if it seemed to be in her best interest. He had yet to be convinced it was, however.

He needed to see her. Soon.

It was unavoidable.

⨯

For purely selfish reasons, Isaac didn't alert Sabrina of Elijah's presence in the clearing. He remained terrified that if she saw him again, history would repeat itself. He didn't know how he would cope if she chose Elijah over him—*again.*

Jealousy alone didn't keep him quiet, though. Elijah posed a danger to her. He'd become a monster, a mockery of a human shell.

Like you're any better?

Well, he didn't want to drink her blood, for starters. He turned into a monster, part of the time. And, hell, part-time would always beat full-time.

Damn it.

If she picked Elijah, she chose to become one of them. A monster. She would also become his enemy, and he'd be forced to hunt them down like the beasts they were.

Kill Sabrina? Over his dead body—which would be easily arranged if he turned traitor. He needed to keep Elijah away from her. And even more importantly, away from *Louisa.* Nothing would stop him from keeping her safe.

Nothing.

Chapter Ten

$\mathcal{M}$arie woke in a much better mood than she'd arrived in, leaving Sabrina relieved. She smiled, laughed, and investigated every square inch of the house excitedly. After seeing the entire house, she asked if they could go for a walk in the woods. The crisp fall afternoon breeze invigorated Sabrina as it whipped through her hair, blinding her each time it covered her eyes. By mid-afternoon, they strolled in companionable silence through the woods.

"You're quiet," Marie commented.

"Am I?"

"Yes. As a matter of fact, you've been quiet for weeks. Ever since you came to England. No, scratch that. You've been quiet ever since you met Isaac. So I could take it in one of two ways. Number one: you're so enthralled by him you can think of nothing else. And as such, are lost in daydream land. Number two: something's wrong."

"Or number three: you're a paranoid pregnant woman who needs to relax," Sabrina teased. "Honestly, Marie, I'm fine. Do I look hurt? Depressed? Obsessed?"

"Hmm. Well, you do look stressed. Like something's bothering you."

"Nothing's bothering me. Now relax and drop it, okay?"

They walked in silence, until she realized they were at the same spot Isaac and she had been earlier. Sabrina paused to look around, suddenly unsure of their position. Something bothered him about this location; she could feel it.

Nothing appeared amiss, though. They were in the forest, but in a spot that looked like it had been cleared, either by man or nature. A bubbling stream ran nearby, making a calming sound. Something tugged at the back of her mind. As if she should *remember* this place.

Sabrina brushed aside her uneasiness and admired the autumn trees turning beautiful shades of red and orange. In the spring, she imagined, the leaves would be a brilliant green, and the ground would be a landscape of budding flowers.

Spotting a fallen tree nearby, she sat down and patted the spot next to her. Marie lowered herself upon the trunk while placing a supporting hand on her stomach. Sabrina sighed and laid her head on Marie's shoulder.

"I know you worry about and love me, but I promise I'm happy. If there were something wrong, you know I'd talk to you," she reassured Marie.

Except about Isaac being an Enforcer, and Elijah being a vampire. Oh yeah, and this other vampire, Louisa, wants me dead because I stole Elijah away from her in another life. And Elijah wants to kill Isaac, and vice versa. But besides that, all is normal.

I promise.

Marie sighed. "Okay, I'll let you off the hook. Part of me feared I'd come here to find you miserable, alone, and ready to come home. Of course, part of me wished it as well," she said shamefacedly. "I miss you, Bree."

She smiled at the use of her childhood nickname before replying, "I miss you, too, sis. I do. But I love it here, and I'm not leaving. I'm sorry."

"Don't apologize. You have every right to be happy. I just want you be careful, too. Don't let this Isaac guy in too far just because you are alone. Don't let him fill a void you feel, simply because you feel it. I know you are not the type to be alone." Marie put a hand up to stop Sabrina's indignant response, and she forced herself to bite back her angry denial and crossed her arms across her chest. "I also know you well enough to know you will latch onto someone you feel is right for you, even if he isn't, because you feel you *should*. So please, keep a distance. Toe the water a bit, before jumping in. For me?"

Sabrina sighed in exasperation before she blatantly lied. "He's not here every day and he's not an obsession or a toy I've acquired. I like him a lot and that's all. Really. I'll even let you meet him."

"Oh, really? When?" Marie perked up and straightened excitedly. Sabrina couldn't tell if she feigned eagerness, or told the truth.

"How about tomorrow night, if he's free? We'll all go out for dinner. I thought tonight you and I could have some time alone," Sabrina explained.

"Sounds perfect to me."

"Good. How long are you visiting?"

"Three days. I leave Friday morning," Marie stated.

"Gotcha." Sabrina sighed. "Well, you ready to head back?"

"Sure. This place is kind of creepy." Marie shuddered.

"You think? I find it peaceful."

Marie snickered. "You have changed. Let's go."

Were the changes really so obvious?

ॐ

Sabrina fought off the butterflies attempting to overrun her stomach. Tonight, Marie and Isaac were going to meet. She knew they would get along great, if Marie let go of her preconceived notions. She also desperately hoped any creatures, be they werewolves or vampires, stayed away. That, she thought as she chuckled, was one side of her life she'd rather her sister not see.

She yawned and rubbed her temples in aggravation. She had tossed and turned on the couch all night long, getting little sleep. Geez, she probably looked like crap. Isaac would think she was a zombie and smite her on the spot. She almost laughed aloud at the thought.

Until she wondered if zombies actually existed.

A knock sounded at the door, and Sabrina—who could feel Marie's eyes studying her every movement—walked demurely to the door to open it. She longed to run into his arms and greet him properly, and see the answering yearning in his blue gaze. It may have been one day spent apart, but it seemed like so much more.

"Come in." She smiled at the mere sight of him. Who knew her happiness could depend so much upon simply being able to set eyes upon a man?

Fascinating.

Her heart raced excitedly, and she felt her cheeks flush with heat.

He stopped at her side to give her a sweet kiss on the cheek and a hand squeeze. "Hello, Sabrina," he whispered in her ear, causing her to tremble.

Gathering her wits about her, she turned to Marie. "Marie, this is Isaac. Isaac, this is my sister, Marie." She swallowed a laugh when she saw Marie staring at him with her mouth hanging open in shock.

Freaking priceless.

Isaac walked over to her and shook her hand.

"Hello, Marie. It's a pleasure to meet you. In the short time I've known Sabrina"—he turned to Sabrina and winked at her over his shoulder—"I've heard so much about you. All good, I promise."

Marie flushed and snatched her hand back. Though Isaac's back faced her, Sabrina would be willing to bet a million dollars he'd just unleashed both dimples upon Marie.

"Nice to meet you, too. I've also heard quite a bit about you. I've been looking forward to meeting you."

Walking to Sabrina's side, Marie snatched her arm. "Shall we?"

"Ladies first," Isaac replied.

"You could have told me he looked so unbelievably gorgeous," she whispered furiously in Sabrina's ear.

She laughed out loud at the anger in her sister's voice.

"Shh," Marie exclaimed. "He'll hear you."

He hears everything we're saying, my dear.

"Okay, okay. Honestly, if I had tried to explain how incredibly hot he looked, I'd have failed miserably. Nothing prepares you for *that*." She made a slight movement of her head, jerking it in Isaac's direction to clarify exactly what she spoke of.

As if it were in question. *Ha.*

"Yeah, well, you could have at least tried."

Sabrina looked over her shoulder at Isaac, only to see him *glowing* with male pride.

"Besides, he's not perfect," she whispered, conspiratorially.

"No?"

She could *almost* hear Isaac lean in closer to them.

"He snores."

೮

In the past few weeks, this restaurant had become a favorite of Isaac's and Sabrina's, and they were seated at their usual table. Soft candlelight flickered on the table and deep crimson curtains hung behind them. The only difference tonight being that they were three, instead of two. Isaac motioned for Marie to order first. She opted for the Chicken Cordon Bleu and Caesar salad.

He arched a brow at Sabrina, and she gave a nod of her head, probably imperceptible to anyone who didn't watch her as closely as Isaac, and closed her menu.

"And the lovely lady and I will each have the filet mignon, baked potatoes, and house salad with French dressing, please. The steaks should be rare, on both." Handing the menus to the waiter, Isaac noticed Marie smirking at him. He glanced at Sabrina in confusion, and she shrugged.

She didn't have a clue what he had done this time. All night long, Marie had been judging him and questioning his every move. She couldn't believe Isaac hadn't snapped yet.

"What, did I do something wrong?"

Marie snickered and replied, "Yeah. Although the gesture is impressive in an old-fashioned kind of way, you ordered wrong." She gloated. "Sabrina eats her steak medium well. You better get the waiter before it's too late."

"Actually, Marie, I've discovered I'm a rare kind of gal," she interjected as she grinned at Isaac. "Why settle for the normal when you can be rare, right, Isaac?"

He laughed wholeheartedly. "Why, indeed."

Marie looked back and forth between them and glowered silently. She muttered something under her breath Sabrina couldn't make out,

123

but no doubt Isaac could. She kicked her sister's shin in an attempt to remind her to be more polite. Marie, ever the drama queen, jumped and yelped loudly. She glared at Sabrina before turning to Isaac with a plastic smile.

"So, Isaac, what do you do?"

"I've been fortunate enough to have acquired a rather large amount of real estate over time. I have several properties spread out here and there, and I rent them out while I am not using them."

"Oh, and what else?" she inquired.

They both froze at her icy tone, neither daring to look at the other.

"I'm not sure I understand your question."

"Well, you can't earn enough to support yourself by simply renting out a few properties. I'm sure you do something *else*, as well."

"Marie, stop it right—"

"No, it's okay, Sabrina," he interrupted smilingly. "I just hadn't understood what she asked me. When I had told you that I own a few properties, I suppose I leaned a bit toward the modest side of my holdings. The land I own would take quite a while to name off. And, I'd rather not, to be honest. I'd come across sounding boastful and arrogant."

"Oh...well...okay...." Marie stammered. Her cheeks flushed, and she took a sip of ice water before settling back in her chair to cross her arms over her chest.

"I also invest in real estate and am always looking for more opportunities. I own a firm that buys, and flips, properties. I'm also involved in an organization that makes sure land stays open in farm areas, and we try to preserve national forests and such. So, I manage to keep myself busy."

"I'd imagine so. You sound like a busy man," she spoke begrudgingly. "I don't know how you've got time to woo Sabrina in-between all of your other commitments."

"Oh, if I didn't have the time, I'd find a way to make some. Your sister is one of a kind."

"Yeah, she is," she agreed. "You know, I'm trying to find *something* not to like about you, and failing." She laughed and met his eyes for the first time the whole night.

He leaned in and whispered with flair, "Well, I've been told I snore."

They all chuckled, and the tension dissipated. The rest of the meal passed minus any hitches, and they were driving home when Marie stated, "Isaac, I'd like to apologize. I know I've been a bit hard on you. I tend to worry about Sabrina, and I want to see her happy. I can see now how much you care for her. So, I just wanted to say I'm sorry."

Sabrina moved forward from her relaxed position against the back seat, straining to listen to the conversation. She'd insisted on sitting in the back, since Marie got carsick so easily.

"There's nothing to forgive. You were protecting your sister. It's an admirable quality to possess."

They stared at each other for a moment and grinned. Sabrina grinned as well.

Now that is what I'm talking about. Everybody getting along. Nothing could ruin this—

"Do sit back, Sabrina. I'd hate for you to strain your neck," Marie said snidely. She giggled, ruining the effect, and Isaac's musical laughter joined in.

Bitch.

Sabrina's smile disappeared, and she pouted as they snickered at her expense. She sat back to stare out the window at the scenery speeding by.

ജ

When they arrived home, Marie winked as she got out of the car. "I'm in need of a bath in your huge tub, so I'm heading straight up. Have a good night, Sabrina. And nice meeting you, Isaac."

"Nice meeting you, too, Marie," Isaac said.

"Night, Marie. I'll be inside in a minute." Sabrina smiled at her sister, who walked to the door and unlocked it. As soon as the door closed, she launched herself into Isaac's waiting arms. He clutched her to his chest and, in an abrupt movement, swung her in a full circle faster than humanly possible.

Oh, right. He wasn't *human.*

She grasped his shoulders and yelped. He chuckled and gripped her hair, giving it a gentle tug so her head tilted toward the starless sky. Her gaze collided with his, and for the first time, she let the love she felt for him show. He drew in a shaky breath, and his eyes darkened.

Unable to resist the temptation any longer, she put her hand behind his neck and tugged until his lips touched hers. Once she felt his breath fanning her lips, she kissed him explosively. Her tongue entered his mouth in a bold movement, and she relished the moan she got in return. Longing shot through her body like molten lava, and, God, she *burned*. Of its own accord, her hand explored his taut body, her fingers trailing across his chest and down his abdomen. She hesitated at his belt buckle before she slid her hand lower to cup his erection. His penis had grown hard, and freaking huge. He pressed against her in encouragement, and she massaged him and let out a breathy moan.

He groaned and moved against her, no longer content to stay still as she had her way. He grabbed her hips and leaned her against the door, wrapping her legs around his hips and pressing against her core in need. She dug her nails into his shoulders, demanding more from him.

She whimpered when he tore his lips away from hers, and he made a tortured sound that sounded inhumane.

"Damn, Sabrina, you pick the most *inconvenient* times to get bold," he teased. His voice sounded husky, and it made her want him even more, if possible.

Crap.

But, unfortunately, he had a point. They couldn't make love on the doorstep while her sister sat inside.

"Sorry," she muttered.

"Me, too. That you had to stop, that is. We could go to my place," he suggested.

Hmm. Tempting.

She'd like nothing more than to go to his house, but knew she shouldn't. Her sister would leave after tonight, and she needed to exercise some control.

"I can't. I should stay with Marie," she said. Regret rang loud and clear in her words, and wind whipped her hair in front of her eyes when he sighed in return. She pushed it away and chuckled. He'd enjoyed himself, if the wind gave any indication.

"Yeah, you're right," he agreed. Yet, even as he did so, he sighed so dramatically that even Marie would be impressed. "Plus, I still have work to do. I have to keep you frail humans safe from the big, bad monsters of the world," he teased. She removed her legs from his waist, and he pulled her against his chest, apparently not ready to let go just yet. His erection pressed against her, and she shivered. The wind whipped around them as she clung to his shirt.

He must have mistaken her shiver for fear, instead of desire, for he soothed, "Don't worry. I'm under control now. And no one's here, just us."

"Did you find Louisa? Or Elijah?"

"I know Elijah's been nearby. I can sense his presence. While hunting Louisa, I found his scent, too. So I think he chased after Louisa, or vice versa. He must have been trying to stop her from harming you. They met up in the forest a few days ago, appeared to have had a fight and separated. I'm not sure where she went, but Elijah headed back this way. I have a gut feeling he's nearby, though. Have you had any dreams?"

"No, none. Just normal dreams. No Elijah or Louisa."

His muscles relaxed under her cheek as he sighed. "Good. I hope it stays that way."

"So, what are you doing tonight?"

"I think I'm going to scout around a bit more, see if I can't pick up a new trail. I'd like to catch up to Louisa." Eagerness added a lift to his words, like a little boy looking forward to his favorite TV show.

Men.

"Can't you just go to bed and watch a movie?" She rolled her eyes heavenward.

His chest shook at his silent laughter. "Sorry, but I *do* have to do my job. Don't worry about me. I'll be fine. I'm more worried about you."

"I'll stay tucked in on my makeshift bed on the couch, safe as can be."

"Now that's a picture I'd like to see."

They both jumped when the door opened and banged against the wall.

"You don't have to stay out there like two teenagers scared of getting caught by their parents while making out. Come in, for God's sakes." Marie's hair looked wet, presumably from the bath she had mentioned going in for, and she'd wrapped herself in a fluffy purple robe. She had no makeup on and held a glass of water in her hand. It became obvious they'd been outside a lot longer than Sabrina had realized.

They both looked at Marie, then back to each other, before breaking out into infectious laughter. "Sorry, Marie. I didn't realize how long we were out here. I should come in, anyway. Isaac was just leaving."

"Yes, I am," he replied smoothly. He shook Marie's hand and brushed his lips across Sabrina's cheek. "Good night, ladies."

She smiled as she watched him trudge his way to the car. His steps were slow and maybe even a little cranky. She knew he hated driving and avoided it as much as possible. He much preferred a more natural way of travelling—running. He would groan when she asked him to drive her somewhere, and she'd always laugh at his disgruntlement.

She turned to see Marie watching her, her eyebrow raised and lips puckered. "Sure you don't want to chase after the car?"

"Oh, shut up already."

They went inside and locked the door behind them. "Did you have to be such a bitch tonight? He's a good guy. I've told you he isn't a loser how many times?"

Marie held her hands up in mock surrender. "Okay, you're right. Take it easy, though. I had your best interests at heart. I had to make sure you aren't falling for the guy out of desperation."

"If nothing else, one look at him can tell you it sure isn't desperation that attracted me to him," she pointed out sarcastically.

"Yeah, I can concede as much." They both laughed, and Marie sobered. "If you had told me how gorgeous he looked, maybe I'd have understood your obsession a little better. And maybe I'd have not come out. He's definitely one of a kind."

"Yup, he is," she whispered. Uneasiness washed over her, and Sabrina tugged on a loose curl. Marie had no idea how true her words were. "But I'm glad you came out. I missed you."

"I missed you, too," Marie said. "You guys are so weird together, though. It kind of freaks me out."

"How are we weird?" she asked. She bit her lip as she awaited the answer. Had Marie, perhaps, picked up on something she shouldn't have?

"When he looks at you, it's like he's known you for years. He seems to know what you're thinking before the thought even crosses your mind. Just like an old married couple, who finish each other's sentences. He's also *very* protective of you. Whenever you move, his gaze follows you to make sure there's nothing new around the two of you that could harm you. If you sigh, his eyes meet yours. If you enter a new room, he positions his body around yours so he's protecting you from all sides. It's like he expects the big, bad wolf to jump out at you and attack." She ended, amusement clear in her voice.

Sabrina got struck speechless. She didn't know what to say to Marie's statement. She hadn't realized she and Isaac were so obvious in their affection toward one another, and she could have slapped herself in the forehead for her ignorance. Of course Isaac watched her like they had been together for fifty years. He'd already lived a lifetime with her—a lifetime cut short by betrayal and murder.

"Well, at least you know I'll be safe around him," she joked.

"I have no doubt about it. I think he would manage to catch the big, bad wolf and tear him to pieces using his bare hands. And you look at him like he's the only thing that matters in your life. But, what I wonder is *how*? It's been a few weeks. Why is it like this, and so soon?"

"He's a good guy," Sabrina said in defense. Her sister was way too intuitive for her own good. Thank the Lord she would be leaving tomorrow.

"He's a good guy, yeah. But is that a reason to look at him as if you need him to *breathe*? It's just weird. It's too much, too fast," Marie insisted.

"Ever hear of love at first sight? Seen, oh, I don't know, like one hundred movies about it? Read a few books?" Sabrina scoffed.

"But those are fake. And they don't involve my baby sister."

"Well, your 'baby sister' is fine, and happy. Marie, I'm finally *happy*. I can see myself by his side. I can picture a life with this guy. Do you understand what I'm saying? I'm letting myself picture it. You, of all people, should know how hard this is for me." Sabrina finished on a whisper.

She'd always had a hard time trusting men. Her former fiancé, Mike, had been a royal ass. She had thought she'd hit the jackpot, but instead gotten a virus—not literally, though it probably would have happened eventually. He banged anything wearing a skirt—or not. He'd been an equal-opportunity-asshole. But even knowing most men were not like him, she held herself back for years from her emotions. No man had proven worth getting hurt over. Until now.

Until Isaac.

Marie went pale and nodded. "Okay, okay. I'll relax. I can't help but worry about you. I love you. I've been your mom since our folks died. It's hard for me to let go." Tears shone in her eyes, and Sabrina swallowed past the lump in her throat.

She hugged Marie, unsure how to respond to what was said, but thankfully got saved from trying by her sister's loud yawn.

"I love you, too," she murmured. "And you've done a great job. You can relax now. I'm okay."

"I'll try. I promise I'll try," Marie assured Sabrina.

Chapter Eleven

*S*he stood in the woods, once more enrobed in purple moonlight, and realized no wind rustled her hair. Utter silence surrounded her, but she could tell Elijah watched her from behind. She spun around to face him and froze at the sight of him. She hadn't seen him in weeks, so she took her time surveying him. His eyes gleamed in the moonlight, his mouth pressed tight into a grim line. He watched her...no, scratch the last statement.

He glared at her.

Oh, boy.

"Why did you bring me here? Where were you?" she inquired as she sat on a fallen tree and sighed.

He looked startled and replied, "I went off to hunt Louisa. We fought and she ran away. She's still out there somewhere, but she isn't here anymore. I can't find any traces of her."

"Are you...okay?"

He snickered. "Oh yeah, I'm great. Never been better."

"I'm sorry," she whispered. She felt his pain as if it were her own. He'd been hurt when she had chosen Isaac, as if he somehow sensed it had been decided.

He cursed and ran his hand through his hair in agitation. He looked so much like Isaac, she paused. "No, I'm sorry. You don't deserve my anger." He sighed loudly and sat beside her. "I always seem *to lose my temper around you. Not the best way to win the girl, is it? Sabrina, I'm sorry about—"*

"Shh. It's okay. I'm sorry I pried. It's obviously a sore subject, for both of you." She didn't want to trigger an angry response from him by discussing what had happened at her house weeks ago. And she certainly didn't want to discuss him killing Amelia.

"Yes, but I should have known you'd ask. And I left because I had to chase Louisa. I didn't want to leave you, I swear. I wanted to explain, to make you understand...."

He stared at her, the longing clear in his eyes, and she met his gaze hesitantly. The same love Isaac showed her—and the same devotion— shone in Elijah's as well. It hurt to look at him, to know she couldn't return his love the way he wanted to. She lurched to her feet, ready to flee back to reality.

"I really shouldn't be here right now. Isaac would be upset if he knew."

"Does Isaac already have such a claim on you that you must worry even about your dreams?" He jumped to his feet to pace furiously, fists clenched at his sides. "You don't know what it felt like, watching Amelia die. It ruined me. It's not a day any of us need to reflect upon, I assure you."

"It's okay, really. I know enough, I don't need to hear about it anymore!" she exclaimed.

"What did Isaac tell you? How much of a monster I am? How I stole the only love of his life, the only thing that mattered to him in the world, and killed her?"

The last came out a growl, and she winced when he gripped her arms so tightly they throbbed.

Her temper swelled and she leaned into his face to jeer, "No, he told me what happened, and the discussion ended. There were no lies, no drama. No raised voices. Unlike now."

He let out a string of curses and released her. "I'm sorry, again. I just get so angry when I think of you two. When I picture you in his arms, I get angry enough to snap, and I do. Unfortunately, it's always seems to be at you. It should be Isaac, though. He somehow discovered my plan to meet you at McGuiness. I hadn't even sensed him nearby."

Sabrina cocked her head, confused by his statement. "What do you mean, he discovered about meeting me at McGuiness?"

"In your dream. I told you to meet me at McGuiness. Do you recall that night?"

"Yes, of course. But it was Isaac, not you...right?"

"It was me in the dream, but him in the daylight," he bit out.

"Oh. So you're telling me you'd intended to be there, but Isaac found out and beat you to me?" Sabrina inquired.

"Yes. I'd seen him go into the tavern the first day you saw him, and I knew he'd seen you. When he came out, looking flustered, I knew I had to act fast. I couldn't go in there to talk to you. The risk was too great. Enforcers swim all over the damn place all day—even the homeless guy is on their payroll. I watched you leave, and wanted to speak to you so bad. But I didn't dare to on their stomping grounds."

Zeke's on their payroll? Why, for the love of God, didn't he have a home? Maybe it had been a front all along?

"Wait...you were the one I saw that day?" She gasped as she remembered thinking she'd seen a man in the shadows. "I saw you, but thought I hallucinated."

"Yes, it was me. I wanted to come to you, but I didn't. Damn it." He kicked a huge rock, and she watched it sail through the air and crash into a tree, denting the rough bark. "So I came to you in a blasted dream, and told you to meet me there when I knew it would be closed. There'd be no risk of running into Isaac or his big oaf, Connor. But you would go to the familiar location, thinking Isaac would be there. And since you hadn't met Isaac yet, it would have been me. *I would be the one in your bed. I would be the one you trusted. Not him."*

She flushed as images of them in bed together played through her head. "How do you know he did it in trickery? Maybe he just happened to show up. He had no way of knowing you were planning the same. And he goes there all the time."

"I don't know how he did it!" he exclaimed in frustration, as he slashed a hand through the air. "All I do know is he's a sneaky bastard who stole you away. And now he reaps the benefits."

"I'm sorry you feel that way. Maybe he did or didn't do what you say. But even if he did, who are you to judge? Need I remind you what

happened to Amelia?"

Elijah sucked in his breath. *"Touché."*

"I'm sorry. You have so much anger in you, it's hard not to fight back sometimes," she murmured. This conversation had gone on long enough. Isaac wouldn't like this—not one little bit. And, yes, she cared about his feelings. How could she not, when she loved him?

She cared for Elijah, too, though. Which royally sucked, since he should be her enemy...since he was Isaac's. But, she felt a pull toward him, some feelings she could not shove aside. His sadness struck her as if it were her own. Seeing him alone in the world hurt. He needed a friend. Couldn't she be that for him, at least?

Would it be so wrong to fill that position?

"Anger over losing you? Yes, I do. Anger over watching Amelia die? Yes, that too. It eats at me, consumes me. I breathe, feel, and live anger and pain. It is all I know. I can't stand knowing I have lost you— again."

"You never had me. I'm not Amelia. You have to understand the difference here. And I love him. Not you. I'm sorry." She ended on a whisper.

"You thought you loved him before. I proved you wrong," he pointed out. Desperation rang out in his tone, and he leaned toward her. His gaze bore into hers, beseeching her to give into his will.

"That isn't me, Elijah. I'm not her. We are two different people," she insisted. *"Why can't you accept I'm not your long-lost love, but only a woman who resembles her?"*

"Damn it, Sabrina. You are *her, and you belong with me, not him,"* he urged.

"No, I don't," she whispered. She felt bad for being so blunt. His love shone clear in his eyes. But she loved Isaac, and the sooner Elijah accepted it, the better off they would all be. *"Elijah, Isaac and I are close now. I know there are feelings you have...you've confused me for Amelia. I'm not her. I know you think you care for me, but—"*

"I think I care for you? I'm sorry, but that's an understatement." He laughed harshly and grabbed her hand to place it on his chest before biting out, *"Do you feel a heartbeat? No? Well, it used to beat for you, and only you. If I had a heart now, it would still beat only for*

you.

"Why does your heart beat faster when I'm near?" He placed his hand on her chest, and she flushed when her traitorous heart sped up. "I can hear your heart beating from a mile away. I hear it speed up as I come near. I hear your breathing get faster as well. Especially when I do this."

Grabbing her chin firmly, he crushed his lips to her passionately. She cringed, afraid she'd feel the same surging emotions she always had in his arms. And to feel anything now would be the worst betrayal to her and Isaac. But she sagged against Elijah in relief when she realized she only had some slight desire toward him. But not love. *Never love.*

He wasn't Isaac.

He seemed to sense she didn't react as she had in the past, for he pulled back to look at her, shock and resignation in his eyes.

She, however, couldn't help but be marvelously relieved. Elijah no longer had a pull over her. For her, Isaac—and only Isaac—would do. She smiled but flinched in guilt as she saw Elijah's distraught face. She cupped his cheek, as she gave him one last tender peck on his lips.

"I'm sorry. You have to let me go," she whispered.

"But, Sabrina—" His words were lost in the howling of the winds whipping in gale-like force around the two of them. Odd, it hadn't seemed windy before....

An invisible force threw Elijah backward through the air. She heard a grunt of pain as he slammed into a tree. Unable to hold straight at the assault, it crashed to the ground. Elijah lay in a heap on the ground at the splintered base of the tree, unmoving for a split second. Leaping to his feet, he growled.

She turned to search the forest, but the furious wind whipped her hair in her face and the thunder crashing overhead told her with frightening clarity who lurked in the shadows.

Isaac.

Her heart lurched to a halt as she realized he had seen her kissing Elijah. He would be mad. No, furious. The dangerous storm attested to as much. They were going to fight over her, and one of them would die.

Oh, God.

"Isaac, no!" She screamed too late. He already soared through the air to crash on top of Elijah. He snarled and grabbed Elijah's head. She gasped when she realized he tried to rip his head off. The next step to killing him, she knew, would be salt water.

He didn't fight to teach a lesson to Elijah—he fought to kill.

She rushed toward the pair and shrieked when Isaac flew through the air and slid across the ground before colliding against a huge rock. Elijah straddled him and lifted his head by the hair to punch him in the face.

Anger surged through her at the assault. "Elijah, no. Get off of him!" He ignored her, and his fist smashed into Isaac's face once more. Isaac struggled to free himself, but Elijah's grip proved too strong to break. They spun in mid-air, defying gravity as each fought to gain the upper hand. Sabrina chased them once more.

Damn it, why the heck can't I fly?

"I'll...kill...you...." Isaac vowed.

Sabrina noticed his teeth glistened in the moonlight, much like Elijah's did. Oh, God, he'd turned into a vampire. She'd never seen him in another form, besides brief glimpses here and there as he left. Which left him vulnerable—and he could die. She had to make them stop this madness.

"Isaac, Elijah, this has to stop, now. Get off him, Elijah!" she shouted as she bolted toward them once more.

Oh, God, what if one of them got hurt—or worse yet, died? She had to do something besides shriek at them uselessly. They came to a halt by an enormous tree, and she wasted no time in reaching them. She was acting foolish, reckless even, to interfere in a battle between two immortals. But she could not—would not—stand by idly.

She leapt onto Elijah's back and yanked his hair as hard as she could. He hissed in anger, but didn't release Isaac. She tightened her grip even more, but he continued to ignore her. She cocked an arm back and punched him as hard as she could on the side of his head. He snarled in response, but continued to pull on Isaac's head. Isaac's eyes were not on his opponent, but instead they focused on her. And he appeared furious.

"Sabrina, get off him!" he shouted. "And leave now."

She glared in response. Leave? Not a bloody chance in hell. She snubbed him as inspiration struck. Her puny strength did nothing to stop Elijah, so she threw her hands over his eyes to blind him. Brilliant.

He roared and arched his back, and reached behind his back to rip her off. Caught in the heat of battle, he tossed her aside. She cried out as her head slammed on the ground. She lay in a daze, staring up at the starless sky. Black spots swam before her vision, and she gasped for air.

Air agonizingly returned to her lungs, and over her desperate breathing, she heard a man cry out in pain before silence descended. A shadow crouched over her, and she recognized Elijah. And Isaac didn't come to her side.

Oh, God. Is he…headless? Had he been a vampire still and therefore vulnerable?

"Sabrina, I'm so sorry. I never meant to hurt you—"

"Isaac? Where's Isaac?" she shrieked. He tensed and glared at her stubbornly.

"Where do you think?" he asked. "I won, as I always did. And always will."

Pain flowed over her body, and she stopped breathing altogether.

He was dead. Elijah had killed him.

Fury encompassed her, and she clutched her hands into tight fists before launching herself at him.

"You son of a bitch. I'll kill you," she shrieked. She raked her nails across his face, feeling the skin tear under her fingers and blood dampen them. She pummeled his chest with her fists, even as tears rolled down her cheeks. "I hate you. I hope you rot in hell."

He grabbed her arms and rolled her beneath him. She shrieked in fury at his grip, and struggled to be free.

"Too late. I'm already there," he whispered brokenly.

Chapter Twelve

*S*abrina gasped and sat upright. She raised her fingers to her cheeks, amazed they came back wet. What the *heck*?

Someone shook her, and she focused on her assailant, still in a daze.

"Oh my God, Sabrina. What's wrong? You were having a nightmare. You kept screaming Isaac's name and yelling at someone named Elijah. Who's Elijah? What's wrong? You were like a woman possessed."

Then…oh God, she remembered.

In an excruciating barrage, the memories assaulted her relentlessly. She clutched her chest and gasped for air as tears welled in her eyes, and she moaned, "Oh no. No, no, no, no, no…."

"It's okay, you just had a dream. Calm down." Marie pulled her into her arms and patted her back in the age-old manner of someone trying to soothe a loved one.

Even though she existed in full panic mode, Sabrina took a deep breath and forced a mask of calm over her face.

One, two, three, oh God…. Four, five, six.

Okay, breathe again. Deep breath. Good job. Now, to get rid of my sister.

When she felt steady enough to open her mouth and speak

coherently, she took one more deep breath. She smiled tightly. "Marie, I'm okay. I-I feel bad for waking you up. Please go back to bed. I-I want to write this dream down before I forget it. Okay?" She managed somehow to hold back the hysteria forming a bubble in her throat as she shooed Marie up the stairs. Sabrina really wanted to pick her up and throw her into the damn bed.

God, could she waddle just a little bit *faster*?

"But what did you dream?"

"I don't want to talk about it, okay? I had a dream about my book, and I need to write it down before I forget it. It will make an awesome fight scene. Good night," Sabrina called. She slammed the door in her sister's confused face, wasting no time before she sprinted down the stairs and into the kitchen to grab her knife. She really needed to get a gun one of these days. She burst through the door and into the night.

She made it halfway across the lawn before she tripped and landed on her knees. Damn it all to hell, she didn't know *where* to go. Clutching her stomach to ward off the pain, she stared sightlessly into the forest. Her throat ached at the tears she held back, but her mind felt numb. Isaac lay somewhere out there and she could do nothing to help him. Possibly headless and tossed in the ocean to dissolve away into nothing.

She wondered if Elijah and Isaac had felt this way that day in the meadow while Louisa had ruined them all. Useless. Lying on the green embankment, watching their loved ones die....

Oh my God!

Eyes wide, she leapt to her feet in determination and dashed into the forest. She knew where to go.

Racing through the forest, she didn't pause until she reached the clearing she had so often dreamt of. No wonder why Isaac hadn't liked her being here in the light of day. Elijah brought her there in her dreams.

She stumbled into the familiar area and spun in a frenzied circle looking for Isaac.

Then she saw him.

He was lying motionless where he had landed in her dream, with his head *on*. She rushed to his side, tossed aside the knife, and surveyed his bloody, pale face. Was he dead? Wait, maybe he still breathed. There! Had his chest just risen?

Before she could investigate further, Elijah stepped out of the darkness he had hidden himself in. She grabbed the knife, jumped to her feet, and shoved him away from Isaac. He stumbled backward and caught his balance warily. "Get away from him. Get away from us. Forever." Anger washed over her like a medicine, and it helped to keep the fear for Isaac's life away. "He's been right all along. You're no good for me, for any of us."

He held his hands up with a comical bewilderment on his face and backed away. "All right. All right. I'm leaving."

She turned her attention back to Isaac and relief swelled over her. Yes, his chest was rising and falling. He'd simply been knocked unconscious. He'd changed into a *human*.

Thank God.

"He's not dead. He changed into human form when I threw you, and I took advantage of his momentary weakness. He's knocked out." He spoke slowly, as if to an imbecile. She kneeled beside Isaac, unable to move.

He's okay. He's alive.

Elijah moved to her side and touched her shoulder. She grabbed his hand and flipped him off his feet. Holy crap, she didn't know she still had those self-defense lessons stored away in her brain. Not wasting any time, she jumped on top of him, held the knife to his throat, pushing in slightly until she drew a drop of blood from his neck. Not satisfied, she drew back and punched him in the eye.

"Damnation, Sabrina! Knock it off, you little hellion!" he exclaimed. He grabbed her arms before she could punch him again and stared at her in horror. She growled and fought to free herself.

She'd kill him.

She brought her knee to his stomach and pushed as hard as she could. This earned her a grunt, and a change of position. He tackled her so all her limbs were useless, and she could only squirm in an attempt to be free, the knife rendered useless by his clutch on her wrist.

The look on his face would have been comical if she weren't so freaking furious. He looked at her like she was a freak of nature—this coming from a vampire.

Hah.

She struggled in his arms until exhaustion came over her, and she collapsed against his chest. "Bastard." She whispered one last attempt at hurting him as he had hurt her.

He laid his head against hers and hugged her to his chest. "I'm sorry. For scaring you like that. I should have told you he was okay right away. Can you forgive me?"

Sabrina pulled away from his embrace and looked back at Isaac's unconscious form, eager to see his rising chest. Instead of seeing him out cold, however, she met his gaze, her own widening in horror at how their position must look. He watched them, fury evident in his eyes, and his body trembled from the force of his rage. He snarled and Sabrina realized he intended to fight Elijah again.

She cried out and ripped away from Elijah to fling herself across Isaac's chest. "Isaac, please don't!" she yelled.

Isaac growled and vowed, "I'll kill you."

"Isaac—" Elijah began as he reached out to pull Sabrina off of Isaac, presumably worried that his brother couldn't control his temper in his current state of fury.

"Touch her and die." Isaac spoke through clenched teeth. In one nimble movement, he stood on his feet, ripped the knife from her hand, and swung Sabrina safely behind him. He held the knife out in a defensive position, and she fleetingly wondered if knives did anything to vampires.

"I didn't want to hurt her. I meant only to protect her, in case you were out of control." Elijah's voice came out so quiet she could barely hear him.

"*I'm* not the one who's dangerous to be around." The slight emphasis on the first word made Elijah flinch. "Step back, and stay back."

She peered over Isaac's shoulder, her eyes fixed on Elijah as she silently pleaded he give in to his brother's demands. She knew he must know what she asked of him. No, what she *commanded*. He stared at her in silent stubbornness, and she waited for him to acquiesce.

She had no question in her mind whether or not he would.

Isaac, seeing where Elijah focused, growled and stepped forward menacingly. Elijah took a step back and snarled.

"I'll leave now. I just wanted to make sure you were okay," he whispered.

"I'm fine, no thanks to you. Don't return. Next time, I *will* kill you," Isaac warned his brother.

Elijah stiffened and stared at Sabrina one last time. All his longing and desire were plain in his eyes. And the look on his face? It would haunt her forever. The despair in his face hurt too much to *ever* forget. He gave a slight nod and left.

Isaac turned to Sabrina, his gaze examining her face. He reached out to touch her cheek, and she flinched at his tortured expression.

"You cry, but the question is, for whom?"

In surprise, Sabrina raised a hand to her cheek. She opened her mouth to reply, but he shook his head, compressing his lips.

"I don't want to talk about it. Not here, not now. Maybe not ever. Let's go."

"Isaac—"

"*No*, Sabrina," he said.

He made it sound like…like they were *over*.

Tears ran down her cheeks, and she blinked in an attempt to clear her eyes. She swallowed heavily and struggled to keep up to Isaac's grueling pace. When she stumbled and almost fell, he gripped her elbow and dragged her behind him.

She'd hurt Isaac, and now he might never forgive her, or trust her. Pain wracked her as she thought of all the things she could have— *should have*—done. She should have slapped Elijah, or not let him kiss her at all, or maybe woken up somehow.

She bit her lip, unsure of how to proceed. If only he hadn't come along when he had. If he had come a mere minute later, she wouldn't have been kissing Elijah.

Oh God, it must have looked horrible from his point of view.

She must have looked like Amelia.

Damn it, she looked just like Amelia.

Isaac glared as he pictured Sabrina in Elijah's arms. He'd entered the scene right when Elijah had pulled her into his arms and kissed her. His heart had dropped, yet he'd held back in the shadows.

Watching.

Waiting.

Hoping Sabrina would pull away and slap him. Punch him, kick him in the balls.

Something.

But instead, she'd returned his kisses. Rage had taken over him until he could bear no more. He'd leapt out of the darkness, somehow changing into a vampire in mid-leap. He'd never done anything like it before. It had always taken a great amount of concentration on his part to make the switch. He usually needed to focus and concentrate to change, and to keep the change. If he ever lost his concentration, he would change back into a human.

But this time, he'd jumped at Elijah, and in a split second, the transformation had been complete. After his instant change, he'd proceeded to attempt to kill his own brother.

Bloody hell.

He'd never felt such anger in his life. Hell, not even when he had come upon Amelia and Elijah. This betrayal caused more pain. It hurt worse. If Elijah hadn't been quick enough, Isaac would have killed him before even realizing he'd begun to do so.

When Sabrina had been thrown across the forest, his concentration had been enough for his transformation to slip—and gave Elijah ample opportunity to knock him over the head using a rock. He winced and probed the aching wound. It still hurt like hell, damn it.

The next thing he had become aware of was Sabrina in his brother's arms again. Isaac wished he'd killed Elijah before they noticed he had awoken. He cursed his damnable honor and kicked a rock as he continued to stalk toward Sabrina's house. Time to get away from here.

Away from *her.*

He'd become plagued by questions that would not cease.

Had she chosen Elijah over him again? Would she even have cared if Elijah had killed him? Or would she be relieved by no longer having to choose between the two men? It would have nicely cleared the way to Sabrina for Elijah, removing obstacles from his path.

Maybe Isaac overestimated his pull on Sabrina, though. Maybe he wouldn't an obstacle at all.

They arrived at her door in complete silence, and she bit her lip when he wouldn't look her in the eye.

"Isaac, please. Let me talk to you," she cried, putting her hands out in a pleading gesture. She struggled to put her thoughts into words and must have hesitated too long, for he drew away from her both physically and mentally. A cold mask covered his features. Ice-man returned in full swing.

"Sabrina, it's late. It's been a long night, and I'm going home," he mumbled.

Isaac turned on his heel to go. It became clear to her he would leave without allowing her to explain. He didn't even want to wait until she'd gotten safely inside behind the locked door.

This was bad. *Really* bad.

Sabrina ran after him, but her weak legs refused to cooperate, causing her to fall clumsily to the ground, on all fours. She ignored the pain and rage building inside her at alarming speeds. She didn't have the time to be angry. Not now.

She swallowed her pride, and cried out, "Isaac. I love you, and *only* you. *Please* come back. Just let me explain."

His back stiffened, and he paused. Hope washed over her. Maybe now he would return and pull her into his arms where she belonged. He spun around, his face flushed bright red. His widened eyes blazed so brightly, she recoiled. "You dare say those words to me now, in the face of your treachery? You *dare?*" he shouted.

"No, it's true. I have been meaning to tell you, I just—"

"Good night, Sabrina," he interrupted curtly. This time he didn't walk. He *ran.*

She gasped and let herself fall to the ground as she watched him run away from her house. And from *her.*

∞

Jesus, her voice wouldn't leave Isaac's head.

I love you, and only you.

Talk about a punch in the gut.

He wanted to trust her. Longed to believe her more than anything in the world. But not minutes earlier, she had been in his brother's arms. It made her declaration a bit harder to swallow.

Maybe he had behaved like an asshole, bolting right after she declared her feelings, but to hear her say the words he'd been longing to hear for so long had been too raw. If she had told him she hated him, it would have hurt less. How could she cling to Elijah and turn and vow her love to him, and only him?

He didn't know what to think. All he really knew was tonight had turned out to be one of the worst nights of his life. And it had been a long life. He needed to get some sleep.

Marie would be going home tomorrow. He'd use that as an excuse to go see Sabrina. And *maybe* he would talk to her.

But, truth be told, he dreaded what she had to say to him.

ა

Sabrina couldn't believe it. He'd left her. And maybe not for just the night, but forever. She didn't cry, but instead watched the scene unfolding in a nonstop reel in her head. Her head had gotten stuck in replay mode, leaving no breaks in between.

Maybe he hadn't believed her? That hurt less than the possibility of him not wanting her love anymore. A shadow fell over her face, and her heart leapt. He'd come back—he *did* still care.

No, no he didn't. Not Isaac. Elijah had returned.

The despair clawed its way over her once more, but she attempted to hold it at bay. She wouldn't break down. Not in front of *him*. She closed her eyes tight, shutting out his concerned face. She clutched her stomach, mentally steadying herself before she opened her eyes and met his gaze defiantly. She searched for her knife, before realizing that Isaac had run off with it.

Son-of-a-bitch.

"What are *you* doing here? Haven't you done enough damage as it is? Haven't we both?" she asked petulantly.

He squatted next to her and brushed her hair back. "You shouldn't be out here alone at night. There are things much scarier than me out there." He motioned toward the dark woods behind them by tilting his head. "Did Isaac leave you out here, alone? Or is he hiding somewhere, ready to pounce on me again?"

"Yes, he left. Big surprise, he didn't exactly want to talk to me after we left you," she said sarcastically. She latched onto the anger: it felt far better than desolation. "Thanks for that, by the way. He now thinks I betrayed him, just like *her*. I hate *her*."

Rage crossed his expression before he looked away from her. Sabrina seemed to have found a sensitive area even where she was concerned. He didn't like her insulting *his* Amelia. He closed his eyes, took a deep breath, and focused on her. "I'm sorry for the trouble I caused. But no matter how angry he felt, he should have seen you safely inside before he left. He does claim to love you, after all."

She inhaled deeply at his words, and her tenuous hold on control slipped. Tears blurred her vision, and she bit her quivering lip as she choked on a sob.

"I'm not so sure he does anymore," she whispered and burst into tears.

Elijah stared at her in horror, unsure of what to do. Or say.

"Oh, good God, don't cry!" he exclaimed in horror. He reached out to pull her in his arms, but hesitated at the glare she shot him. He cursed and yanked her into his arms anyway.

She didn't have the energy to fight him, so she let him smooth the damp hair off her face and kiss her temple. She knew she should protest at the familiarity, but didn't bother. Who cared any more, anyway?

He carried her inside and went into the living room. It probably should have surprised her he knew where she slept, but it didn't. Nothing surprised her anymore.

Chapter Thirteen

*T*he next morning, floorboards creaked overhead and Sabrina groaned to herself. Marie woke up already? Did the sun even come up yet? The creaking continued toward the stairs as Marie began to descend them.

Oh, crap. Do I look like hell?

In a flurry of sudden activity, she ran her fingers through her hair to remove any twigs and rocks that would make it obvious she'd been outside last night. After removing all the debris she managed to get her fingers on, she lay back down on the couch to pull the blanket over her head.

Please think I'm sleeping. Please think I'm—

The scratchy wool blanket tickled her nose, and she scrunched it in an attempt to ease the itch. Marie ripped the covers off of her head, down to her hips. Forgetting to look freshly awoken, she glowered at her sister in resentment.

"You never were capable of faking sleep. Give it up, already," she said smugly. She placed her hands on her hips.

"That was rude, even for you," Sabrina grumbled.

"Well, I do have a plane to catch today…."

Sabrina sat upright and gasped. "Oh my God, already? What time, again?"

"We have to leave in an hour," Marie responded in a slow voice.

"Crap. Let me go hop in the shower."

"Are you okay?"

"Yup, I just forgot. I'll get ready real fast so we can spend some time together before you go. All I need is five minutes."

She sprinted up the wooden steps to the bathroom, and made quick work of brushing her teeth and showering. She threw her hair in a messy ponytail and dressed in a black shirt and black yoga pants. It suited her today. It matched her dark mood, she concluded, as she nodded in the mirror.

Miss Daisy Sunshine, I am.

She ran downstairs and accepted the coffee her sister held out to her. "Thanks," she mumbled. "Do I look as tired as I feel?"

"Worse, probably. You had quite the nightmare, huh? I thought someone was killing you."

She cringed and cursed herself for mentioning her lack of sleep. "Sorry, I have nightmares when I'm writing. I should have warned you. I tend to blend my book into real life. After you went to bed, I calmed down," she lied. "I wrote down the scene, and went back to sleep."

Marie raised an eyebrow and asked, "Is Isaac in your book? And who, exactly, is Elijah?"

"No, Isaac isn't in it. But Elijah is a character in my book. In my dream, Elijah tried to kill Isaac, and it upset me. It's all silly, in the light of day." She plastered as much of a smile as she could manage on her face. Hopefully, she didn't look demented. Now she'd have to add an Elijah to her book, or tell Marie she'd changed the name.

Great.

"Yeah...silly," Marie agreed. Sabrina could hear the confusion in her sister's voice, but also knew that though her story didn't quite add up, Marie couldn't guess the truth. It was too damn unbelievable. "Really, do you think I'm an idiot? What's going *on*?"

She groaned and buried her head in her hands. "Please, for once can you just *let it be*?"

Some of the desperation in her voice must have gotten to Marie, for she floundered for a good ten seconds, opening her mouth and closing it as she shook her head. Sabrina watched as her sister battled every instinct that screamed at her to question Sabrina further, and won.

"Fine," Marie griped. "But this is not over."

Her sister's eyes probed hers, silently asking to be told of the secrets she kept. Sabrina returned the stare, content in the knowledge she would not find the answers she sought.

"Fine. Question me all you want tomorrow when you're home. But for now, please, just enjoy the last few minutes we have?" Deciding upon a quick change of subject, Sabrina asked, "So, are you all packed?"

"Yeah, I woke up early. I miss Sam. And my husband, of course." Excitement shone in her sister's eyes, and Sabrina fought back the pain that coursed through her. She had nothing to be excited about any longer. "But I miss my baby more."

"I bet. She's growing so big. Those pictures you showed me are adorable. I'll have to come out to visit, once my nephew makes an appearance." She reached out a hand and rubbed Marie's protruding stomach. She gasped in awe when she got kicked in her palm. She laughed and forgot for a brief moment about Isaac.

Very brief.

"You made him excited, see? He can't wait for his favorite aunt to come visit him."

"I'm his only aunt," Sabrina teased.

"Inconsequential."

She met Marie's eyes, and they each smiled. A knock on the door caused them both to jump in alarm and grin at the other's show of surprise.

Sabrina trudged to the door with a racing heart and trembling legs. She couldn't help but feel like a prisoner walking to her execution. She feared it was him, and yet dreaded that it wouldn't be. Wiping her sweaty palms on her pants, she took a deep breath and opened the door.

Isaac's lips were compressed, and his brow furrowed, but damn it, he looked as gorgeous as ever. His searching gaze roamed over her face, seemingly taking in every little detail, until she glared at him in frustration. He flushed and shifted on his feet. He looked away from her to focus upon Marie, who had come up behind her.

What the hell was he thinking? Why did it have to be so hard to figure out his feelings? Was he mad? Angry? Betrayed? Or did he not care anymore?

He hid them too damn well.

Anger flowed through her blood like a drug.

Well, screw him.

"I came to say goodbye. I knew you were leaving early. I hope I'm not intruding." His voice sounded warm, but Sabrina noticed his clenched fist and his hard eyes.

"No, it's good to see you again," Marie reassured him. "Thanks for coming."

"Well, I'll leave you girls alone, but I'll talk to you later, Sabrina?"

She stared at him in stubborn silence, unsure how to answer. Why did he want to talk to her, anyway? She didn't plan on agreeing to anything right now, thank you very much.

"I'm sure she'd like that, right, Sabrina?" Marie nudged Sabrina's calf using the tip of her foot. Sabrina glared at her sister wordlessly, who shrugged in confusion, and turned to Isaac to explain further. "She had a rough night last night. She isn't herself. Don't mind her."

"Oh?"

"Yeah, she had a bad dream," she stated. "You don't know anything about that, though, do you, Isaac?" she asked slyly.

Isaac looked from Marie to Sabrina in confusion, and Sabrina lifted a shoulder in response. She had no idea what her sister had gotten into now. And she didn't give a damn either.

"Um, no I didn't," he stammered. Shifting on his feet, he looked at Sabrina for help. She frowned in return and sighed in irritation.

"Let's go, Marie. I could use some more coffee on the way," she said before stomping out the door and holding it open for her sister. Isaac motioned Marie forward, collected her bags, and followed her out the door. Glaring at his retreating figure, she barely resisted the urge to throw her keys at his head.

But...maybe she had a better punishment. Biting her lip to hide her pleasure, she followed Isaac and Marie to her car. She waited as he said his goodbyes, speaking only when he started to climb into his car.

"Isaac, could you drive us to the airport? The traffic will be horrendous, and it will take *forever*. Hours, I'm sure. I'm too tired to concentrate." She added a big, loud yawn for Marie's benefit. It didn't take much effort to bring one on. Her body barely had the energy to move, yet alone think.

But if Isaac hated anything more he despised than cars, it would be traffic. She almost cackled in glee at his disgruntled expression. He glared at her before forcing a polite smile to his face.

"Certainly, Sabrina. *Anything* for you."

He slammed his car door shut, stalked back to her side, and snatched the keys out of her hand.

Maybe today wouldn't be so bad.

ໂບ

The silence in the car on the way to the airport sounded louder than a gunshot…and just as uncomfortable. Isaac and Marie chatted occasionally, but Sabrina remained silent in the back seat, quietly basking in her revenge. The ride proved to be as long as she'd suspected because they hit rush-hour traffic. Sabrina could practically feel the impatience flowing off Isaac's tense shoulders. She chose not to dwell upon the fact that his anger stemmed from finding her kissing Elijah. She much preferred to focus on her anger at his treatment of her last night.

Marie glanced over her shoulder and Sabrina forced a tight smile. Obviously, her sister sensed the tension in the air. She kept glancing between Sabrina and Isaac, as if trying to see some sort of invisible sign on their foreheads that blinked, *we fought, and here's why.*

Eventually, even Marie fell silent.

Arriving at the airport came as a bit of a relief to all of them, Sabrina suspected. They exited the car, collected the luggage, and her and her sister walked side by side while Isaac followed with the bags. She felt Isaac's eyes glaring at her from behind and resisted the urge to look his way. The anger that kept her going all morning no longer held her up. The pain had returned. She didn't want to look at him, terrified of what was—or wasn't—in his eyes.

Lost in thought, she got taken off guard when Marie turned and said, "Okay, this is where you leave me. Security and all."

"But we need to check your luggage!" Sabrina cried, causing Marie to stare at her in confusion.

"We just did," she said slowly, as if she were talking to Sam, her two-year-old daughter.

"You must have been so distracted over your sister leaving, you were in a daze," Isaac said sympathetically. His face softened, and he put a hand on her shoulder. She almost cried at the tender gesture. Almost.

Get a hold of yourself, Sabrina.

"I'll miss you so much," she vowed. She shrugged Isaac's hand off her shoulder under the guise of pulling her sister into her arms for a tight hug.

"I'll miss you, too, Bree," Marie whispered, tears in her voice.

Sabrina turned to hurry away. She became forced to stop, however, when she realized Isaac didn't follow her. A glance over her shoulder revealed he'd been held back by Marie's hand on his arm.

"Go ahead, Sabrina. I just want to ask Isaac a quick question."

She groaned, immediately on guard. What now? "Marie, you promised to behave."

"I am. I want to ask him something. I'm being good, I swear." Marie smiled at her and motioned for her to walk away. Sabrina stomped away and leaned on a nearby pillar. She glared at the pair and crossed her arms over her chest. Though she'd give them privacy, she'd be damned if she wouldn't watch.

Isaac watched Sabrina retreat to glare off in the distance before turning to Marie. What happened now? Another interrogation?

He hoped not, because he didn't bloody feel in the mood. She smiled at him, and he returned the gesture in an attempt to look relaxed. When he was anything *but*.

"Okay, what happened last night? You guys have a fight when you came over?" she inquired.

"I don't understand what you mean." Confusion made his voice sharp as he reminded her, "We didn't fight at dinner."

What the bloody hell is she talking about, anyway?

"Last night, Sabrina had a nightmare. She kept screaming in her sleep, yelling your name, and sometimes the name 'Elijah.' He's a character in her novel she's working on. When I finally woke her up, she was still crying her eyes out, and kept repeating 'No.'"

"Hmm, sounds like a bad night. No wonder she looks so tired." He clenched his fists and gritted his teeth in an attempt to stay calm.

Fucking Elijah again. God, he hated him sometimes, brother or no. He forced himself to focus on Marie's words and to push down the anger for later. Much, much later.

"Well, after she put me back to bed like a child, she ran outside. She doesn't know I saw her, but she took off like a fire chased at her heels. I wanted to go after her, but I had no idea what direction she'd gone. So I sat in the kitchen and waited for her to return. I figured a pregnant woman wondering around in dark, unfamiliar woods isn't the best idea.

"It must have been a while, because at some point I fell asleep leaning on the island. When I woke up, you were carrying her inside. I waved to you, but I figured you didn't see me since you didn't wave back. You took her to the couch and held her."

His whole body clenched in fury, agony, betrayal. She'd spent the night with Elijah. After he'd been up all night stressing over his words, and his actions, she'd spent the night in his brother's arms.

Doing what, exactly?

The thought proved too much to bear, and he bit back a curse. Marie stepped back as if she feared him. Well, hell, he probably looked pretty bloody scary to her. He felt manic. A loud bang of thunder shook the airport, and she ripped her eyes from his livid face to gape outside. It had been cloudy, but dry, earlier; now a storm gathered outside. Seeing Marie's distress forced him to take a deep breath as he plastered the most sincere smile he could manage on his face.

He had a feeling he seemed less happy...and more maniacal.

Isaac held his pleasant expression for Marie's sake, but not easily. His whole body ached to be released from this sham—to howl in his fury. Elijah had brought Sabrina into her home? Had held her? What, had he waited for him to leave before swooping in and bringing Sabrina inside? Had they kissed—or worse, *made love*?

He'd gone to sleep last night feeling ashamed, as if he had wronged Sabrina in his anger. But he hadn't misunderstood the situation after all.

She'd chosen Elijah.

He ground his teeth behind his smile and tightened his fists into balls.

I'll kill him.

"Oh, no," she groaned. "I hope they don't delay my flight."

Across the room, Sabrina's eyes widened in horror as she hurried toward them, pushing her way through the crowd of worried travelers, eyeing the sudden change of weather. If she so much as *opened* her mouth, he'd snap. Time to end this conversation—now.

"Yeah, I left my windows open at home. Didn't realize a storm would be coming," he muttered. "Sabrina and I are fine. I feel bad I appeared in her nightmare. I'd hate to cause her to lose sleep." He gestured outside using his hand. The rain had stopped. He glared at Sabrina over Marie's head as she approached, and smiled when she faltered in step and paled.

Yeah, your secret is out, my love.

"Wow, it's calmed down already. Good!" Marie exclaimed.

"What's going on over here?" Sabrina demanded as she took a furtive glance at his face. She paled even more as he glowered behind her sister's head, only to smooth his face into a carefree expression when Marie turned back to look at him.

"Nothing. We're done talking," he responded. Smiling at Marie, he grasped Sabrina's elbow. "Have a great flight. You better get going now. They're starting to board."

"Yeah, goodbye you guys." After one last curiosity-ridden look at them, she left. Once Marie disappeared out of sight, Sabrina turned back to Isaac. He scowled at her curious expression.

"What now?" she probed.

He growled and dragged her behind him as he stalked out of the airport. She had no choice but to run to keep up to his brisk pace, so it came as no surprise when she stumbled over her feet. Isaac caught her before she hit the ground but put her away from his body as soon as she steadied herself. He did *not* want to feel her pressed up against him right now.

"Isaac, slow down. I can't walk as fast as you!" she cried breathlessly from behind him. He didn't release his iron grip upon her arm or acknowledge her plea, but he did slow his speed by a fraction. "Why don't you just leave me the keys, and go away. I can drive myself. Or do you enjoy growling at me too much to leave me in peace?"

"Yes, that's exactly it," he snapped in response. She dug her feet into the floor and refused to move another inch. She yanked her arm hard, and he saw her clench her teeth against the stinging pain where his grip remained. Isaac steeled himself against her discomfort and growled. No way in hell would he release her.

Ever.

She arched an ironic eyebrow at him at the noise, causing him to flush and growl once more before leaning close to her face, nose to nose, and snarling, "Unless you want to make a huge scene in the middle of the airport, one that'll probably bring along a storm such as you've never seen, you'd better follow me. Now."

As if on cue, a loud rumble of thunder boomed overhead. She followed him, no longer attempting to speak.

Thank God for small favors.

ɞ

Sabrina glared out the window of her car. The scenery sped by way too fast, but the last thing she cared about right now was whether or not Isaac got a speeding ticket. As a matter of fact, she'd *love* to see it. Except she'd have to be near him longer. And she wanted to get away from him.

Now.

Really, his actions were ridiculous. If he wanted to be an asshole, why did she have to be forced to put up with it? Couldn't he just sulk off to some corner and pout like men always did? Or go chase a mongrel or something? After a couple attempts at getting him to tell her why he'd gotten so angry, she crossed her arms and vowed not to speak to him ever again.

Always the drama queen, aren't we?

But what had Marie told him to make him so angry? He hadn't seemed mad when he'd first showed up at the house this morning. If anything, he'd looked worried about her. But she couldn't mistake the fact that he remained pissed him off. When he shut off the ignition, she noted with surprise that they were already home. She glanced at him, only to see him glaring out his window.

She cleared her throat in an attempt to get him to look her way, but only the tensing of his shoulders told her he heard her. So, he wanted to play, did he? Well, fine. But she didn't need to sit here and suffer in silence. She unbuckled her seatbelt, opened the door, and slammed it behind her before leaning into the open window.

"I'm done playing these games. I'm not a child, and won't be treated like one. Come talk to me when you grow up, okay? That is, if you ever *do*."

She grabbed her keys out of his hand and stomped her way to the front door, not caring if she'd managed to piss him off even more. She went inside, locked the door, and gave it a kick for good measure. Her toe throbbed in protest, and she glowered at the offending door. For a brief moment, satisfaction at her fabulous exit made her smirk. Unfortunately, it didn't make her anger and hurt go away.

Unable to contrive an easy way out of her predicament, she went to the kitchen and grabbed a glass of wine and her second-favorite knife. Next time she talked to him, she'd demand her damn knife back, too. Damn it.

She stalked to the living room, placed both items on the table next to the couch, and sank into its soft cushions. She settled herself comfortably into its pillows, and began her wait.

But what she waited for, she had no idea.

৪৩

Isaac watched her retreat, and gave a bemused shake of his head. He knew he acted like an ass, but he hadn't wanted to have a discussion anywhere in public. Or while driving. And now that he'd gotten to her house, he had no bloody clue what to do.

Should he follow her inside and attempt to talk some sense into her, or would he be wasting his time? If she wanted Elijah so bad, what gave him the right to say no? They could run off into the moonlight together and live happily ever after in the land of the eternally damned, for all he cared. Until Enforcers hunted them down and killed them, anyway. His fist tightened involuntarily at the thought.

Hell no.

He just needed to show her how unsuitable Elijah was for her, no matter how much she thought she loved him.

Isaac loved her, and she could grow to love him, too. She'd forget all about Elijah, given time. And if not, well, he loved her enough for the both of them. It would have to be enough.

It had to be, damn it.

He exited the car and made his way up the walkway to the front door. He took a steadying breath and reached for the doorknob, only to have it refuse to budge. She'd locked him out?

Son of a bitch.

"Sabrina, let me in," he growled.

A slight shuffling sound came through the door. "Who is it?"

"It's me. Open the door."

"Who? I'm sorry, but I must make sure. You could be either Elijah, or Isaac. So, which is it?"

Which are you hoping for, my dear?

Teeth gritted, he snapped, "It's Isaac. Let me in. Now."

Dead silence met his ears, and he stared incredulously at the door as he wondered if she would actually refuse him entry. He measured the strength of the barrier, computing where it would be best to deliver the force of his impact to crash it open. Within seconds of breaking it down—he'd even backed up in preparation—she unlocked the door. As soon it swung open, he pushed his way inside. Not a chance in hell he would give her time to change her mind.

Sabrina studied Isaac's angry face and promptly walked away from him. Judging by his scowl, he didn't look any more agreeable than he had earlier. If he wanted to talk to her, he'd follow. She'd had enough of trying to explain what had happened last night. It was his turn.

He sat beside her. She turned to him and arched an eyebrow. She didn't have to wait long.

"Were you planning on keeping me out? If so, I should warn you a simple door wouldn't stop me if I didn't want it to." His chin jutted out in defiance, and his eyes glittered. "And the knife is useless, too."

"Maybe so, but it would still be damn satisfying to make you bleed right now." She toyed with it in her hands, spinning it in slow circles. Okay, maybe she didn't want to actually *stab* him, did she? "I didn't know you were going to be coming in, first of all. You haven't been in a talkative mood today. Second of all, you once yelled at me for opening the door before I made sure it was you. So I was being careful. Isn't that what I'm supposed to do? And last but not least, I want my damn knife back."

He flushed and refused to meet her eyes.

Score one: Sabrina.

"Yes, you're right. I'm sorry. I seem to be capable of doing nothing but yelling at you today." He ran his hand through his hair and took a deep breath. "And the knife is at my place. I'll get it to you as soon as possible."

"Fine. Make it soon. And yelling seems to be something I bring out in people," she drawled.

"I'm sorry, okay?" he snapped. "Is Elijah here, hiding?"

She stared at him in surprise, caught off guard by the change of subject. Not to mention the loud clash of thunder shaking her house. "Elijah? No, why would he be hiding here?"

"Seeing as you seem to have fallen in love with him, I figured he'd be here to gloat. Well, he can come out, and I'll tell him right here and now I—"

"Stop it right there, buddy. First off, calm yourself down. Second, where did you possibly get the ridiculous notion I love Elijah? Did you think I'd somehow mistaken the two of you last night when I told you I loved you? When you *ran* away from me?

"Because, call me crazy, but a man who runs when a woman declares her love for him really has no right at all to even *attempt* to be angry over what he thinks is her love for another." Her voice shook at the force of the emotions inside her, and by the time she finished her tirade, she'd poked him in the chest to emphasize her words.

Isaac stared at her in a mixture of admiration, anger, and shock.

"I don't know. I'll tell you what I do know, though. I know I found you kissing Elijah. I know we fought. I know he pushed you and took advantage of my distraction to knock me out. I know when I awoke, you were in his arms, again. I know after I left last night, he came *here.* That's what I know."

When he mentioned Elijah being inside her house last night, her mouth dropped open, and her face must have betrayed her shock. "How did you—?"

"How did I know? Oh, what a cute story. You see, your sister told me all about the nightmare you had, and how you were yelling my name, and some stranger's name. Whose could it possibly be?"

"Oh, knock it off," she grumbled. She gripped her knees in an attempt to stop the shaking of her hands.

"I remember...Elijah. How *ironic*. And after you sent her to bed, you left. She tried to wait up for you, but alas, she fell asleep in the kitchen. Imagine her relief when I, being the loving man I am, carried you inside and snuggled you until you fell asleep. Isn't it abso-fucking-lutely heartwarming?"

"But wait just a minute.... I went home last night. I went to sleep worrying about whether you were okay. So that means I couldn't have been here, holding you in my arms. Which leaves only one other person who could have been. I don't think I need to say his name. Nor *will* I," he snarled.

She cringed, but glared. "Maybe if my *loving man* hadn't left me alone on the lawn, he wouldn't have left room for another to sweep in and comfort me."

Isaac paled and whispered, "What?"

"Did you really think I would just shrug and walk away after you left me? I told you I loved you, and you ran *away*."

"You didn't even mean it!" he yelled. His clenched fists rose to his chest before he lowered them. "It was nothing but a lie, a guilty gesture at best."

"Oh really? You're a fool."

"I won't argue that. Just look where I've ended up with you—twice now. Jilted."

She sucked in a deep breath at the way he couldn't separate her from Amelia. For the love of God, what would it take to make these men see she was not her? Tears filled her eyes, but she refused to allow them free rein. She turned her back to Isaac, swiped an errant tear away, and faced him once more.

"Now it's my turn to tell you what I know, and you'll sit and listen. Got it?"

He sat down, glared, and with an imperious motion for her to begin, crossed his arms over his chest.

Gee, thanks.

"I had a nice night with my boyfriend. We went to dinner and came home. I went to bed, smiling when I thought of him. In case you're confused, that's *you*."

He glowered, and she smiled bitterly. "I fell asleep, and for the first time in weeks, I dreamt. I dreamt about my boyfriend's brother, who *thinks* he loves me. I can't help but care for him, as well, though I'm not sure why. Maybe because he looks like you." She shrugged. When a distant rumble of thunder accompanied his scowl, she snapped, "Oh, calm down."

"Calm as can be. I promise."

"Let me continue. I feel a pull toward Elijah, but it is minuscule in comparison to the pull I feel to *you*. I tried to explain this to him, but he got angry when I mentioned you." Her pointed look in his direction, she knew, spoke louder than simple words could. "When I tried to explain to him how much you mean to me, he decided to kiss me to prove me wrong.

"Yes, I should have slapped him. Yes, I should have said no. But I'll admit part of me felt curious. Would his kiss still pull me toward him as much as it once had? Would his kiss make me forget you? I decided to let him kiss me, and I'd find out the answers."

She watched him hesitate before he asked, "And did it? Make you forget?"

She knew it had to be one of the hardest things he'd ever asked. She put a hand over his clenched fist and squeezed. "No, it didn't. His kiss felt good. Breathtaking, even. But it wasn't *you*. He must have sensed the change, because he pulled away. He opened his mouth to talk…then he'd disappeared, and you were there.

"Watching you two try to kill each other has got to be one of the worst things I've ever seen. It hurt so badly. And I knew I could do nothing to stop it."

"Nothing but straddle Elijah's back and get thrown across the forest for your efforts," he grumbled.

"I wanted to get him *off* of you!" Sabrina shouted.

"Next time, stay back. I appreciate the sentiment, but your human powers are comparable to a fly landing on his arm. You feel it, but it doesn't hurt."

"Gee, thanks." She frowned at him and crossed her arms over her chest.

"Anyway, I'll shut up again." He mimed himself zipping his lips shut before he leaned back on the couch. She glared at his show of drama.

"So after I get thrown off Elijah, I open my eyes to see him leaning over me. I knew you would be there too, if you could, so I assumed you might be headless. Or worse—dead. At this lovely moment, my sister wakes me up. Suddenly, I'm back in my house, knowing you were lying out there somewhere and I didn't know where I'd find you."

"Oh, Sabrina. I'm—"

"Shut up. I don't want to hear a word. So *after* I manage to get my sister off my back, I somehow realize why I always thought the clearing in my dreams seemed familiar. It's the place in the forest by my house. It appears different in my dreams, but I thought the similarities were close enough to make it a feasible location. I was desperate to do something to find you.

"So I run off to the clearing, and sure enough, there you were, still lying on the ground. I figured out you weren't dead, just knocked out, and I attacked Elijah. But he easily warded off my *puny* human efforts and tackled me to the ground."

"You *attacked* him? Are you insane?" he asked in horror.

"Heck yeah, I did. And it isn't the first time, thank you very much. I gave him a black eye, too."

"You gave…a vampire…a black eye?" he questioned incredulously.

He swallowed hard, and she wondered if he tried not to shout or laugh. Yet again, his face proved impossible to read. Stinking ice-man.

"I did. Now, where did I stop? Ah yes, I wanted to throw myself into your arms when you woke up, but you glared at me, yelled at me, and left."

Isaac grabbed her hands earnestly and looked into her eyes. "Sabrina, I'm sorry. It's just, seeing you in his arms, it brought back dreadful feelings. Hatred. *Betrayal*. It was too much to bear. When you told me you loved me, all I could think of was you and Elijah, making love. It hurt too much."

"I didn't make love to him," she reminded him sternly. "I am not *Amelia*." Her voice rose in frustration at the end of her sentence. She tired of being accused of feelings she did not have. It infuriated her. She glared at him and stood up. "Well, now you've heard my story, and you can leave."

He gaped at her, clearly shocked. "Excuse me?"

"Leave," she stated.

"You're kicking me out?" He whispered.

The pain in his eyes looked so gut-wrenching, she longed to retract her words but didn't. She couldn't let him constantly mistrust her, and accuse her of betrayal. It just wouldn't work.

"Yes. It seems to me all you and Elijah are capable of doing is waiting for me to betray you. Like *her*. You'll never realize I'm not the same as her. So, I want you to leave. Now." It broke her heart to say it, but she needed him to trust her. Against all odds, he needed to know she loved him and wouldn't leave him. "Just because I look like her, doesn't mean I *am* her. I love you, and *only* you. And because I love you so much, I won't cause you pain, or anger. Not even false feelings of betrayal."

"Sabrina, wait. I understand—" A shake of her head stopped his plea, and he stared at her finger pointed at the door.

"It's my turn to say we won't discuss this today. Maybe not ever. Go."

His shoulders slumped as he walked to the door, but he strode back to grab her by her neck and kiss her. He clutched her so tight she almost couldn't breathe, and he crushed his lips to hers with a desperation that called to her. She almost crumbled into tiny bits and pieces of herself. She clung to his shirt as his lips moved over hers, demanding a response. When he pulled away, she gazed into his eyes, refusing to budge.

There were no words to be said, no words she would say.

He hugged her one last time, and she heard him take a deep breath before he cursed and walked away without looking back. Once the door shut behind him, she collapsed on the couch, put her head in her hands and burst into tears.

Chapter Fourteen

*I*saac sat down outside her door, feeling curiously weak. He needed to learn how to control his stupid temper. And he needed to stop comparing her to Amelia and unfairly judging her. Just because she looked like Amelia didn't mean she'd act like her. No more so than he would act like Elijah because they were identical. The thought seemed ludicrous to say the least. So why should her case be different?

Bloody hell, she was right. He acted like an utter asshole.

Even so, why should he expect her to pick him, instead of Elijah? He'd always been honest enough to admit Amelia had been drawn to Elijah. From what he'd seen, Sabrina had felt the same irresistible pull. Is it actually possible through her love for Isaac, she no longer felt drawn to Elijah?

He hoped so. He debated returning inside to grovel for her forgiveness when he sensed Elijah's presence. He hid nearby, and he seemed to call out to Isaac.

As if he wanted to be found.

Did Elijah want Isaac to kill him? Or did he assume Isaac would just let him go, since he was his brother? He focused in an attempt to pinpoint Elijah's location. It looked like he waited at the clearing.

Of course. Where the hell else would he be?

ಶ

Elijah grew more desperate with each passing moment. Louisa hovered constantly in the area, and he had yet to track her down. The time had come for them to have a one-on-one, him and his little brother. The same brother who hated him so much, he wanted to kill him. The thought depressed him. Hopefully, Isaac wouldn't attempt to kill him again. But if he did, so be it. If Isaac did manage to finish him off, his time in Hell could be over. Sabrina had made her choice, and it hadn't been him she'd chosen.

He needed to be strong enough to step aside.

Isaac approached from behind, and Elijah spun to face his twin. Isaac had looped around to the south end of the woods, only to come in from the opposite side of Sabrina's house to approach.

"There's no one else here. This isn't a trap. I wish to speak to you."

He got caught off guard by Isaac's fist plowing into his nose. He'd seemed so calm, not as if he were ready to attack.

Son of a bitch.

His nose throbbed, and he cursed.

Just goes to show you can never trust appearances.

"That's for Amelia," Isaac stated before an uppercut to his left eye. "That's for me." He picked Elijah off the ground and threw him across the forest. He slammed into a tree and rolled to safety as the tree crashed to the ground. "And this is for Sabrina."

"Sabrina can take care of herself," he muttered, remembering the punch she gave him. "She might be little, but the lady can fight."

"It's true? She punched you?" Isaac asked as he quirked an eyebrow.

Elijah tensed then relaxed. At least he had stopped the beating, if only temporarily.

"She's a hellion. Damn near scratched my eyes out—and gave me a black eye!" he exclaimed in horror.

Isaac studied him and threw his head back in laughter. "You, a vampire, brought down by a tiny human. Absolutely brilliant," he choked out over his mirth.

"Yes, bloody hilarious," Elijah mumbled before arching a brow. He winced when pain shot through his head at his action. Thank God he healed fast. "Are you finished?"

Isaac hesitated and replied, "For now."

"Good, because as much fun as this has been, we need to talk."

"Sabrina is—"

"Sabrina is yours. We both know it. What I want to talk about is Louisa. She wants Sabrina. She is looking at duplicating history." Thunder crashed overhead, and the wind blew as Isaac hissed. Elijah nodded before continuing. "Yes, I know. I've spoken to her, and she made it very clear to me. If we were to combine forces, your powers and mine, we stand half a chance of beating her."

"*Combine?* Are you insane? I am the Ruler of the Enforcers. The Protector. You expect me to team up with my enemy, who I am, by all rights and purposes, sworn to kill? Do you know what will happen if anyone finds out I didn't kill you last night? Or if anyone finds out I am here, meeting you now, and not trying to kill you? I would be hunted down, ostracized. I would be, in short, one of you. That is not acceptable."

"Not even for Sabrina?"

"Especially for Sabrina," Isaac insisted. "The last thing she needs to see is me hunted down and killed. She'd try to stop them—to save me—as you saw last night. She could get hurt. I'll not allow that. We'll have to discover another way to defeat Louisa, because we sure as hell won't be working together. We should never see each other again, unless it is a battle to the death."

"You think I want to be a monster, Isaac? You think I enjoy this life? This *Hell?*"

"You were a monster before you ever became a vampire," Isaac swore.

"You want to kill me? Please, do it. I won't even fight you. Just *do* it."

"Go to Hell."

"*Why* can no one see I've been there all along?" Elijah asked in exasperation before leaping on Isaac. They flew through the air clasped in battle and landed on the ground, Elijah on top of Isaac. Isaac hissed when rocks and twigs dug into his skin. Elijah smiled grimly and took advantage of the moment by slamming Isaac's head into the ground.

"Do it, Isaac. Finish what you have been dreaming of all along. Rip my head off my body. Let's go." Elijah even tilted his head to the side to allow easier access.

Isaac stared at him oddly before he flung Elijah off of his chest and jumped to his feet. "Elijah, I'm leaving. Stay away from me. And stay away from Sabrina. Just leave us *alone*."

Elijah stared at his brother in frustration. He'd told Isaac to kill him, yet here he stood, unharmed and untouched. In a last effort to get Isaac to return and end his personal Hell, he called out, "Next time you break Sabrina's heart, you might not want to leave her outside. You never know what kind of night creature will stumble upon a woman who is lying outside for two hours."

Isaac stiffened and swung around to look at him. He'd gotten a reaction indeed, but not the one he wanted. "Two hours? She lay outside for two bloody hours?"

Elijah started and then nodded. "Yes, she did. Probably would have been longer, but I got her and brought her inside. So next time, see her inside before you leave her, please."

Isaac glowered at Elijah, and replied, "There won't be a next time." And he left.

Elijah cursed and sprinted away. He needed a good run to clear his head. He ran until he reached the edge of the cliffs towering over the ocean. He wished he could jump into the water and end it all. Salt water mimicked acid to his kind. It would be painful, but at least it would be over.

Unfortunately, when the devil made vampires, he'd decided not to let them be capable of offing themselves. He found this ironic, since suicide had always been a sin. His existence was a sin. Yet, no matter how hard he commanded his muscles to move, to jump into the swirling abyss below, they wouldn't obey. He'd tried many times before, and he knew it would be useless to try once again.

But he still tried.

It was impossible to accept. There had to be a way to get out of this Hell, once and for all.

He had only to discover it.

ༀ

Isaac also ran, but to Sabrina's. His mind had become overrun by thoughts of his brother. He hadn't expected Elijah to be so miserable, so *suicidal*. He'd tried to make Isaac kill him. Even though he killed vampires every day, he cringed away from the idea of killing his own flesh and blood. If his people discovered he'd had a prime opportunity to kill a vampire, yet didn't, there would be hell to pay.

Elijah's suggestion regarding teaming up against Louisa made sense. It would probably work, but it couldn't be possible. Enforcers didn't trust, nor work beside, monsters. It just didn't work that way. He may as well go bite a human and join the vampire ranks, for that's what would happen in the end. He'd be even worse than the average vampire, since he would have betrayed his own kind and their principles.

He shook his head to clear it of all thoughts of Elijah. When he got to Sabrina's, he listened for any signs of crying. Everything sounded quiet. He leaned against the door, trying to determine if she was upstairs or downstairs.

Apparently Sabrina had been awaiting his return, because she opened the door at the first sign of his arrival. He stumbled inside and quickly righted himself. He tugged on his shirt and smoothed his hair in an attempt to appear natural. He knew he failed.

Well, that was smooth.

Sabrina paled as she scrutinized his disheveled appearance. Hopefully, she'd been too distracted by his uncharacteristic sloppiness to see his entrance.

"Are you okay?"

"Yes, I'm okay. I just had a minor...altercation."

"Connor told me he sensed Elijah, and you had run off. He's in my living room," she said, warning clear in her eyes.

Isaac craned his neck to find Connor eyeing him.

Shit.

"Connor, thanks for watching Sabrina."

She scoffed at his phrasing, and he cringed. He'd hear about his careless phrase of words later. *If* he got lucky enough to get a later.

"Did you catch him?"

Connor examined him, seeking any signs of a fight. In a pretense of setting his sunglasses down, Isaac turned so Connor would see his back. Sabrina gasped at his injuries, causing him to wonder at how bad they really seemed. "I did. We fought, and he managed to get me on the ground. I scraped up my back pretty good, and hit my head. He took advantage and ran. I tried to find him, but he'd already left. Or he'd blocked my abilities to find him. I'm not sure which." Connor stared out the window, and Isaac watched his eyes scan the forest for signs of life.

"I can't sense him. I wonder why you could find him before? It's like he wanted you to find him. But why?"

Isaac cursed Elijah inwardly and forced a shrug. Connor being suspicious of his actions didn't bode well for him. "I haven't a clue. But he's gone now, and that's all that matters. Now, if you'll excuse me?"

Isaac stared at him until Connor jumped to his feet. "Yes, of course."

"Let me look at your back, Isaac," Sabrina stated. Connor seemed to relax at the physical evidence of an altercation.

Thank God.

"I'll keep an eye out for any trouble, Isaac."

"Thanks. Especially Elijah," he added for good measure.

Connor nodded and left, and Sabrina rushed after him to lock the door. Isaac motioned her to wait when she tried to question him. "Okay, he's gone."

"What happened?"

"Elijah made himself traceable, and I went to him. He wants us to join forces to defeat Louisa."

She gasped. "What did you say?"

"I said the only thing I could. No. If I were to join forces with a vampire, I'd be betraying everything I stand for. My people would turn on me, and kill me. We're enemies. I can't form such an alliance. It wouldn't matter to them if he's my brother, or even if we were trying to defeat a more evil vampire.

"I would become something worse than a vampire, I'd be a *defector*. They would search for me more avidly than any vampire or werewolf. I would be the priority for all of my kind, the number-one objective to kill. Especially since whoever had the pleasure of finding me would become the next Ruler, which is a bit of an added incentive. And if you were beside me, you could be hurt. If you were not, they could use you to catch me, and you could be hurt. They are smart enough to know I wouldn't allow anything to happen to you. I can't be around Elijah. It just isn't safe for any of us."

She stared at him in dawning horror. "Oh my God, so if they knew you met him, and didn't try to kill him—"

"They'd kill me," he finished. "Those are our rules. The rules I have been required to enforce over time as well. If we do not follow the rules, the waters become murky, difficult to navigate. We would be lost at sea within moments."

"I understand." She put her hand on his shoulder and squeezed. "Elijah has to stay away. Surely he sees it now?"

"I hope so." He ran his fingers through his hair and stared at her in determination.

She shifted on her feet, uneasy at the scrutiny. Now that the urgency of finding out what had been going on was gone, she remembered all too well why she had kicked him out earlier. "Well, maybe you should get going."

"Sabrina—" he pleaded.

"What, Isaac? What more could you have to say to me? I'm certain it won't change my mind."

"I'm sorry. I shouldn't have acted the way I did. I fucked up. Can't you forgive me? Give me another chance?"

Put so prettily, it seemed hard to say no. But she didn't want to give in yet. He'd been wrong, and he damn well should suffer for a bit before she forgave him. "Maybe someday. But not now." She shook her head and tried to pull away from him. "I need time. And I think you do, too."

"No," he insisted. He yanked her toward him and stared intently into her eyes. "Time away from you is never a good thing. I *need* you," he whispered.

Oh, God, he'd pulled out all his cards now. She'd always been a forgiving person, always the first to let go of her grudges. But this time, she really didn't want to give in, hence the reason she had kicked him out in the first damn place. To resist his blue eyes pleading at her felt like more than she could bear. Seeking a respite from the force of those suckers, she spun him on his feet so she could study the wounds she'd noticed earlier. At least his eyes would be hidden, and she could maybe think clearly. "Let me see your back." She lifted his shirt and drew in a quick breath at the sight. "It's *gone*."

"Yeah, remember how I told you we heal fast? Exhibit A, in front of your eyes."

"Oh my God."

"Yeah."

"How amazing." She exhaled, running her fingers over his smooth skin. The faded red marks that remained were the only sign he'd ever been hurt, and even those disappeared before her eyes. His muscles clenched as she trailed her fingers over his skin, and a stab of desire shot through her. There were at least a million reasons why she should step away from him and kick him out again. A million reasons to resist the urge to find pleasure in his arms.

But the need to feel his lips on hers, to feel him inside her, overcame all rational thought, and moaning at the torture, she pressed her lips to his back and wrapped her arms around him from behind. She gently dug her nails into his taut abdomen and scratched his skin through his chest hair. He gave a low curse and turned to grab her shoulders. No sooner did his arms close around her than his lips were on hers in a thirsty need for satisfaction. No longer was it an issue of stopping if things got out of control for them. She could feel it in his kiss, and she could damn well feel it in herself. This wasn't about desire anymore; it was a matter of life and death. To live, they needed each other. To breathe, she needed his kisses.

Her legs buckled under the force, and he cradled her in his arms as they collapsed to the ground. He gripped her hips to pull her against him before grinding against her. She whimpered as liquid warmth flowed through her and settled between her legs. They both ceased to breathe out of sheer pleasure when she wrapped her legs around his hips. They ripped at each other's clothing in their eagerness to be naked, for the erotic feel of skin meeting skin in all the right places. The only sounds besides their harsh breathing were the sounds of clothing being torn.

As he ravished her mouth, she dug her nails into his shoulders and thrashed beneath him, desperate for something solid against her fingers. The marks would be gone by the time they finished, so neither paid much heed to them. His lips burned a hot trail from hers and down the side of her neck, where it focused. She shuddered and grasped him even tighter.

"Isaac…."

He tore his mouth from her neck, and she breathed a deep sigh of relief. She couldn't handle the wait; she needed to feel him inside her now. Normally, she would be all about the foreplay, but if he didn't hurry the hell up, she'd burst into flames. Lust licked at her in hot bursts, causing her stomach to clench and her legs to wrap around him in desperation. When he pulled back from her neck, she thought her wait over, but he only teased her, as he kissed a trail of hot kisses to the other side of her neck. She couldn't take any more of this sweet torture, surely she couldn't.

Oh, sweet God.

His lips closed around her nipple, and she lost all thought. She arched her back in frenzy, needing to get closer to his mouth, to give him free rein over her body. His tongue bathed her sensitive nipple, and a jolt of liquid desire shot straight to her clitoris. She almost came, then and there. She'd done this before; she was no innocent. But never before had it felt like this. Like she could explode at a single touch. Seriously, just one touch from him, and she'd surely burst into a million pieces.

He moved to her other breast, and she trailed her fingers down his smooth back. She skimmed her hand over his buttocks and moved around to the front of his body to run her fingers over his tight abdomen, and smiled in pure satisfaction when his muscles clenched at her touch. She heard him take a swift intake of breath when her hand closed around his hard shaft, and she moved suggestively beneath him while gently stroking him. A drop of moisture gathered at the tip of his penis, and she rubbed it over the head of his shaft. He groaned and crushed her lips beneath his again, plunging his tongue inside much as she would like him to do with his penis.

He positioned himself between her legs and threaded his hands through her hair. Triumph swelled inside her, and she pulled demandingly at his hips. At the point of entering her body, he paused to look outside. The wind howled, and the skies were turbulent. He took a calming breath, uncertainty clear in his features.

Oh, hell no. They weren't stopping now. She didn't give a damn if a tornado came and killed her while he came inside her or not—the time for waiting had ended. Sabrina grabbed his face in both of her hands.

"Focus on me, look at me."

He followed her command, and she stared into his eyes. His desire burned as clearly as his insecurity, laid bare for her to see. The world outside calmed as his breathing slowed. "I love you, Isaac."

"God, I don't deserve you, but I love you, too."

He kissed her and entered her in one swift thrust, all the way to the hilt. He filled her completely, stretching her as far as she could go, and she had never felt better. Any other time she had done this became a pale imitation of making love. This man brought new meaning to making love. It should always feel so good. So right. Sabrina tensed, and widened her eyes as she instantaneously climaxed when he touched her clitoris. The combination of him inside her and his fingers proved too much to bear. And oh, God, he hadn't finished. Not even close to it.

He continued to move in her as he stroked her. Pressure built up inside her again. She would die. But man, it would be the best. Death. Ever. She cried out and met his every push as burning need encompassed her, the greedy need to feel more pleasure, to fall to pieces once more. He cried out her name, and as she watched his face as he climaxed, she let go of herself and joined him, allowing satisfaction to overtake her once more.

Lightning flashing illuminated her closed eyes, thunder boomed, and the house groaned under the force of the winds outside, but neither occupant noticed. She was too busy staring at him in awe, and he did the same.

When they both crashed back to reality, she giggled as she realized a freak storm had wiped out the power. Apparently, the darkness that had overcome her during sex turned out to be more than a climax. It had been a power outage. Isaac groaned in despair and hid his face.

"Oh, don't do that! Obviously, we did a good job if we caused that to happen." She wiggled her eyebrows, but he still looked bashful. "Don't make me hurt you, boy," she warned.

She finally got a reaction out of him, even if it had come from laughter at her weakness. "Now, that is a funny thought," he teased as his lips quirked. His eyes were sparkling.

"Oh, you think I'm amusing, do you?" She jumped on him and tickled him, but only got a grunt for her efforts. Okay, not ticklish. She studied him, determined to get a reaction. "I have other ways of torturing you, you know," she whispered in his ear. Her fingers trailed down his taut abdomen, and when he realized her intentions, he bolted into a sitting position. She giggled at his reaction.

"Oh no, you don't." He gripped her wrist firmly and pulled it close to him, making her drape across his chest even more closely. "Let's give England a break from the storms for a little while." He kissed the tender inside of her wrist and smiled at her.

God, she loved him.

"We'll figure it out, don't worry. We just need more practice. Given time, we can probably avoid the storms entirely, and instead it'll be sunny out."

"I don't think you'll ever not cause storms with me." He smirked. "The weather reflects my emotions, and how I am feeling at a particular period of time. When I am inside of you, I do not feel sunny and calm."

She laughed. "Well, I guess I shouldn't strive for sunshine, huh?"

"Hell, no," Isaac mumbled. He tackled her beneath him and pressed his lips to hers. When it started getting too passionate, she regretfully pulled her mouth away from his. This didn't deter him; he just kissed a trail down her neck, and suspiciously seemed to be heading for her breasts.

"I thought you were giving the people of England a rest from the storm." She breathed deeply as her heartbeat quickened and her legs trembled.

"Screw the people of England," he muttered. A low rumble of thunder boomed in the distance.

"Well, in that case…."

His moan matched the loud boom of thunder outside as she flipped him over on his back and straddled his hips.

"Let's give them a show," she whispered.

ॐ

The storm passed, and the sun shone brightly. The weathermen of England were completely mystified, and even more so frustrated. Sabrina, on the other hand, had never felt happier, or more deliciously, perfectly, completely satisfied. The lights flickered and turned back on, and she wiggled her eyebrows and asked, "Wanna go again?"

He laughed and smacked her butt. He jumped out of her reach and declared, "I need food first. I wouldn't want to be found lacking due to hunger."

"Ow, that hurt." She pouted as she lurched to her feet and rubbed her butt while grimacing. It didn't *really* hurt, but if he thought it did, maybe he'd kiss her to make it better. She sneaked a peek at him, only to see him pulling on his pants with his back to her. She sighed and gave up her show of pain, and dressed before following him into the kitchen.

As they prepared dinner, Sabrina studied Isaac as he strolled around the kitchen. He wore only a pair of jeans, and every movement of his muscles taunted her. She found it hard to focus on cutting boring potatoes. He looked like much more fun to watch. His chest muscles flexed as he prepared the steak with seasoning, and his arms contracted as well.

Mmm, she'd love to run her fingers over those arms, to kiss his chest….

"Here, give me the knife before you cut off your finger," he joked as he pulled it from her fingers, effectively ending her delightful fantasy.

She jabbed his shoulder with her finger, scowled, and asked, "Why are you always taking my knives away?"

"Why are you always carrying them, and not paying attention?"

"Hey, I'm distracted, what can I say? It's not often I have a half-

176

naked immortal cooking in my kitchen." Expecting him to laugh, she got surprised instead to see him turn somber. Oh boy, here comes the talk.

Crap, take a sip of wine, girl.

"I'm sorry for how I acted. I have no excuse, except to say I love you so much. Sometimes my thoughts are nowhere near rational when it comes to you."

"It's okay. I'm sure I would have been upset if I walked in on you kissing someone else, too."

"Yeah, but for me to have left you like I did. I didn't even stop to see if you got inside. It's unforgivable," he whispered.

"Really, it's okay. I didn't stay out for long." She flushed when he arched an eyebrow. "Or, it didn't seem long. I honestly don't remember."

"I got told two hours."

"Oh." She inhaled.

"But when I came across the two of you, I have *never* been so angry in my life. I felt ready to kill him with my bare hands. Even when I found him and Amelia naked together, I didn't get *so livid*."

"You were angrier over me? Is it wrong of me to say it pleases me to hear that?"

He laughed. "No, I think it's fine. Natural, even."

"Good, because it does." She kissed him and trailed a hand down his chest to rest upon his heart. His heartbeat accelerated at her touch, and she smiled.

"How about we make a pact?" he drawled.

"A pact?"

"Yes. How about from now on, we only kiss each other. At least, until one of us decides otherwise."

"Oh, I'm not gonna change my mind," she whispered. "You're stuck with me."

"Is that a promise, lass?"

"Aye, it is." She mimicked his soft accent.

He chuckled and replied, "Music to my ears."

Chapter Fifteen

*L*ater that night, Sabrina jerked awake and gasped for air. Isaac's pale face hovered over hers, and she groaned as she covered her eyes. She tried to jump to her feet, but collapsed on the floor. Pain coursed throughout her body, and she felt paralyzed.

Isaac rushed to her side and pulled her into his arms. "What's wrong? What did you dream this time? Is it Elijah again? Louisa?"

She clung to Isaac, needing the feel of his arms around her to assure herself he hadn't been hurt. Last time she'd seen him had been in her dream, and he'd been on the ground, dead for all intents and purposes. She never wanted to see anything even remotely like it ever again.

"I saw it," she whispered against his chest. "I saw Amelia die. I don't know why, or how, but I saw it."

His muscles tightened beneath her cheek at her words. "How could that be?" he breathed.

She relaxed against his body and sighed in relief. The pain faded rapidly from her body, and she moved her fingers in careful consideration. Yup, definitely better. Now, if only the horrors she had been forced to witness would leave so easily as well.

"I don't know. I got trapped in Amelia's body. I saw it all—felt it all. The pain. Oh my God, the pain. It felt *horrible*."

"What did you see?" he whispered. She had the distinct impression he didn't really want to hear what she had to say, but felt he should. "I can tell you how accurate it sounds."

"The sun shined down on me, and in the dream, I actually became Amelia. So everything Louisa did to Amelia, she did to me, too. Does that make sense?"

"Yeah," he said in a broken voice.

He ran his hands down her back as he listened to her, and she felt her body relax into his even more. His fingers were pure heaven. Pulling her thoughts away from his tender ministrations, she resolved to get the story told as fast as possible, and hopefully she could begin to forget it as well. "My nose hurt—turned out it was bloody. Louisa came over. It surprised me to see her. I remember worrying about whether you were there, too." She paused and looked at him. "She worried about how you were doing, if you had found out already."

"You or her? You keep switching back and forth." Isaac pursed his lips and studied her.

"It doesn't matter." She waved her hand in front of her face. "In my dream, we are interchangeable. I became her." At his tight nod, she continued. "Louisa grabbed me by the hair and threw me. I landed at Elijah's feet. When I looked past him, I saw you. You looked dead. Your neck had been twisted to the side, and it looked broken." She covered her eyes and moaned. "It hurts to see you there, Isaac. I can't stand having the picture in my head."

He squeezed her. "It's okay. Try not to focus on it." He smoothed back her hair and kissed her forehead. "I'm here."

She took a calming breath. "I asked if you were dead, and Louisa laughed. She said she had other plans for you, but by the end of her fun I'd be dead. Elijah tried to keep her from me, but she grabbed him and shoved him against a tree. She broke another smaller tree, and slammed it through his shoulder so he'd be stuck there. Forced to watch."

"Jesus," he whispered as his face paled.

"First, she broke one arm, followed by the other, before I passed out. I could still feel the pain, and hear everything going on. Even unconsciousness didn't give me any relief.

"I heard Louisa go to Elijah and bite him. I think she worried whether he bled too heavily and would die," she said in an afterthought.

"Probably. It wouldn't be any fun for her…if he died when she didn't pay attention, he wouldn't get to live through eternity with her." Bitterness laced through his tone, reminding her of all the evil woman had put him through.

"Yeah, it makes sense. Anyway, she broke both my legs and I looked at Elijah. She tried to focus on him as she died. Elijah screamed, and my chest hurt. I looked down and saw a dagger sticking out of it."

Isaac paled before asking, "Do you remember what it looked like?"

Remember? I'll never forget.

"It looked silver, and had a jagged edge. One of those really lethal-looking weapons you see only in movies? On the hilt it had two blue topazes side by side. Above them was a ruby, and below, a diamond."

Isaac cursed and nodded. "The two blue topazes are me and Elijah, the ruby is my mother, and the diamond my father. We each received one on our seventeenth birthday."

She couldn't help but be shocked Louisa had used Elijah's treasured gift as a weapon to finish off Amelia even though she'd proved herself to be a ruthless monster. "I see. Well, after that she died. And I woke up. I could feel the pain as she felt it. It hurt. It was excruciating. And the look on Elijah's face. It killed me. So horrible."

She shuddered and buried her face against his chest, inhaling his scent in a plea for sanity. God, the pictures would not stop barraging her. Isaac lay on the ground, neck bent; Elijah crying out her name while pinned to a tree; Louisa taunting her as she broke her apart, bone by bone; the dagger sticking out of her chest. And the pain—oh God, the pain.

Isaac pulled her against him again and tucked her head under his chin. "Yes, it was."

"Where is the clearing? Is it the one you don't like me being in? The one where I found you the other night? The same one from my dreams?"

Isaac sighed, and replied, "Yes, it is. In your dreams, Elijah is showing it to you like Amelia remembered it. It was a meadow we often visited."

"So you all died there?"

"Yes," he stated.

"But if you were there, then you lived near here? And so did Amelia?"

He tensed and looked away. "I lived down the road," he admitted sheepishly.

"And now?"

"Still do," he replied.

"And Amelia?"

"Are you sure you really want to know?"

"Um, yes?" She wondered why she *wouldn't* want to know.

"A few thousand feet from here."

"Excuse me?"

"You're living in what used to be Amelia's father's barn."

"Oh. My. God."

"Yeah, I know. I couldn't believe it when you told me where you lived. Unbelievable. Why did you pick this place?"

"I don't know, it just seemed…right. Like it had been made for me." She caught the look of amusement on his face and glared at him. "Oh, shut up."

"Sorry." He laughed.

"What happened to the house? I'm trying to remember. Oh, right, a tornado took it down." Isaac blushed and looked away. "Are you blushing? Why in the world would you be blushing?" And suddenly, it dawned on her. She gasped out loud and exclaimed, "It was you! You caused the tornado, didn't you?"

He grimaced and nodded. "I hadn't yet learned how to control my emotions. I'd been moping about the house, and the next thing I knew, a tornado came ripping through. Luckily, no one had been inside."

"Don't feel bad. It's not your fault. It's not like you do these things on purpose."

"No, I don't."

"*Can* you do it on purpose? Cause tornadoes?"

Isaac paused and studied her. "I've tried to create tornadoes here and there. I've gotten close, but it's not easy. It takes a lot of energy to produce a storm from willpower alone. When I'm angry it just kind of happens. That's when it's dangerous, because I'm not in control of the situation. When I'm purposely causing a storm, or wind, I can decide how strong I need it to be. If I lose control, or my emotions cause storms, it can be devastating."

She paled, and bit her lip nervously. "So that's what made you nervous earlier."

"Yeah, I didn't want to bring a tornado on our heads."

She nodded. "Is there anything I can do to help?"

"Hmm...not look, or feel, so good?"

She scoffed. "Not possible, sorry."

He smiled. "I didn't think so. Now, back to bed for you. Hopefully your dreams will leave you alone for once."

Sabrina's head spun busily with all the new information she'd learned. And he wanted her to sleep? Was he *insane*? "I'll never fall asleep. Are you crazy?"

"I think you'd be surprised. Lie down and close your eyes. If you can't sleep, I'll stay up, too. Just try for me?" he pleaded.

"Fine," she gave in. "But it's not going to work, so be prepared for a late night."

She fell asleep as soon as her head hit the pillow.

ജ

Elijah studied the turbulent waters below as he perched on the edge of the cliff. It's not like he needed to worry about falling in. Hell, if only it were so easy.

Hunger gnawed at him, yet he didn't feel in the mood for hunting. He liked to wait as long as he could, to deny the beast in him what it most wanted.

Blood.

It tortured him alone, yet he still persisted. He enjoyed the pain it brought about, enjoyed feeling *something*. Something besides the misery that always plagued him over the loss of Amelia. And now, Sabrina too. She had chosen Isaac, and he'd been left to wander the world alone and miserable once more.

When she had come back into his life, he had seen a light at the end of the tunnel. He had pictured a future, bright and sunny, by her side. He'd change her into a vampire, of course, because life without her would be meaningless. He damn well wouldn't have watched her die again. Hell no, he'd seen it already. And never, ever again would he watch that.

But in one sure move, she had ripped those dreams from him by falling in love with Isaac. And really, he couldn't blame her. Isaac had always been much purer of heart than him. He was a monster, after all. One who should die. This brought him back to his earlier thought—death.

He stiffened as he studied the water. Someone approached, and he knew exactly who. He'd recognize her stench anywhere.

"Come to push me in, Louisa?" he asked, not bothering to turn around to face her.

Her laughter tinkled through the air as she approached. She stopped just short of arm's reach. She might be confident, but she was not reckless enough to stand on the edge of the cliff.

Not like him.

"Now, why would I do that, Elijah? To ruin a beauty such as yours would surely be a sin."

"The fact we exist is surely a sin," he growled in response.

"You always say the same things. Can you not accept your lot in life?"

"If I had a life to accept, maybe I would. But I'm not alive, Louisa."

"You aren't?" Her voice shook as she cried, "Do you get angry? Sad? Can you still love?"

"Do not speak to *me* of *love*, Louisa." He stepped toward her, ready to pound her into the ground.

"I happen to know for a fact you can, and so can I. So you tell me how we are not living right *now*?"

"Hatred for you doesn't make me feel alive," he insisted.

"Maybe if you allowed yourself to feel happy every once in a while, to care about something other than your dead whore, you'd feel more alive."

He whirled on her, nostrils flared. "Don't even speak her name."

"Ah, now you look animated. The mere mention of her existence and you perk up. It's sick, you realize that, right? If this who—" She broke off at the look he shot her way. "If this woman is so worth it, if your undying devotion is so warranted, where is she now?"

"Dead, by your hand," he declared. He locked his hands in fists and deliberately ignored her reference to Sabrina. If she didn't know he loved her maybe, just maybe, he'd stand a chance of convincing her to let Sabrina live in peace.

"By my hands? Or yours?"

He snarled and launched himself at her. She swung up on a nearby branch and kicked him in the face. Pain exploded in his nose. He flew backward, away from the bloody cliff edge.

Pity, that.

She followed him and straddled his hips. She pressed herself against him, and he gritted his teeth to keep his desire at bay. He hardened against her moist heat—Jesus, he could feel her through their clothes—and she laughed. She stroked a hand down his chest to the waistband of his jeans, and he drew a deep breath as she traced his erection. He captured her hand in his steely grip and fought back the desire fighting to overcome him.

It had been too long. Too *damn* long. Hell, at this point, he'd probably screw a tree.

For a moment, sadness crossed her features. He studied her as he struggled for control. As quickly as the sadness had appeared on her face, it disappeared. In its place came an evil smirk and her eyes glittered at him.

"Don't overreact, Elijah. I merely pointed out a fact."

He growled at her and threw her off of him. She landed on the balls of her feet. He didn't bother to attack her again, simply glowered his hatred.

"Are you forever destined to desire what your brother has?" Her question sounded soft, and for once, there no anger laced through her words. "Will you always deny what happiness you could enjoy in life, those things in your reach, only to yearn for those you cannot achieve?"

He stiffened and sighed. "I can't be happy with you, *ever*. I might feel the normal attraction and pull toward you every vampire has for their maker, but I will never love you. You need to accept that, just like I need to accept I will always be a monster. A monster you made."

"Of course you can't ever love me," she said sadly, "because you are too obsessed with her. The new whore."

So much for keeping Sabrina out of the conversation.

"Sabrina doesn't want me, so you can leave her alone. She wants Isaac. She is innocent of Amelia's sins. She looks like her, but she can't be held at fault for something out of her control. Leave her and Isaac alone. She means nothing to me."

She moved behind him and whispered in his ear, "Now, Elijah, what would be the fun of that?"

Her laughter taunted him as she fled, and he howled into the wind.

No one heard him.

Chapter Sixteen

As Sabrina sat at her computer checking her e-mail, the phone rang. She answered, not bothering to glance at the caller ID.

"Hello."

"I made it home in one piece." Marie's voice sounded tired to Sabrina.

"Well, that's good to know." She rubbed her eyebrows and leaned back in her chair. She dangled her head back against the top of the chair and stared at the ceiling. A yawn escaped her, and she blinked rapidly to clear her vision. Maybe she should take a nap.

"Yeah. How are things? Did you and Isaac kiss and make up?"

Sabrina winced, but didn't bother to deny they'd fought this time. "Yes."

"Good. Your puppy-dog sad faces haunted me the whole way home. It was awful."

"Ha-ha," Sabrina drawled.

"I'm serious. It was terrible to watch."

"Sorry."

Marie laughed. "It's okay, I forgive you."

"Gee, thanks. Now I'll be able to sleep again." She cringed as soon as the words were out of her mouth.

Here come the questions....

"Have you had any more nightmares?"

"No, I'm fine. How's Samantha?" Hopefully the quick change of subject would confuse Marie. It worked, and Sabrina smiled as Marie launched off on her favorite topic: Sam.

They chatted for a few moments before hanging up. She shifted in her seat and tapped her fingers on her desk. All morning long she'd attempted not to think about the one thing on her mind even now, her dream. The clearing they had all died in taunted her mercilessly, and she yearned to compare it to its current state. She needed to see it again, but also knew Isaac wouldn't want to take her.

Not only did he not like her going there, he didn't enjoy going there either. That much had been clear when they had been there a few days ago. And she knew if she asked him to take her he'd feel compelled to do so, even though he didn't want to. So while she didn't want to make him go, it didn't mean she couldn't go check it out herself, did it? Screw it. The desire proved too strong; she needed to go.

The dream from last night tormented her endlessly, assaulting her with images she had no desire to see. She cringed as she remembered it once more.

"I love you, Elijah." Amelia whispered.

"I love you, too, Amelia." Love shone in his eyes as he leaned down and kissed her.

Then pain exploded in her face, and the world faded to black. When Amelia came to, Louisa hovered over her. What in the world happened? And where did Elijah go?

She groaned and rolled to her side, searching for signs of him. She didn't see him anywhere. She sat up and tried to calm her rolling stomach.

She wet her dry lips and croaked out, "Where's Elijah? What happened?"

"Hmm, maybe I can help. You are a harlot, and Elijah is a bastard who can't keep his hands to himself. Caught up? Good, because off you go."

Louisa grabbed her by the hair and threw her. She felt too stunned to even cry out from fear, or from the pain of her hair ripping out of her head. In an excruciating collision, she hit the ground and lay motionless as she attempted to catch her breath. A shadow fell over her, and she whimpered in fear.

She opened her eyes, sure she'd see Lady Harding, and instead saw Elijah.

Oh, thank God.

"Elijah, help me," she whispered.

"There's your whore, Elijah. Have any final words to say to her, before I kill her?"

She struggled to sit up, and Elijah shook his head at her.

"It need not be like this. We can leave together, just the two of us. Come to me, and we shall leave."

Louisa sneered. "I have a much better plan, Elijah."

Louisa stalked toward them, and Amelia sat up to search for an escape route. There had to be a way out.

Her eyes caught sight of a familiar face, and she drew in a horrified breath. "Good Lord, is Isaac—"

Louisa followed her line of vision. "Dead? No, he's very much alive. See, I have plans for him. But you, my dear, will definitely be dead when I am finished."

Elijah jumped in front of her, presumably to protect her. Louisa threw her head back and laughed. "Oh, Elijah. You are positively hilarious." Louisa picked him up and slammed him against a tree before breaking another tree nearby. She forcefully drove it through Elijah's shoulder and into the tree behind him. He let out a cry of pain, and Amelia shrieked. Louisa dusted her hands off and laughed. "Ready for the main show, Elijah? You surely will not wish to miss it."

She stalked to Amelia, who in turn whimpered in fear. "Lady Harding, I am sorry, but please don't do this. You have hurt Elijah. Look at him!"

"Have you never been told not to frolic under a promised man? You are a shameless harlot, Amelia." She shook her head and smiled. "This is going to be marvelous. Prepare yourself for a broken arm."

She grabbed Amelia's left arm and snapped the bone in two. Amelia cried out and sobbed as pain wracked her body. Elijah strained against his prison and yelled her name.

Even as Amelia reeled from the injury, Louisa grabbed the other arm and repeated the action. Mercifully, Amelia passed out from pain.

Next thing she saw, Elijah had blood oozing from his neck. His eyes looked drugged, as if he had imbibed too much brandy. His eyes met hers, and she was startled to see the tears running down his cheeks.

The pain of her leg snapping made her tear her eyes from Elijah, and she screamed in agony. Before she processed the pain, a new one exploded in her other leg. From a distance, she heard Elijah call out her name. She tried to hone in on his voice and conjured up a picture of his face when he had first kissed her.

It had been worth even this agony. She could have no regrets.

Amelia turned her head and focused on him. She could tell he grew weaker, and sobs wracked his body. She latched onto on her beloved's face and waited for death, mercifully, to take her away. Surely Louisa would finish her off soon.

Pain burst through her chest, and she involuntarily looked down. Elijah's dagger protruded from her. She choked on a strange liquid and realized it was blood.

She couldn't breathe. She would soon die.

Thank God.

Sabrina walked out of the house in a daze, focused on the dream until she reached the clearing and examined it under her new insight. She could see all the similarities now, the silly things she'd missed before. She found and studied the tree Elijah had been pinned to, and pictured with perfect clarity the startling red of his blood against the bark. In a trance, she stumbled to the tree and touched its rough surface, and saw a scar on the tree's surface in the exact spot where Elijah had been speared. The same spot he'd suffered, fought, and died.

She looked over her shoulder and recognized where Isaac had lain motionless. Not far from the tree she leaned against now. He had been so close to them, so close to saving them and running. But instead, he had been cut down like a savage beast. By a savage beast.

The bitch.

She wandered toward where Isaac had landed and froze. And here, here was where Amelia had died. Where they had both lost the love of their lives. Everything had changed drastically that day, both emotionally and physically. Though both immortal, they could no longer embrace each other as brothers. They were on opposite sides of the battlefield, forever locked in a ferocious war that would only end in death.

Her fingers were still on the tree when Elijah walked up behind her. She turned to him; his gaze locked on the scar on the tree, strangely fascinated with the spot where he had died long ago. He tore his gaze off of the tree to focus on her, and the pain in his eyes spoke to her without words. His face looked the same as it had the day Amelia had died. "Oh, Elijah, I'm so sorry. I saw it all happen last night. It—no one should have to go through that. Ever."

"You saw it?" he whispered. "But, how? I didn't come to you last night."

"I don't know. But I did, somehow."

"Oh, God." He looked away from her and sighed deeply. "I'm so sorry you had to see it. No one should ever see what happened that day, what I did that day." His brow furrowed, and his eyes were lost in shadow as he stared off into the distance.

His pain hit her as strongly as if it were her own, and her heart ached from the force of it. Though she couldn't love him the way he wanted her to, she *did* love him. She yearned to heal the hurt bottled inside him, and it seemed natural to open her arms to him. He immediately took her offering of comfort, and she wrapped her arms around him and rested her cheek on his chest.

The oddness of the lack of beating heart beneath her cheek struck her, making her bite back a smile. Instead, his chest was still, immobile as stone. She noticed the oddest things at the most inopportune times.

He didn't move, and she did her best to do the same. They stayed in their frozen embrace for an unknown amount of time. When he finally spoke, pain wracked his voice and broke her from her silent thoughts.

"I loved her so much." He sighed.

"She loved you, too."

"I love you, too."

She paused before whispering, "I know."

"And you love Isaac."

"I do."

He sighed and inhaled the fragrance of her hair. "Let me enjoy this, just one moment longer."

She laughed and glanced up at him as she conceded, "Okay, *one* more minute." She had a moment's warning as he stared at her lips, before he went to take the kiss he could apparently no longer resist. She flinched and shouted, "No, Elijah! Don't do it, or I'll have to punch you again."

He groaned and closed his eyes as if deep in thought. "Damn it, Sabrina, it might be worth another black eye."

She laughed and stepped back from his arms. "Oh, Elijah, you really need a—"

Clap, clap, clap.

Oh man, someone watched them, and she knew it would be Isaac. And, of course, he'd found her in Elijah's arms again. However innocent the embrace had been, it would look anything but to Isaac, who already felt insecure about his brother.

Her heart lurched, and she took a deep breath before turning to face Isaac. This was going to suck royally. Her eyes widened in fear and she found herself wishing it had been Isaac. But it looked far, far worse. Across the clearing, Louisa glared at her.

"You know, you almost had me convinced the girl could *live*. Clearly, you were lying through your teeth last night, Elijah. Didn't anyone ever tell you lying to your maker is frowned upon?"

"I didn't lie to you." As Elijah spoke, he positioned Sabrina behind him. "We aren't lovers. I already told you as much. She loves Isaac, not me."

"She has an odd way of showing her love for Isaac. For if I'm not mistaken, it's you she embraced. Not Isaac," Louisa sneered.

"I only comforted him. That's it. He was grieving over what you did to him and all the people he loved," Sabrina replied in a rush of anger. She should be terrified of this woman—this *monster*. But instead, hatred flowed through her veins and gave her a heady sense of power.

"Oh, how darling. I'm sure that is what Amelia was doing as well. Comforting him," Louisa said, sarcasm oozing from her voice.

"Sabrina, be quiet." Elijah shushed.

"I will *not*!" she exclaimed. "She doesn't scare me."

"Louisa, knock it off. She is innocent. Leave her be."

"Once again with the broken record. Don't you ever say anything new?" She took a step closer to them, and Elijah snarled in response. She seemed to take heed of the warning, because she paused and raised her hands in a gesture of peace. "Did you like the dream you had last night, Sabrina? It's one of my most shining acts of all time."

Sabrina gaped at her and completely forgot her bravado. "You showed me the dream?"

"But, of course. Who else?"

"Which dream?" Elijah interjected.

"Why?" Sabrina questioned.

"Well, what would be the fun of killing you, if you didn't remember the last day in detail? I have always been somewhat dramatic, and I love my scene to be set perfectly, in all ways. As a matter of fact, I'm still not quite ready to kill you yet. We are missing one key factor."

"Isaac," Sabrina breathed. "You leave him alone, bitch. He has done *nothing* to you!"

"Oh, you're a delight. I'm here merely for informational purposes today, which is the *only* reason you're still safely tucked away behind dear old Elijah. Otherwise, I'd be snapping your bones in two. Like I did before."

"I think you're wrong there, because I'm not *her*. I have information for you, too."

"Oh? And what would that be?"

Sabrina stepped around Elijah's protective stance and moved to walk up to Louisa. Elijah grabbed her, so she settled for leaning forward to hiss, "I'm not scared of you."

"Are you trying to get yourself killed?" Elijah snapped as he pushed her back behind him. Sabrina ignored him, and so did Louisa.

Louisa laughed. "Oh, my, you are fun. Too bad I have to kill you."

"I *have* to breathe. You don't *have* to kill me. How about we just call it a day and you crawl back to whatever little hole you came from? M'kay?" Even as she taunted the dangerous creature in front of her, she knew she played a dangerous game. But, she couldn't seem to help herself. Seeing Louisa brought out feelings that overwhelmed her. Hatred. Fear. Sarcasm.

"Oh, I disagree. As much fun as you are, seeing your face makes me ill. Seeing him moon all over you again makes me even sicker. I'm going to kill you the same way I killed her: slowly, and happily."

Sabrina shuddered at the promise, because Louisa would love to do just that. But she would be damned if she'd show any fear in front of the bitch, and so she forced a sardonic laugh.

"Bring it, bitch." Sabrina stuck up her middle finger. Louisa's eyes widened and she threw her head back and laughed.

"You are *so* going to be fun to kill. So much fun," she said.

Elijah snarled, and she felt his muscles tense in preparation to defend her. Yet somehow, she didn't think even he would be enough to stop this madwoman. She would die—and soon. It sobered her.

Louisa shook her head and said scathingly, "Down, boy. I'm not going to hurt her yet. But I want to talk about the day Amelia died. Sabrina woke up too early, and I didn't get to show her everything. I think it's time for her to find out who really killed her."

"I know who killed Amelia. You," Sabrina argued. "And don't think I'll be so easy to get to this time. I'm no cowering weakling, Louisa. You don't scare me. And I have Isaac's protection this time."

Louisa stared at her before throwing her head back and laughing. "Oh God, you believe you can conquer me? How amusing." She laughed and winked in Elijah's direction. "She's got much more fight in her than your whore Amelia. Too bad she doesn't want you. She didn't even mention you as one of the weapons in her arsenal."

Elijah roared in anger, and Sabrina cried out when he shoved her backward and lunged at Louisa. She stumbled to her feet and watched in horror as he rolled on the ground fighting her.

"Run, Sabrina. Go to Isaac," he yelled as he held Louisa down. She bucked against him and growled as she struggled to free herself. Sabrina tore her gaze from the fight and forced her feet to flee in the direction of home. Hisses and snarls filled the air around her as she sprinted away. She worried about Elijah, but also knew she had to get away. Her being there actually made him *weaker*.

It annoyed her to admit it. But that didn't make it any less true.

The house lay in her sight when she got grabbed from behind, and she screamed in terror as arms clasped around her. She fought against her captor, fear giving her the strength to fight for her life. A hand slapped across her mouth, and she kicked harder to make up for the loss of sound. A grunt came from her captor when her foot succeeded in kicking its target, and the arms tightened around her even more, cutting off her breath.

"Jesus, Sabrina, stop it. It's me, Isaac. Calm down or we'll have Connor running to see what is wrong," he whispered urgently in her ear.

Hearing the familiar voice, she sagged in his arms and attempted to catch her breath, which still came out in harsh pants from her struggles. Isaac, sensing she'd stopped fighting him, removed his hand from her mouth.

"What happened?"

"I went to the clearing, and Elijah came to see me." She took a deep breath, "Nothing happened, I swear. He got upset and I consoled him. Nothing more."

"Shh, it's okay. I trust you, Sabrina. What happened to make you run?"

His statement gave her pause, but she forced herself to continue. "Louisa came along. She taunted me, telling me how she'd kill me like she had Amelia. She also told me I needed to know the truth about how Amelia really died. Elijah pushed me away and told me to run. They were fighting when I ran away."

"Shit." He ran his fingers through his hair and cursed under his breath, presumably warring at the desire to bring her inside to safety, and his equally strong desire to rid her of the threat of Louisa. "If I go and try to get her now when she's off guard, I might stand a chance of beating her. But it could be held against me later. If I don't get her, she could hurt you. I *have* to do something."

"Not that!" she exclaimed. "Never that. You can't risk yourself. There'll be another day to get her. *Without* breaking any rules," Sabrina insisted.

She could tell by the look in his eyes his mind had already been made up, and not in the way she wanted. She shook her head, but to no avail.

He kissed her hard. "Go. I love you."

"Isaac, no," she cried. But he vanished out of her sight before she could take a step in his direction. Fear and fury warred inside her, each trying to claim a stronger hold over her than the other. Though it killed her to do so, she ran toward the house. She'd reached halfway across the lawn when she slid to a stop. Screw this. She needed to find out what happened.

Sabrina bolted back, desperate to help in some way. She refused to cower in fear while Isaac broke every rule he'd ever followed—every rule he'd ever *made*—for her. She pressed herself harder than she had ever done before to get to Isaac before it was too late to do something, anything, to help. When she finally reached the clearing, she doubled over, grabbing her knees as she attempted to catch her breath, while simultaneously scanning the area. Isaac *was* there, but alone. He stood still, head cocked to the side. Deciding he looked safe enough for the moment, she backed away silently, hoping to return home unnoticed.

Please don't let him see me; please don't let him—

"I should have known better than to assume you would go home, shouldn't I have?" His voice had a resigned tone to it, laced with equal parts amusement and frustration. He turned to her and raised an eyebrow, and she flushed.

Son of a bitch.

"I couldn't just leave you."

"You left Elijah," he pointed out.

"You're not Elijah," she stated.

His eyes widened, and he studied her so intensely her heart stalled.

"What she means is I can take care of myself, but she doesn't think you can," Elijah spoke from above their heads.

Her eyes widened in shock, and she tilted her head back to scan the trees above. Did he want to get himself killed? She found him crouching on an impossibly high branch, and Elijah jumped down and landed on his feet, in a crouched position upon the ground.

"I don't think so," Isaac grumbled. "Still hiding from me?"

"I didn't know if you wanted me to show myself."

"Better than spying on us from above."

Thunder crashed in the distance as he glared at his mirror image. He apparently did not like the image of Elijah lurking in shadows, watching them. She couldn't blame him; neither did she.

"Isaac, calm down," Sabrina warned. They didn't need another Enforcer interfering in this mess, so he needed to keep his emotions in check.

He nodded and pulled himself together. "Where's Louisa?"

"Gone. She ran away after Sabrina left. You should really get her in her house now. Or are you going to leave her outside in another endearing fit of jealousy?" Elijah asked hopefully, perking up in his excitement. "I'd be happy to escort her."

Isaac growled, and Elijah laughed.

"Knock it off, Elijah," Sabrina snapped. "It's not funny."

He sobered at her admonishment and gave a curt nod of his head. "Go now, before she decides the stage is set nicely and returns."

"Elijah—" she started.

"Sabrina, go. Now." He stared at her, love in his eyes, and she tore her gaze away.

Isaac grasped her hand and dragged her away. She looked over her shoulder, and her heart broke a little at Elijah's face. Isaac squeezed her hand and she met his eyes. He gave her a reassuring smile. He paused and turned to Elijah. "I've changed my mind. We'll work together. Meet me here at ten o'clock tonight so we can work out the details."

Sabrina gasped in horror as Elijah nodded.

"Oh, hell no!" she shouted in fury.

"Oh hell, yes," Isaac insisted, his jaw set stubbornly.

Not allowing her the decency of a proper fight, he pulled her into his arms and ran full speed to the house. In seconds, they were behind the locked door. She wasted no time turning on him in rage.

"Isaac, you can't *do* this. What if the others find out?"

He tensed and looked out the window. "I can't let her hurt you, and not do everything in my power to stop her."

"Letting you kill yourself over me is not in my power." She pushed his chest. "Look at me!"

His eyes collided with hers, and his jaw hardened even more. Not a good sign. "Watching you die is not in mine."

"Your life will be forfeit if you do this," she argued.

"My life is forfeit without *you*," he cried in frustration. "I won't budge in this. I need you to be safe. I am willing to take the risk of discovery, so long as I know you are alive and free from Louisa."

Sabrina glared at him. "I will not let you destroy yourself for me. What kind of person would I be if I allowed you to do this? I'll leave here right now, if that is what it takes to get you to stop this nonsense. Not killing your brother is one thing, but joining him? It's *treason*."

Isaac growled low in his chest, and pinned her between the wall and his hard body. "You will not leave me, do you understand? You are *mine*."

Her eyes widened in apprehension at this new side of Isaac. Unsure how to proceed, she nodded and watched him nervously. Dare she argue more? He dropped his forehead against hers and pulled her into his arms.

"I can't bear even the thought of you not in my life, so please don't threaten me like that. Ever." His voice wavered.

Remorse came over her. "I'm sorry, Isaac. I won't do it again."

She laid her head on his chest and breathed in the scent of his skin. She bit her lip in an attempt to hold back her tears. The time for arguing was over. He had made up his mind. No amount of arguing on her part would change it.

He remained quiet as well, probably plotting how he and Elijah would team together to overcome Louisa and keep Sabrina safe.

Sabrina, however, schemed to stop him. No matter what he said, her priority would always be *his* safety. And the plan he'd agreed to didn't allow for him to be out of harm's way.

In fact, it put him directly in its path.

Chapter Seventeen

Sabrina and Isaac were curled up on the couch, sipping White Zinfandel, when she remembered something Louisa had said to her earlier. How had she neglected to tell Isaac about Louisa having sent the dream to her?

"I forgot, Louisa told me she showed me the dream last night, so I would remember what had happened."

Isaac gawked at her before shrugging. "It makes sense, I suppose. She's sick," he said in disgust.

"If she showed it to me, how did I get in Amelia's head? I heard her thoughts; I felt every broken bone she received." She shuddered at the memory.

Isaac looked troubled for a moment, before shrugging. "Maybe it's how she chose to show you the memory? I really don't know what else it could mean. Unless if you *are* Amelia reincarnated, and you were therefore remembering it as it happened to you?"

She scoffed. "Do I even act like her?"

He pondered her question before answering, "In some ways, yes. You have the same smile, same laugh. You get the same determined look on your face when you decide upon a course of action. But you are a lot braver and stronger than she was and a *hell* of a lot more stubborn, too." He quirked an eyebrow at her. "And you didn't screw my brother."

She swatted his arm and debated whether she dare ask him the question that pulled at her heart daily. "Do you love me because you think I'm her?"

She lay on her side, her legs curled to her stomach. At her question, he sighed and leaned over her, rested his cheek upon the curve of her hip, and draped his arm around her legs.

"No. I'll admit it's what drew me to you originally. But it's you I love, more than I have ever loved another. I can't breathe fully if you aren't near, I can't sleep. And life? Meaningless. You are my life. Without you, I simply wouldn't exist. There is *nothing* I wouldn't do to keep you safe. By my side."

She drew in a breath and stroked a hand over his shoulders. "I feel exactly the same."

He looked troubled at her statement, instead of pleased. "Sabrina, are you planning something? There's nothing you need to do, nothing you can do, to keep me safe. I'll be fine. I don't need your help. You'll only weaken my defenses. Can't you see that?"

She looked in his eyes and lied. "I'm not planning anything. I was thinking about how long it's been since you kissed me." She tugged his hair until he rose over her, smiling.

"I mean it, Sabrina," he warned with a growl.

"I know, I know," she whispered as she kissed him lightly. He succumbed to her demand, and when he tried to pull away from her, she clung to his neck. She didn't want him questioning her, dreaded he'd see it in her eyes that she'd lied. "Let's make a storm." She trailed kisses down his neck and pushed his shoulders until he lay on his back. She flicked her tongue over his skin, and she worked her way down his firm stomach.

He took a deep intake of breath as she caressed his erection, and a boom of thunder shook the house when her lips closed around him. His penis felt so silky smooth and hard against her tongue, a contradiction at its finest, and she couldn't help but moan throatily as she took all of him in her mouth. He threaded his hands through her hair and brokenly whispered her name. The sound made Sabrina squirm in anticipation.

Apparently, he could take no more of her sweet torture. He threw her on her back and rose over her. In one movement, he entered her and they both groaned in satisfaction.

He thrust inside her, and her hips rose in a dance as old as time itself, until they both climaxed and collapsed into each other's arms.

They remained in their lovers' embrace until the alarm on Isaac's phone went off, and he sighed and left her arms. He kissed her goodbye, and murmured, "Stay here, I won't be long."

She nodded and closed her eyes against his scrutiny, feigning exhaustion. He didn't seem fooled, however. Hell, acting had never been one of her skills.

"Please, stay here," he pleaded. "I'd tie you to the bed if I thought it would make you stay."

"I'd like to see you try." She grinned at him in challenge. He drew in a breath, and his eyes darkened at the mental image she must have planted in his head.

When in doubt, distract with sex. Works every time.

"Hmm, maybe another day?" he suggested. "Could be fun...given the right circumstances."

She didn't answer him, and he gave a frustrated sigh, leaving the room.

When the door shut, she counted to sixty and hopped off the couch. She dressed faster than ever before. She didn't want to miss their meeting.

Chapter Eighteen

*I*saac scanned the clearing for his brother and found him draped across a giant boulder.

"So, what are we going to do?" Elijah asked without preamble.

They both knew they couldn't waste time on niceties. Nor did Isaac care for them. He had a job to do, pure and simple. He had no desire to forgive his brother, or to become friends. Hell no, he did this for Sabrina and Sabrina *only*.

Isaac cocked his head. "We need to set a trap for Louisa. When one of us is distracting Louisa, the other can try to sneak up on her. No, that won't do at all. She will see us coming, and know what is happening. Louisa's *impossible* to beat. We'll never—" He paced in agitation as he ran a hand through his hair.

Elijah interrupted him. "No, I may have a plan. It came to me earlier. She's always lusted after me. We can both attest to as much." Isaac gave a curt nod of his head and met Elijah's eyes. More than likely, Elijah also remembered just how much she had desired him, and how far she would go to get him. "I can entice her, make her think she has a chance. Distract her using kisses and caresses. That's where you take advantage of her distraction. If you know what I'm saying."

"Will she fall for such an old trick, after all this time you've spent hating her?" Isaac scoffed. Louisa would believe that all of a sudden,

Elijah couldn't keep his hands off of her? Not bloody likely.

Turning red, Elijah looked away from Isaac's scrutiny. "There have been moments of weakness. We have—"

Isaac's eyes widened as he realized what his brother alluded to. He glared and snapped, "You've had sex with the woman responsible for killing Amelia, the same woman responsible for making us what we are? Is this what you're telling me?"

"Oh, spare me the righteousness of Isaac, if you will." Elijah snarled as he made a dismissive gesture of his hand. "We vampires don't exactly have a whole lot of choices out there, unlike you. If we try to take a human, they usually die in our arms. You, however, can have anyone you want, minus the repercussions. So don't judge me."

"Some people just do without," Isaac argued. His cheeks flushed when Elijah studied him, and he avoided his gaze and shifted on his feet. He hadn't meant to let that slip. "So you keep her otherwise occupied. Then, what, I run up behind you and snap her head off?"

"Precisely," Elijah drawled.

"How would we arrange the time, and place? We'd also need a signal, one no Enforcers would catch on to." Isaac tensed, and shouted, "God damn it, Sabrina!"

Elijah stared at him in confusion before he, too, sensed her presence. He whipped his head in her direction, and they both glared at her as she walked into the clearing. She held her head high, and her chin set stubbornly. Her eyes flashed in the moonlight as thunder boomed overhead. She had never looked so gorgeous, and he had never been so goddamned furious.

Once, just once, could she listen to him? Isaac rushed to her, pausing only to glower at Elijah when he headed toward her as well. Oh, hell no. Sabrina belonged to him, and Elijah needed to remember it. Now.

Elijah, heeding the unspoken warning, instantly halted, though his fists remained clenched.

"What the hell are you doing here, Sabrina? Are you crazy?" Isaac whispered.

She glared and answered, "No. *I'm* not. *I'm* not the one risking my head for treason."

Isaac opened his mouth to retort, only to be interrupted by Elijah. "Perhaps she's here for a reason, Isaac."

That earned a hiss from Isaac, but he did manage to ask using great control, "*Is* there something wrong, Sabrina?"

She hesitated and her gaze darted from him to Elijah speculatively. She looked terrified of what she wanted to say, but her chin jutted out nonetheless. If she was scared by what she had to say, he had a feeling he wouldn't like it either. At all.

"I'd like Elijah to change me," she stated.

Not like it? Understatement of the century.

Thunder crashed overhead, and Isaac found himself incapable of words, so he sputtered. The wind whipped around the trio at hurricane-like speeds, and Sabrina braced herself against a tree to fight the force of the winds pulling at her.

"Isaac, you need to calm down!" Elijah yelled as he approached Sabrina, presumably to help keep her from floating away in the wind. He got rewarded for his admonishment when Isaac pushed him, slamming him into the boulder he had previously rested upon.

The message, Isaac felt certain, came out loud and clear. Isaac stalked away from them both and punched a tree. The tree proceeded to shudder, and a cracking sound filled the air it crashed to the ground. Sabrina screamed, and Elijah hurried to her side to put a soothing hand on her shoulder. *This* did not help his anger very much.

Apparently the message hadn't been as clear as he had thought.

Anger oozed out of his pores like a sickness as Isaac stalked toward them, but he halted when he saw how petrified Sabrina looked. He growled and sat down to hold his head in his hands in an attempt to calm himself. She'd asked to be bitten. She'd actually *requested* to become a monster, to become his enemy.

He concentrated on calming his fury, and attempted to steer away the mental images of Elijah sinking his teeth into her neck. Although vampires liked the sensitive spot on the inside of the thigh, too. Elijah would probably much prefer that spot over a measly neck bite.

No, those types of thoughts wouldn't calm him down.

Get a grip, man.

When Isaac finally felt calm enough to confront Sabrina, he raised his head and glowered. Elijah still stood by Sabrina, but had wisely removed his hands from her. If he even so much as touched her right now, Isaac would lose the small bit of control he had. "And what, my love, would you accomplish if you got your way? Have you changed your mind, and would you like to live with Elijah instead?" he bit out. He ground his teeth together in an attempt to stay calm.

Sabrina ran to his side, halting Elijah's panicked attempt to stop her with a glare of her own, and crouched down beside him. "No, Isaac. I love you. I thought maybe if I weren't so weak—"

He laughed somewhat hysterically at her line of thought. Shaking his head in bemusement, he sneered, "You thought you would become a big, strong vampire and defeat Louisa, and we could live happily ever after?"

Sabrina blushed, but scowled at his condescending tone. "Yes, but God knows why I would want to be with an asshole like you." They glared at each other, neither backing down from their icy stance.

"Do you realize if he bites you, you would always be a part of him? That you'd have loyalty and attachments such as you've never known? Even Elijah feels drawn to Louisa, and he despises her."

She looked to Elijah for confirmation, and he nodded his assent.

"Oh well, if it helps us all out of this mess, so be it. I'm strong enough to resist," she insisted.

"Even if that were true, it would take at least a week until you were able to fight Louisa. Until then, you'd be lying in bed, wracked with pain. Useless. You don't become an invincible immortal right away."

"It's true," Elijah added softly from behind them. "It's not something you should wish for, Sabrina. It is no way for anyone to live. You'd be better off dead, just as I should be."

She gasped and glared at him. "Knock it off, Elijah. You may not be a mortal, but you're no monster."

Elijah scoffed at her words and looked away from her probing eyes.

"Sabrina, you're forgetting one fact," Isaac interrupted. She swung her gaze back to Isaac and arched an eyebrow. Isaac continued, "If you become a vampire, we couldn't be together. I'd be your *enemy*. We'd be apart forever, or damned and hunted down if I went to you. It's no way to live."

"You'll be damned and hunted down for pairing with Elijah as well, which doesn't bother you. So why not be damned and be rid of Louisa's threat in the process? I wouldn't be a weak human, and we could be together forever."

Isaac let his breath escape in a hiss. "No. Absolutely not."

Sabrina crossed her arms and turned her attention back to Elijah. "If you won't do it, Elijah, I'll find some other way to make it happen. I won't sit by and let Louisa hunt me down and kill me. I will *fight*."

"You will not!" Isaac yelled.

Elijah interrupted once more, insisting. "Isaac, you need to get her inside. I know Louisa is nearby, and we don't want to risk tempting her any longer. Go argue in the house, where I don't have to listen."

Isaac nodded his head and grabbed Sabrina's arm.

She pulled back and drawled, "Yes, let's hide the poor human girl. We wouldn't want her to stub her toe."

Elijah hid his smile, feigning a cough, while Isaac growled.

"Knock it off, Sabrina."

She glared at him and spun to Elijah. "Elijah, please...." His eyes softened, and Isaac picked her up in his arms.

"Don't even *think* about it, or I'll kill you right here and now."

"Do you promise?" Elijah taunted.

"Absolutely."

He turned his back on Elijah, and ran home.

❧

They were back at her house in seconds, and she opened her eyes to see him glowering at her.

"This is unacceptable."

"No, my becoming a vampire isn't unacceptable. Me staying a human, however, is," she insisted.

He sighed and ran his fingers through his hair. She knew he was frustrated, but no longer furious, since no storm brewed outside. He clutched her to his chest and kissed the top of her head as he sighed.

"Sabrina, I'll keep you safe. I promise you, if it's the last thing I do, I'll kill Louisa."

She whispered, "I can't accept the risk. I won't allow it to be the *last thing* you do."

"You becoming my enemy will solve nothing. It'll just serve to keep us apart. If you are a vampire, and I follow the rules I, myself, enforce, I can never see you again. If I go with you, knowing you are my enemy, I sign both of our death warrants. A leader can't just do as he pleases and expect his followers to stay in line. The chances of them discovering anything about me and Elijah are a lot lower than them finding out I'm in love with our enemy. You might as well kill me now, and save me the pain."

"We can still be together. It will have to be in secret. But still, it's possible. We could find a way."

"Stealing away at midnight for a romp in the forest? Not my style, thank you," he said sarcastically.

She rolled her eyes, and replied, "So you'd rather screw a seventy-year-old woman?"

He looked at her in confusion. "What in the *world* are you talking about?"

"I'm going to get older. You'll always be twenty-seven."

Laughter filled his eyes, and she knew she had lost the battle. "I'm sure you'll be a delicious old lady."

She growled. He nibbled her ear and laughed harder. "I won't allow you to become my enemy because you're afraid of a few wrinkles. There's always Botox," he joked.

"I'm going to die sometime. You realize that, right? If I remain human, eventually you'll have to hold my hand as I die. It's inevitable. It might be in a few days' time when Louisa gets her hands on me, or it might be in fifty years. But regardless of when it happens, it will."

Pain flashed over his eyes as he contemplated her words. It became obvious to her he'd never thought of this unavoidable fact.

"Yes, of course. And there's nothing I can do but make sure you live a full mortal life. I can do no more," he maintained.

She glared at him and bit her lip. He looked into her eyes and pulled her into his arms again.

"This will pass soon, and Louisa will be gone. Now isn't the time to be making rash decisions."

"Now is the perfect time to make decisions," she insisted.

They both knew they wouldn't agree on this issue. He would keep her safe, and *human*, at all costs. She remained determined to keep him alive at all costs. They shared a common goal, yet had different plans on how to achieve victory.

They were on opposite sides of the river, and neither would step foot onto a boat to cross to the other side.

There was nothing more to say.

&

"Hello," she murmured.

He smiled at her, his eyes both cynical and self-depreciating in the purple-strewn darkness. "I had to speak to you. I have to explain our conversation in your house. I haven't had a chance to tell you why I killed Amelia."

Sabrina tensed, and stared at him in confusion. "You didn't kill her. Louisa did."

Elijah looked away before turning back and holding his hand out to her. She put her hand into his, and they wandered to a fallen oak tree to sit.

"I don't understand, Elijah. I saw Louisa stab Amelia with your dagger."

"No, you saw Amelia with my dagger sticking out of her chest. My dagger I kept by my side, always."

"Of course it would be by your side, how else would she get it?" When he stared into her eyes, she comprehended the meaning behind his confession. "Oh."

"I killed her. I took her life—"

"You did it out of love, Elijah. You have no idea how much pain she felt." Sabrina shuddered. "She'd have thanked you if she could. I promise."

He stared at her and swallowed heavily. "How I wish I could believe you. It haunts me, the look on her face as she stopped breathing." He put his head on his knees and moaned.

Her heart twisted at his words, and she put a comforting hand on his shoulder. "I got put inside her head. She loved you even after the stabbing. The last thing she thought of, the last thing she saw, was you."

He studied her intently and nodded, wonder in his eyes. "I think I believe you."

"You should, it's the truth."

"I love you more than he ever will," Elijah stated.

She rolled her eyes at his brazenness and jumped to her feet, ready to go home. "Be free of needless guilt, Elijah. I know why you did what you did, and I approve. Were I her, I would demand the same. You remember that."

He shook his head. "I'll not take your life again."

"Even if I want you to?"

"Even then."

She sighed and knelt in front of him.

"Elijah, you did the right thing. Please don't feel bad anymore."

"I do feel a little better, and I'm glad you understand. If only...."

She put her finger on his lips to silence him. "Don't, please. I have to go. I don't want to worry Isaac."

Anger passed over his face, and his fists tightened by his side, but he stayed seated. She knew it couldn't be easy for him.

She looked at him one last time before walking away. She knew he followed to ensure her safety, but he kept himself hidden in the shadows.

හ

Sabrina awoke at the bottom of her steps inside her house. Isaac gripped her arm tightly and glared at her. She gasped in confusion and stared at him in question.

"What are you doing?" Isaac demanded.

"I-I don't know. I d-d-don't even know why I'm *down* here," she babbled. "Why am I down here? What happened?"

He glared and pointed at the door. She looked at it and turned to him in question.

"Look next to the door, Sabrina," he spat.

She followed his directions and saw her shoes sitting there, coated in wet grass and mud. "Oh my God," she muttered. A glance at her feet showed traces of grass and moisture as well. Her legs weakened and her heart raced. It brought to mind the dream she'd had where she woke up and found her feet muddy, and her bed covered in dirt.

She'd never sleepwalked before in her life. Why would she start now, of all times? Had the dream happened, or had she imagined it while sleepwalking?

"I don't understand," she whispered.

"Where did you go, and who came there?"

She told him of her dream, and he glowered at her another moment before he melted and pulled her into his arms. He breathed in her scent and moaned. "You scared the shit out of me when I woke up and you were missing. I ran downstairs, only to find you walking inside and removing your shoes. I didn't even realize you were asleep at first."

"I'm sorry. I've never done this before, I swear. I don't know what happened." She wrung her hands, mutilating her pajamas in the process.

"Actually, you have. Once before." He shifted on his feet, not meeting her eyes.

She cocked her head and studied him before his meaning suddenly dawned on her. "That night wasn't a dream? When I woke up with sticks in my hair?"

"You fainted. I made sure you stayed unconscious, cleaned up your sheets, and washed your hair. I cleaned you and tucked you back in. I didn't want you to be scared." He shrugged and grinned ruefully.

She drew in a breath and stared at him in horror and surprise. "You stripped me naked and *washed* me?"

Isaac grinned. "My eyes were closed the whole time."

"Really?"

"Absolutely not," he chirped. His lips quirked as if holding back laughter. She tried to resist the laughter trying to burst out and failed. He lost his own silent battle and joined in.

"Pervert," she quipped.

"You wouldn't have it any other way." Isaac smiled at her, and the smile dissipated. "We need to be more careful, though. There are dangerous things out there, and you need to stay inside. We need to keep you safe."

"Me and my frail humanness?"

"Is humanness a word?"

Sabrina cocked her head and glowered at him. "Does it matter?"

He grinned, sweeping her into his arms. "No, I guess not."

Isaac carried her upstairs, and she pulled his face down to hers for a kiss. Isaac swept in a breath at the desire clenching him, and he deepened the kiss. He grew hard, his cock seeking the warmth only Sabrina could give him.

He set her on her feet and removed her shirt over her head. Watching her delicious body appear inch by inch proved to be more torturous than anything else in the world. Her nipples hardened in the cool air, and they taunted him to take them into his mouth and plunge inside her. But he forced himself to continue his slow seduction, pulling her pants down using soft caresses on her legs, before allowing his hands to roam back up to her inner thighs.

Her legs quivered, and she let out a small breathy sound as he grew harder yet. What she did to his body equaled pure insanity; surely he'd die from the pleasure one of these days—immortal or not.

She clutched his shoulders with unsteady fingers as his hands caressed her inner thigh and moved inward to her moist heat. He laid her on the bed, and he couldn't miss her sigh of relief as he rose over her.

But he hadn't finished yet. She'd have to wait for him to enter her. Whether she liked it or not.

Ignoring the primal instinct to thrust himself inside her, he instead took her nipple into his mouth, like he'd been longing to do since he'd bared them. His other hand caressed her clitoris, causing her to squirm in delight.

Jesus, she was wet and ready for him.

It tortured him to feel her heat beckoning him and, moaning her name, he plunged a finger inside. Her hips rose off the bed as she arched her back and whimpered his name. Her small sounds of pleasure urged him on, and he kissed a hot path to her stomach and down her left leg. From there, he traveled to her inner thigh as he caressed her sensitive nub with his thumb. Her body jerked off the bed, and he pressed her back down. He closed his lips around her clitoris to savor the sweetness of the intimate spot.

Jesus, she tasted like summer and sunshine. She moved against his mouth urgently, her hands gripping his hair. He deepened his caresses against her sensitive bud and felt her whole body tense as she neared her climax. His senses heightened from knowing he had mere seconds until he could thrust inside her body. She let out a cry, and her whole body froze. He tore his lips from her intoxicating taste, and thrust inside her. Her muscles squeezed him as she climaxed again, and he lost all control.

After a few more thrusts, he threw his head back and yelled hoarsely, collapsing on top of her. She trailed her fingernails down his back, and kissed his neck tenderly.

"I love you," she breathed in his ear.

Her hot breath made him harden once more, and reflexively, he pressed himself further inside. She moaned and moved her hips against his, making his heart quicken in response. He thrust again, and soon got carried away by passion. She flipped him onto his back and straddled him while grinning naughtily.

"My turn," she whispered as she kissed his neck and traveled down to his nipples. Her hand trailed down his abdomen until it closed around him, and she stroked him exactly the way he loved it.

Jesus, she might really kill him.

ം

The next morning, Isaac left Sabrina at dawn. He told her he had a merger meeting to go to, and she knew he lied to her. He may have "work" to do, but it had nothing to do with real estate, and probably everything to do with evil vampires.

She twiddled her thumbs for a few hours, even picked up her latest knitting project she had been neglecting, before deciding to visit Connor at McGuiness's. Her hatred of being alone had caught up to her and slowly drove her insane. Though Isaac had reminded her to stay home, he couldn't truly object to her going to see another Enforcer, could he? She and Isaac came there often to enjoy the quietness of the tavern before opening hours, and Connor's divine omelets.

She'd be perfectly safe.

Her decision made, she hopped in the car and drove straight to the tavern, windows cracked despite the coolness of the autumn breeze. She inhaled the fresh air, feeling a sense of rejuvenation. The outdoors always brought her to life. She hated being trapped inside. And she'd spent way too much time there lately. Once this whole mess ended, she'd sleep outside, just because she could.

As she drove the winding roads through the hills, she racked her brain for any possible solutions to get her and Isaac out of their current predicament. It seemed a hopeless endeavor. She'd only been able to come up with one suggestion, and it hadn't gone over well at all. She shuddered as she recalled Isaac's anger upon hearing her plan.

Arriving at the tavern, she hopped out of the car before heading inside with a light skip to her step. Zeke lurked nowhere in sight, causing her to wonder if the homeless act had indeed been a front all along. He probably lived in a flat somewhere with a wife and kids, she snorted. She made a mental note to ask Isaac about it later on. The tavern might not be open, but she knew Connor would be there. He was always here early if he wasn't at her house.

The door had been left cracked open, a piece of cardboard jammed in the lock, like it always was before hours, and she walked to the kitchen unannounced. The scent of eggs cooking teased her nose, and her stomach growled in eagerness. She paused mid-stride when she heard low voices. Smiling smugly, she recognized Connor and Sheila's voices. Maybe she'd been right about them. Hopefully she wouldn't interrupt a rendezvous.

Tiptoeing, she crept silently past the empty tables and flickering lights to approach the pair and decide if she should leave. However, once she got close enough to hear them, she froze in her tracks, all thoughts of leaving gone.

"I know Elijah is out there, and I'm positive he and Isaac have communicated. I've seen it in his head, and Sabrina's. There's no doubt," Sheila said.

Sabrina's blood ran cold. *They knew.*

"Sheila, you don't know the whole circumstances." Connor sighed.

"I know he's the enemy, and as such, should be killed."

"It's his brother. It's not so cut and dry," Connor insisted. "He's not a huge danger to humans. He mostly feeds off of animals. He uses blood banks, for Christ's sake. He's only lapsed a few times as a vampire. If Isaac wants to leave his brother alone, who are we to judge? I can't say I wouldn't do the same."

"His brother is a menace to humans because of what he is. And what about Sabrina? She's in the middle of a love triangle. Isaac and Elijah fight over her like two dogs with a bone. They think she is their long-lost love, reincarnated." Her voice held a tone of disgust.

Sabrina's fists tightened at her sides as anger rushed through her blood. She longed to jump out and defend Isaac against Sheila's bitter words.

"Sabrina loves Isaac, Sheila. Maybe Elijah has feelings for Sabrina, but I have no doubt Sabrina is loyal to Isaac." He paused. "There were a few fights in the beginning, but they're happy now."

"And what will he do about her?"

"What do you mean?"

"She's *human*, Connor. We all know relationships with humans don't work. They get old and die, or they get killed. It's not natural. We need to stick to our own kind."

"There are only two female Enforcers in existence, Sheila. It's not a whole lot of women to throw around," he said ironically.

"There's nothing wrong with dallying among humans," Sheila insisted, "but to love one is disastrous."

"What makes you such an expert on the subject?"

From Sabrina's hiding spot, she saw Sheila blush and look away from Connor's scrutiny. "I fell for a human once. I was so happy, I debated doing the forbidden by changing him myself."

"Sheila—" Connor began.

"I know, I know. But we were going to do it, and run and hide. I had the perfect plan. We were going to run away to some exotic island while I changed him, and we would go to the United States via false ID, and hide in a big city there. We've always had such a hard time tracking down our enemies in big cities. I figured I'd use that.

"So, we had our plane tickets bought, our bags packed. I sent him out to get some books for me to read on the flight. He never came back.

He got hit by a car. Dead on impact. Isaac came and told me. He'd been there when it happened. I've often wondered if he'd somehow taken care of a *sticky* situation, if you know what I mean."

Connor shook his head as Sabrina stifled her gasp beneath her hand. "I don't think Isaac would kill your boyfriend, Sheila. That's crazy."

Sabrina paled, trembling at the force of her fury. She longed to jump out and slap Sheila for her accusations.

"He looked at my bags, looked at my face, and said, 'Sheila, I just saw Neil. He'd been crossing the street, and got hit by a car. He's gone.' He came over to me, and said, 'I'm going to pretend I don't see those bags over there, and I'm clueless to what you were going to do. Consider this your warning.' Then, he turned around and left. No words of comfort, nothing except the news of Tony's death."

Connor sighed and seemed to surrender. "Maybe he did take care of the situation, in the best way he knew. Maybe he didn't want to have to have to punish you. You know the penalty for treason is death. For both you and your boyfriend."

"We'd have run, and hidden. I'm not an idiot."

"We would've found you. Don't fool yourself," Connor insisted.

"He shouldn't have killed him!" Sheila exclaimed. "He could've spoken to me—"

"And you'd listen?"

Sheila's stubborn silence seemed answer enough.

"Sheila, you have to understand he did what he thought best, as ruler. At least he didn't kill you, too, even knowing you had planned to commit treason."

Sheila glared at Connor, and finally sighed in dejection. "You're right, of course. But if I even catch wind of him thinking of doing anything to make Sabrina immortal, I'll bring it to the Council. I'd love to see how he would react. Would he run and try to hide, knowing we would find him, or would he kill her to save himself?"

"Sheila, Isaac won't change Sabrina, I assure you. He loves her too much."

Sheila remained silent for a brief time before she finally insisted, "Time will tell, Connor. Time will tell."

Sheila and Connor whirled, and their eyes widened.

"Sabrina, how long have you been there? I didn't sense you." Connor rubbed the back of his neck and peeked at Sheila. They both stepped toward Sabrina. Connor looked apologetic; Sheila, triumphant.

Sabrina shook her head, and held out her hands to stop the pair. "Just—just let me go."

Her hands trembled so badly it took her three attempts to open the door and slip away.

She bolted to her car and pulled away from the tavern. She couldn't believe all she'd heard. Sheila seemed convinced Isaac had killed her boyfriend. Would he have done such a thing?

Would he have decided this man held too much of a risk to the Enforcers, that he could not lose Sheila? And in deciding this, had he removed said risk and warned Sheila to stay in line?

It did not seem like it could be possible for Isaac to behave so coldly...so cruelly.

Those are our rules. The rules I've been required to enforce over time. If we don't follow the rules, the waters become murky, difficult to navigate.

A chill ran down her back as she recalled the words he'd spoken to her the other day. Maybe he could be capable of murder—and if he was, this Isaac held no familiarity to her boyfriend. The Isaac she knew and loved had never once made her fear for her safety.

Now, however, she wavered.

Would he kill her to keep his place as ruler, to show he, as well, would always be held susceptible to the laws of the land, or would he fight the rules for her sake, damning them both?

No, surely he couldn't *kill* her. He loved her. Which led to another problem altogether. He was immortal; she never would be. In time, she would grow old, and he wouldn't. What if he decided it worth the risk of death and damnation to change her so they could live together forever?

She may have begged to become a monster yesterday, but she saw now why he'd refused to allow Elijah to change her. And for him to do it?

Even worse.

They were doomed, no matter what.

Their love risked too much, for them both.

Maybe, for the safety of Isaac, and the Enforcers he ruled, they shouldn't be together at all.

Maybe it would be best for everyone involved if she just left.

Forever.

ℰↄ

When Sabrina arrived home, she moved quickly. She didn't know how much time she had left for a successful escape, and urgency overcome her as she sprinted up the stairs. She winced as she thought of what would happen when Isaac discovered she'd left.

There would most likely be a storm incomparable to any ever seen before.

She only took the time to grab a few articles of clothing and the necessary toiletries. She spent too long deliberating over the note she knew she must write to Isaac.

In the end, she wrote only four sentences.

I love you, Isaac. I'm sorry I broke my promise, but it's for the best. Please don't follow me. It's just not meant to be—you need one of your own kind to love.

Love always, Sabrina

She wiped a tear from her cheek, and left the house, not bothering to lock the door. Isaac would get inside anyway, and she had no more energy left to care about anyone else entering, either.

ℰↄ

Anxiety crept up Isaac's spine as he approached Sabrina's house. He wasn't sure why he felt that way, but he slammed his foot on the gas nonetheless. He'd learned long ago his instincts rarely failed him. He found himself wishing he'd run instead of driven, but tonight he planned on taking Sabrina out to dinner. He would provide plentiful amounts of wine and get her drunk.

Because when she got drunk she got drowsy, among other things.

He needed her sleepy tonight. Tonight, he and Elijah were going to conquer Louisa.

Hopefully.

He'd be gone all night, and he wanted to be sure she didn't come anywhere *near* them when they fought. He'd also acquired a sleeping pill, should he find it necessary to use such methods. He'd rather not drug her, but he remained resolved to do so if he deemed it crucial.

He pulled up to her house and cursed when he saw her missing car. He jumped out of his TVR Cerbera. His heart pounded in his ears as he sprinted to her door.

Where the hell did she go? Is she insane?

"Sabrina?" he called. Even as he searched for her, he knew he wasted his time. He couldn't sense her presence.

He searched the house, observing a few articles of clothing thrown about, and she'd taken her toothbrush. He growled and bolted down the stairs, only to stop when he noticed the white sheet of paper on the foyer table.

He scanned it and threw his head back and yelled her name. Thunder crashed overhead, and the wind howled so strongly that the door banged against the wall with a loud crack. In a rage, Isaac flipped a table across the room. It banged against the wall, shattering upon impact. The sight of it breaking into pieces sobered him, and he sank to the steps. His emotions were whirling unleashed, and it showed in the weather outside. A tree blew over from the sheer force of the wind, and it crashed onto the Sabrina's roof. The house shuddered under the impact, and he wished it would fall down on him, and put him out of his misery.

If only he weren't freaking immortal.

She'd left him after promising always to remain by his side. Now she was alone, and he couldn't protect her from Louisa. He needed to find her; he needed to protect her from herself, because she'd created the perfect opportunity for Louisa to kill her.

She'd just signed her bloody death warrant.

Chapter Nineteen

*E*lijah awaited Louisa by the cliff's edge. They had one chance, and one chance only, to get her.

He inexplicably felt guilty for using her desire for him against her in such a way. He hated her more than anyone had ever hated anyone, or *anything*. But she had created him, and in doing so, she'd connected them for all eternity. He'd always feel an odd sense of loyalty toward her, as well as a grudging affection. And it killed him.

He needed to end this twisted cat–and-mouse game they'd been playing for over one hundred years. He'd finally be free of her power. About damn time, too.

He whirled in shock, his nostrils flaring when he smelled Isaac. "What are you doing here?" he hissed. "Louisa will see you, and know it's a trap. Get out of here." When he saw the pain and worry echoing in Isaac's eyes, he questioned, "What is it? What happened?"

"Sabrina's gone. She's left me. She's obviously trying to keep me safe, and she thinks it's the only way to save me. And in doing so, she's now—"

"Easy to get to. Son of a bitch."

"I'm going to find her. I can only hope she's still in the area, maybe in a hotel. So our plan tonight's off. Louisa will live to see another day. Unless, God help us, we're too late."

"I'll help you search," Elijah whispered. Images of Sabrina being broken like Amelia ran through his head in a disturbing montage.

Isaac hesitated before nodding briskly. "You can check the airlines, see if she booked a flight. I'm off to search hotels."

They both headed off in separate directions, but Isaac froze. Had a shadow rushed past him? No, it must have been Elijah. He ran toward the city and tried to block the images of what could be happening to Sabrina even now.

જી

Sabrina glowered out the window in her hotel room as she watched the ocean's turbulent swirl. A horrible storm had hit England and unleashed a tornado, of all things, upon the innocent citizens. She winced as she thought of it, grateful no one had been hurt. Isaac obviously discovered her absence, and his anger swept over the country. No, anger would be putting it mildly.

He felt fury, devastation, *betrayal*.

It hurt to even think of him.

The tears welled up in her eyes again, and she wanted to scream out of sheer frustration. How could she have any tears left? Sabrina had done nothing but cry since she'd left him. She'd even needed to pull the car over to the side of the road after leaving her house. She couldn't see well enough to drive through the steady gushing of tears. She'd broken into tears in front of the receptionist as she had checked into her hotel, and had sobbed into the phone as she had booked a flight out of England for tomorrow morning.

She was a wreck. A weeping, snotty, red-eyed wreck.

Ugh.

She walked away from the window and curled up on the bed in a fetal position. It hurt too much to sit anymore. The ache in her heart overpowered her every sense. It throbbed constantly and gave her no rest. She didn't know how she'd get through the trip home tomorrow— let alone live the rest of her life—without him. The tears rolled down her cheeks and she closed her eyes.

Please God, let me sleep.

౭ఎ

Elijah finally discovered some useful news. Sabrina had booked a flight the next morning at ten. He'd needed to use vast amounts of charm upon a numberless amount of hapless booking agents, but it had paid off. But now that he had news to share, he realized he and Isaac hadn't set a meeting point at which to rendezvous. So, while his search had indeed borne fruit, it would be useless unless he could locate his brother.

He stood outside Heathrow, trying to pick up Isaac's scent. He found him easily and ran almost full-speed toward him. He paused when he saw a family staring at him. The pretty mother had wide eyes, as if she sensed something was wrong, and the husband glared at him, probably because his wife stared at him. The little girl clutched her mother's fingers and smiled at him cheerfully, and he felt a responding grin come to his moth. He'd always wanted children, children who had curly brown hair and bright green eyes....

Another impossible dream.

He forced himself to walk calmly away from the crowds of people surrounding him and stopped in his tracks. He flared his nostrils at the familiar stench. Louisa definitely hid close by.

Did she somehow know Sabrina had run? Did she know she was unprotected?

Blast it all to Hell.

He hesitated as he agonized over which direction to take. If he went after Louisa, he could try to stop her and lose. If he went after Isaac, they could save Sabrina and later band together and defeat Louisa.

His decision made, he headed in Isaac's direction.

౭ఎ

Isaac already tried three hotels and stood inside the fourth of the evening. He had four people in front of him in line, waiting impatiently, when Elijah found him.

"Louisa's here."

He blanched and gripped Elijah's arm. "In this hotel, you mean?"

Elijah shook his head, and reiterated, "No, but she's in the city. I don't know why, but I'm scared she's doing the same thing we are."

"Shit."

"We have to find her first, Isaac."

"I'm *trying*, Elijah. I'm hardly twiddling my thumbs here. Did you discover anything?"

"She has a flight at ten in the morning."

"Can you smell her? I know my senses are stronger than a human's, but they are nothing compared to yours," he whispered so quiet it would be inaudible to the human ear. It killed him to ask Elijah to search for her, but he needed to brush jealousy aside tonight. Saving Sabrina won out over his petty feelings, and his sense of smell got ruined by the crush of people in the city. He *hated* cities.

"I can smell her, but it's hard to tell if she's here. I think she's very close by, however."

"You found me...can't you find her the same way?" Isaac asked somewhat impatiently. He gave an irritated sigh and stepped forward another place in line.

"It's not the same. I've tracked your scent for over a hundred years. Sabrina's, I've only known a few days," Elijah snapped.

This statement came out a bit too loudly, and earned them both an odd look from the couple in front of them. Isaac gritted his teeth and glared at them, until they turned around and whispered fervently to each other. They took a step farther away from them, and he grunted in satisfaction.

Nosy humans.

"Oh," Isaac said with some surprise. He hadn't realized a vampire could sense people better once they were better acquainted with their scent, so to speak. He wondered fleetingly how often Elijah had tracked him, as he'd never seen him until Sabrina appeared. "Well, at least she's still local," he exclaimed while he ran a hand through his hair. He *barely* resisted the urge to reach in front of him and throw the people out of his way as they laughed in front of him in line.

"How about if I help out by checking some of the other hotels? Where have you gone?"

Though he didn't want Elijah to be the one to discover Sabrina, he also knew time was of the essence, more so than ever before. Reluctantly, he named the hotels he'd visited and watched as Elijah ran off to aid him in his quest for Sabrina. For once, he didn't feel jealousy rip through him at the thought of Sabrina being brought back to him in his brother's arms. He needed to find her too badly to care how she it got accomplished.

He shifted his weight to his other foot, and relieved to see he finally stood next in line. He sighed as the couple in front of him chatted nonsensically at the receptionist. He resisted the urge to knock their heads together and throw their motionless bodies to the side.

When the couple *finally* moved toward the elevator, he quickly told the receptionist his concocted story of how his wife had come somewhere in England, and he knew she had to be in this town somewhere. He didn't know what hotel she'd chosen, but wanted to surprise her since he'd come to England early.

The other times this earned the appropriate *oohs* and *ahhs* of appreciation from the recipient of his story, but this time it merely got a stern look.

"I'm sorry, but I can't give out that information."

"Not even for her husband?"

She shook her head. "Not even then."

"Okay, I'm sorry for bothering you." Isaac smiled, walked around the corner, and closed his eyes. He created a gust of wind that blew the doors to the back employee entrance open. The startled receptionist rushed to investigate the bang of the doors, and Isaac ran to her computer.

A few quick movements of his hands, and he yearned to shout in delight. She was *here*. She'd be safe now because he'd found her.

Thank God.

He heard the receptionist returning and went to the other side of the counter with a smile plastered on his face. When the confused receptionist returned, she jumped to see him standing there once more. "Sir, I told you—"

"I got a hold of her! She's here, Sabrina Hodges in room 215. So, I'm going to go up to her room now."

She perked up. "Oh how nice!" She pursed her lips and shook her head. "Oh, she must be the crying lady," she informed him.

The sheer intensity of the happiness washing over him made his legs feel weak enough to collapse on the floor in relief. He laughed hysterically and forced a calming breath when the receptionist looked at him warily, like she worried he might be a little mad. He smiled at the receptionist, resisting the urge to pull her into his arms and kiss her.

"Yes, she thought I'd been delayed. She'll be quite happy to see me, I assure you."

The receptionist smiled. "Elevator is to your left, when you get off on the second floor, take a right, and a quick left."

"Thank you, ma'am."

"Would you like the spare key?" she asked.

"Yes, that would be wonderful."

The receptionist beamed at him, clearly happy in her role as co-conspirator, and handed him the plastic key. "She's popular, your wife is. A girlfriend of hers stopped by an hour ago as well."

He got halfway to the elevator before her words registered in his brain, and he stopped dead in his tracks. His blood ran cold, and his heart clenched in his chest.

He slowly turned. "A friend?"

"Yes, a pretty girl, about your age. Perhaps you know her as well?"

He wasted no more time or effort on the receptionist and bolted to the staircase. His legs were faster than any elevator could be.

"The elevator's quicker, sir," called the desk clerk from behind him, confused.

He arrived at her doorway in seconds, but the sinking dread in his heart told him she'd already be gone.

Or lying on the floor completely drained of blood.

He threw open the door and searched for any signs of Sabrina. The covers were wrinkled where someone had once lain, but the bed lay empty. He recognized her unopened overnight bag on the chair by the window. A pillow lay to the floor, and the bedside lamp had gotten tipped over. Of Sabrina, there was no sign. He growled in his throat and turned around. He ran out of the hotel room and through the lobby, not caring if anyone saw his mad dash.

The time for appearances had ended. He needed to find Sabrina before he was too late.

He didn't stop to search for Elijah—he couldn't afford the delay. Every minute wasted added to the minutes Sabrina would be scared, hurt, tortured, or even killed.

He ran faster than ever before, pausing for nothing. He could barely even see where he ran, his speed too fast to concentrate on anything. But that was okay, for he knew where he needed to go. Normally he would at least *attempt* to calm his raging emotions, to lower the risk of any unwanted injury or damage from the storm he had unleashed.

But not tonight.

Tonight, he welcomed the damage he caused. Tonight, he embraced the danger with open arms, relished the sound of trees crashing to the ground. Let the storms take down the whole country of England and everyone in her. He didn't give a damn, as long as he could save Sabrina.

Every step he took, he saw her cry out in pain as Louisa broke her arm, broke her fingers, and broke her neck. He roared and amazingly, his speed increased. A cracking sound met his ears as a tree broke and collapsed to the ground in front of him. He hurdled it effortlessly and continued on.

Nothing would stop him.

ॐ

Sabrina lay upon the bed sleeping when she heard the light knock on the door.

"Housekeeping, please open the door."

"I don't need room service. Go away," she mumbled sleepily. She rolled over and tried to go back to sleep. Sleeping helped her forget what she'd done. Sleep was necessary for her sanity.

Another knock sounded, and it was more insistent. She heard the shuffling of the cart the maids always pushed through the hallway and glared at the door.

"Housekeeping, ma'am."

"Can you please leave? I don't want to be disturbed." She sought and found the stupid sign on the door where it hung on the inside doorknob, and she cursed.

"Housekeeping," the voice repeated.

She gave an annoyed sigh and glowered at the ceiling. It was nighttime. Why would there be someone knocking on her door at this hour? Maybe they did things differently in England. To be honest, she didn't care; she just wanted to be left alone to wallow in her misery. She might as well let the bothersome maid in, and maybe she would leave.

Swinging her feet out from under the blankets, she rolled lazily out of bed. The pillow fell off the bed, and she stared at it for a moment.

Let the maid earn her salary. She can pick it up.

Shaking her head at the laziness of such an action, she nevertheless walked to the door, leaving the pillow where it lay. Not pausing to look at the maddening maid, she unlocked the bolt, turned the knob, and swung it open.

"Come in." She stomped back to the bed in a huff. Her hands were braced on the bed to climb in when the maid spoke.

"Thank you, Sabrina. You made it even easier than I thought it would be."

She froze in horror, and a chill ran down her spine. She knew the voice behind her all too well—and she didn't want to hear it when alone in a hotel room.

And she'd just invited her in.

Idiot.

"Surprised, I see? Well, I don't know why. You didn't actually think your pathetic plan to leave Isaac would save you, or him, did you?"

She growled in a paltry imitation of Isaac and stepped toward Louisa. "You leave him alone! He's done nothing to you. He never did anything to deserve what you did to him. He was innocent in all this. He still is."

Louisa laughed, lounging comfortably against the closed door. She looked so calm, so relaxed. *So normal.* But looks were deceiving more often than not, and Louisa couldn't be farther from normal. She'd come with one purpose and one purpose only: to kill her.

It chilled her.

"Oh, Sabrina. You're so funny. It will truly pain me to hurt you." She grabbed her heart, a pained expression on her face.

Sabrina stiffened. "How about you don't? I'm leaving. Elijah's staying. Even Isaac is staying. Why do you feel the need to do this?"

Her mind raced as she attempted to stall her enemy. She knew Louisa to be a formidable opponent, impossible to beat. But, she wouldn't let the bitch kill her while she begged for her life.

Hell no.

She'd done this to herself. Stupidly, she now knew, she'd flown the relative safety of her home and ran straight into the waiting arms of her enemy.

Now, she'd die.

"They won't let you leave, you know. You're stupid to even think your plan would have worked. Isaac won't stand by while you leave him. Neither will Elijah. Even if he can't have you, he won't let you leave. You're his one and only love. It's disgusting." She glared at Sabrina in spite and continued. "I don't know what it is you do to cause this unwavering devotion. You must be incredible between the sheets. You certainly aren't much to look at."

Fury overcame her, and she forgot her fear. She glared and spat, "Go to hell."

Louisa laughed. "Maybe someday, but first I will personally see you get there."

The small talk obviously over, Louisa stalked toward her. Sabrina forced herself to cower until she reached the foot of the bed. Sabrina knocked the lamp off the bedside table, plunging the room into darkness. She launched herself over the bed to land on the other side. She ran for the door as fast as she could, and felt the cool brass knob under her hand before Louisa threw her backward through the air. Painfully, her head slammed on the floor and the wind whooshed out of her lungs, leaving her gasping for air. She attempted to roll to her feet, but the heel pressing down on her throat halted her.

Louisa smirked down at her. "Nice try, Sabrina. Impressive, even. You'll be so much more fun than that weakling Amelia. I bet you won't even faint from the pain." She spoke with a far-off look on her face, as if she thought of the torture to come.

Sabrina clawed at Louisa's foot, desperately trying to free herself. The world turned black, and still she fought until her hands fell to the floor beside her head, and she fought no more.

Chapter Twenty

*L*ouisa picked up her useless bundle and snuck back outside. Once there, she didn't pause until she'd reached the clearing. And when she and her unconscious guest arrived, there had been no time to waste in setting the scene.

A glance up poured rain down on Louisa's raised face. The clouds covered the sky so densely that not even the moonlight could be seen. The only light illuminating the forest surrounding them were the intermittent flashes from lightning strikes. The resulting effect was gloomy and shattering. Sabrina watched her as she approached and crouched down beside her.

Louisa laughed, mocking her. "This is too much fun, Sabrina. I can't wait for the show."

Sabrina locked her jaw and refused to look at her. It hurt like hell to talk through her bruised throat, and she didn't feel the desire to amuse Louisa. Stuck on the ground like a sacrificial animal waiting to be slaughtered, she knew she would soon die. She only wished she didn't have to break Isaac's heart in the process. Losing her would kill him.

Louisa hissed and slapped her. "Look at me."

Though her cheek stung from the force of the blow, she still refused to look at Louisa. She stared into the moonless sky, allowing Isaac's storm to wash over her. It gave an odd source of comfort, as if he were there by her side, holding her hand.

The excruciating pain in Sabrina's legs cleared her head, leaving her unwillingly aware of every detail. When they had arrived in the clearing, the storm raging above knocked down a nearby tree. Unfortunately for Sabrina, it had given Louisa the wonderful idea to put the tree on top of Sabrina—*better drama*, she had said. Sabrina had fought, to no avail. It seemed impossible to win against Louisa's inhuman strength.

Not a big tree by any means, it still proved heavy enough to effectively render her motionless. So, she'd gotten pinned down to helplessly await her death as her tormentor mocked her. But she'd be damned if she gave her the satisfaction of seeing her cower in fear. Even if it *did* paralyze her with its force.

Apparently Louisa had suffered enough of Sabrina's silence, for she cursed and in a fit of anger, reached forward to grab her arm threateningly. Sabrina tensed, but managed to glower in stubborn silence. Louisa flicked her wrist, and a snapping sound met Sabrina's ears. Pain shot up her arm, from her wrist to her shoulder, and she felt the arm drop, useless. Sabrina flexed a finger, testing it, and clamped her jaw tight to stop herself from crying out from the pain.

Jesus, that hurts like hell.

Pain—remembered pain from her dream the other night—coursed through her. In a way, it helped her get through this. She knew what to expect, and just how bad it would be.

God help her.

She stiffened and bit her lip, but managed to keep her silence. Louisa growled at her unresponsive victim and twisted the tortured arm under an agonizing squeeze until finally, Sabrina cried out. Tears rolled down her cheeks, and blood ran from the spot she had bitten to keep her cries silent.

"Not so tough now with a broken arm, are you?" she taunted.

"You're...nothing more...than a bully. Like a teenager ripping wings off of butterflies for fun," Sabrina managed to get the words out in a steady voice.

Louisa hissed and tightened her fist one last time before jumping to her feet. She leaned over and stroked Sabrina's cheek. "Stay here, doll. It's showtime." She laughed, and stepped on Sabrina's broken arm as she walked away to hide in the forest.

ᗩ

Isaac paused short of the clearing to assess the situation. He could sense Louisa had been here, and probably still hid somewhere. He strained to catch Sabrina's presence: her perfume, her shampoo, anything.

There! A hint of lavender. His nostrils flared as he latched onto her signature scent. Heart pounding, he approached the clearing.

She was here.

As necessary as he knew his caution to be, it still hurt to go so slowly when he knew she was out there, hurt or…dead.

No, he would know if it she were dead. He would feel the absence deep inside him. She had to be alive, and he needed to save her. And when he finished rescuing her, he would kiss her senseless and wring her little neck for putting him through this torture.

He peered into the clearing from the cover of the trees, all senses finely attuned for any sign of ambush. The rain came down so heavily and the wind whipped so severely he couldn't see anything. Aggravated at yet another setback, he forced himself to take a deep breath and concentrate on reining in his emotions. Slowly, the wind died down, and the rain dissipated.

He couldn't see anyone in the clearing, neither Louisa nor Sabrina. He began to doubt his intuition, thinking he'd been wrong, when through the silence of the night, he heard a soft sob. Pausing, he cocked his head toward the noise. It had sounded like a tiny whimper, as if someone were trying to remain silent in fear of discovery. But it couldn't be Sabrina. Why wouldn't she want him to find her, rescue her?

To save him.

She probably tried to make him leave, the little fool. She would kill herself to keep him safe. Didn't she know he had no life worth saving if she died?

It was too damn dark. He closed his eyes and concentrated. It took a lot of energy from him, but a long, bright flash of lightning struck.

When it did, Isaac opened his eyes to scan the clearing. Only a fallen tree lay in the clearing. Perhaps one last lightning bolt, mostly to be sure the cry had been a figment of his imagination.

Then he saw her.

His heart stopped dead.

Chapter Twenty-One

*G*od, everything looked so dark. She could hear her breathing, erratic and uncontrollable. Each breath took an immense amount of effort, sounding unbelievably loud in her ears, easily drowning out the sound of the storm raging above her. She wanted to cry out, to yell out her despair to the forest that surrounded her, but instead bit her lip until she tasted blood.

Her arm hurt like hell, and the excruciating pain in her legs kept her way too alert for her liking. They were *almost* numb at this point, which she supposed couldn't be a good thing. Not like it mattered anyway.

Soon she would be dead.

The sound of her gasping breaths was interrupted every once in a while by a sob escaping her lips, but she tried not to cry. She couldn't let them find her. They didn't need to witness this again.

But her hopes were dashed when his face appeared over hers, ghostly white against the black night. His voice washed over her like a healing balm, and some small part of her hoped he could save her, but the larger, and *louder*, part wanted him to leave.

Now.

"S-Sabrina," he whispered. His blue eyes met hers, and she saw his eyes were bright with unshed tears. "Oh, God, what have I done?" he cried.

The anguish on his face hurt her so much she tried to reach out to touch him, only to gasp as she got reminded, all too painfully, that her arm had been broken. Isaac gazed at her arms, and her face, with tears in his eyes.

"I'm so sorry, Sabrina."

"Not...your...fault," she managed to force out through her swollen throat.

His gaze fly to her neck, and he blanched at her bruised skin. "What else is hurt?" he asked urgently.

"My...arm..." she muttered between her clenched teeth. "But Louisa—"

As she spoke, he cursed and probed her broken arm. She gasped in pain, and he withdrew his touch.

"I'm going to take the tree off of you, and get you out of here. I'm sorry, this is going to hurt...."

Pain laced through his voice, and his eyes apologized for the agony he needed to cause. She looked at him, ready to assure him she didn't give a damn, and cried out instead. Louisa smiled at her over his shoulder as she raised the rock and knocked him over the head. Isaac went down without a fight. He hadn't even seen Louisa coming since he had been so worried about her.

"You bitch," Sabrina snarled, finding strength in her fury. "I swear to God I am going to kill you."

Louisa laughed and slung Isaac over her shoulder. "I'm certain you'd love to do just that, darling."

Fury swelled over Sabrina, and she fought to free herself using the few unbroken body parts she could still move. Unfortunately, she remained trapped beneath the tree so she watched in dismay as Louisa propped him against a tree and punched him in the face. Though he jerked at the abuse, he didn't awaken even as blood gushed out of his nose.

"That was fun." Louisa laughed. She turned away from Isaac and looked at Sabrina. "Everything's coming together perfectly. Thank you for your help."

Sabrina swallowed roughly and glared at her enemy.

"Go to hell."

Louisa smiled and stalked over to her. "What did you say? I didn't hear you." She came over to Sabrina's unharmed arm and grabbed it. "Did you say something, hmm?" Leaned into her face, she arched a brow and watched Sabrina, smiling delightfully—with pure evil. Excitement shone in her eyes, and lit up her face in a sheer mockery of joy. Sabrina knew if she opened her mouth, she would receive another useless limb as an award for her efforts. But she no longer cared.

"I said, go to hell, you nasty bitch." The pain of her arm being broken came immediately, and she bit her lip without a sound. She felt her teeth rip through her lip and tasted the metallic flavor of blood on her tongue, but she refused to budge. The pain doubled when Louisa twisted the arm at an unnatural angle. Still, she didn't cry out. It was the only thing in her control at the moment, and by God, she'd remain silent.

Louisa studied her with wide eyes, and exclaimed, "What the hell is *wrong* with you?"

It would have been almost laughable in any other circumstance. The woman who made a habit of torturing women and breaking bones asked what was wrong with *her*. But the irony got lost when Louisa released her arm and ripped the tree off her legs to throw it at Isaac. It landed against his chest, the thick crunching sound causing Sabrina to cringe. The tree rolled to a stop at his feet.

His eyes were open, and he looked *pissed*. He'd changed into a vampire; it showed in the hard lines of his face. He roared, murder written in his eyes, and threw the tree off of himself. He jumped up and charged at Louisa. He halted when Louisa grabbed Sabrina and held her in front of her like a shield. Louisa had one hand on her head and another on her shoulder.

"One more step, and you can say goodbye to her head," she warned. "You'll never be able to save her if she's headless, no matter what beast you become."

"Don't listen, Isaac. She'll kill me no matter what you do."

"Shut up, you insignificant human." Louisa growled in her ear. She turned to Isaac and taunted, "What a predicament, Isaac. What should you do? You can't come save her. She'd be dead before you even get close to me. And if you don't come to her rescue, she'll die anyway.

"So will you step forward now, knowing she will be put out of her misery quickly, like a dog? It's what your brother did to Amelia—stabbed her like a sick animal. She didn't *deserve* his mercy. Or, do you wait, holding out hope that some way, somehow, you will overcome me? Now, that's a laughable prospect."

Isaac hissed. "I will kill you, Louisa. Have no doubt."

"You are such a man, all talk and no action. All these promises you men make to women, but never follow through. Love, honor, respect—revenge." She sneered in an unnerving imitation of humor. "I'm sure you swore to keep Sabrina safe from me. Yet here she is. Broken and bloodied. And soon? Dead."

Louisa backed away, and Isaac took a casual step closer. She glared at his movement. "Stay back."

He obeyed her command, holding his arms up in a gesture of peace. "Louisa, we can work out a deal, I swear. I'll let you walk away, if you just give me Sabrina," he said in soothing tones. "We can make this work...."

Louisa sneered at him. "No, and don't move again." She looked behind him and her eyes widened in horror. Isaac whirled around to see what stood behind him, only to see nothing but the gloomy forest. He cursed and spun back around. He'd fallen for the oldest trick in the book, damn it.

She'd left.

ജ

Louisa looked down at her bundle in disgust.

Weakling.

Though even *she* had to admit she had been impressed by the strength Sabrina had shown thus far. She'd refused to give in to Louisa, and she knew Amelia wouldn't have been so strong. She would have been screaming and crying like a baby long ago.

Sabrina had hardly uttered a cry the whole time, and she'd been much rougher on her than she had been Amelia. Louisa felt a reluctant respect for this woman, this mere human. She didn't want to feel any kind feelings toward her, but found she did.

Louisa almost wished she didn't have to kill her. She reminded

Louisa of how she, herself, had been, so long ago. Stubborn, strong, beautiful. Even with broken bones throughout her body, Sabrina's strength and beauty shone through into the night.

She ignored any and all feelings of pity or sympathy for Sabrina, and increased her speed. She almost made it to the cliffs when something hit her from behind. She fell on top of Sabrina and heard another bone break from the force of her fall.

Maybe I killed her.

She jumped to her feet, but before she could reach a standing position, she got hit from behind and thrown back on the ground.

Elijah launched off the tree at his side and landed on Louisa, snarling. She twisted within his grasp, her hair whipping around them, and they rolled around the ground in a battle for control. Their breathing came out in harsh pants as each fought to get a grip upon the other, a grip that could give an advantage. They slammed into an old tree near Sabrina, and it shuddered from the strength of the impact.

Louisa fought against his hold desperately and kicked him in the stomach. He soared through the air and bounced off an enormous boulder. She leapt to her feet and sprinted for Sabrina.

Isaac only spared a cursory glance at Sabrina before he joined in the fray. Her biggest threat wasn't lying alone in the forest; it was Louisa. And Louisa ran straight for her. He growled and launched himself at her.

The tree shook under the force of the blow, but she whirled around the trunk and climbed the tree. He followed suit, gaining speed as he got higher and higher. As Louisa reached the top of the towering tree, she froze. Her eyes looked from where Elijah perched on the outside of the thick branch to where Isaac stood on the inside. She'd gotten trapped between them, and judging from the panicked darting of her eyes back and forth between the brothers, she knew it.

Isaac took a step closer to her in unison with Elijah. She growled as they took another step. Isaac looked at Elijah, and Elijah nodded imperceptibly. He would lunge for Louisa, and Elijah would rip her head off while he held her captive in his arms. Isaac roared and jumped at her. His arms groped thin air, and he plummeted to the ground below.

He heard Elijah cry his name as he bounced off of branch after branch. He tried to grab the branches as he hit them, but still got beaten in the face, back, and side by the unyielding bark as he flailed for a stronghold.

Blackness threatened to overcome him, and he cursed when he realized he'd changed back to human form. He needed to start controlling his emotions better so he could in turn control his changes. He spent the rest of the short fall trying to concentrate on changing back into a vampire, or a wolf, or anything.

He failed.

He crashed to the ground below.

Chapter Twenty-Two

"*W*ake up, Isaac."

He heard Elijah's voice as if it came through a train tunnel, as though he yelled from the other side. He moaned and opened his eyes to stare at his brother for a moment, then his eyes widened.

He jumped up and under obvious effort, and Elijah followed.

"Where's Louisa?" Isaac grunted.

"I think she's left. Let's get Sabrina out of here. She needs to be examined by a doctor."

Isaac blanched as he remembered his brief glimpse of her lying broken on the ground. He whirled and sprinted back to where Sabrina had been. He stopped, spinning wildly in a circle as his heart raced. She wasn't there. She couldn't possibly move on her own, so it left one person.

Louisa.

He cursed. "Louisa!"

"Over here," she called sweetly.

They turned at the sound of her voice. And both froze in horror. She perched at the cliff's edge, holding Sabrina over the edge by her neck. Her feet hung useless, like a rag doll's. The cliffs towered above the ocean at intimidating heights—the same cliffs that had killed many a person foolish enough to approach too close to the edge. Louisa practically glowed in triumph.

241

Isaac looked at Louisa's face, and at Sabrina's lifeless body, and *knew* what she would do. It showed in the evil smile that lurked on her face, the excitement shining in her eyes. He yelled out in fury and ran. He sprinted faster than he ever had before. But he still arrived too late.

Louisa hurled Sabrina over the side of the cliff. She plunged toward the water at an alarming speed, soon to sink into the dark, cold, turbulent seas below. Isaac dove over without breaking stride, and after impossibly long, breathless seconds, knifed into the water.

He searched frantically, looking for any signs of Sabrina. He caught sight of her head and saw her take a gasping breath. She sank below the surface, and he took a deep breath and went down after her. He swam in the direction he'd seen her sink, hoping against all odds he would find her in the treacherous waters.

His hand brushed against something, and he immediately latched onto it. Seaweed. Damn it. He had the benefit of being able to hold his breath longer than a human, and he'd never been more grateful for the gift than now. He swam deeper, and each stroke brought more despair over him.

He had to find her. He couldn't live without her.

⁖

Elijah yelled Sabrina's name and sprinted to the edge of the cliff. He tried to follow into the water out of instinct—he *had* to save Sabrina—but his body forced him to stop at the edge.

He watched Isaac dive neatly over the edge and cursed. He studied the water, trying to see her head, her body, anything.

There. There she is.

She sank below the surface, her red curls disappearing below the dark water once more, and he watched in helpless frustration as Isaac swam toward her. He kicked a rock lying near the cliff's edge, and it rolled into the ocean, where he, himself, could not go.

Damn, what a useless piece of crap he'd turned out to be.

Laughter came from behind him, and fury overcame him.

"That held a nice touch, don't you think? This time, there's no way you can save her. You *can't* save her. Again."

He roared in anger and lunged at her.

"No, Elijah!" she shrieked.

Even as she screamed at him, he collided against her and they went flying backward. There was no chance to grab onto the side of the cliff, no chance to stop their deadly fall. They catapulted over the side.

He'd found a way to conquer the barrier from death. He had to attack another without *intending* to go over the side. Life finally felt good. When he hit the water, it would make him die as it ate his skin and body away until nothing existed.

He'd be free. Finally free.

He saw Louisa reach for him, and he attempted to jerk back. He didn't want to die while touching *her*, but she had always been older and stronger than Elijah and managed to grab his arm anyway. She swirled in the air and threw him toward the cliff wall using all her strength.

He smashed into the cliff and grabbed on the rocky sides, hanging in mid-air. Elijah clung to the side and threw his head back as he let out an agonized yell. She'd saved him from dying. He turned his head and watched with horror as his maker hit the water and dissolved. The last to go was her head, and she kept her eyes on him the whole time. He watched, mesmerized, as she finally melted away to nothing.

Why? Why had she saved him, and not let him die? Had she had done it out of some misguided devotion toward him? Or had she simply done it to deny him what he had wanted most in that moment, which was his death *and* hers?

He studied his hands on the rocky wall, commanding them to release the wall and allow him to drop to his acidic grave, but instead they climbed the cliff of their own accord until he could leap nimbly over the side, and onto safe ground.

The one chance he'd stood of plunging into the water was gone; she'd ruined it. Like she'd ruined everything else in his life, including him.

ဢ

Isaac was losing hope when he saw something float in front of him. He reached a hand out, and latched on. It was hair. Curly hair.

He clutched it and pulled. He hoped it was Sabrina and not an old corpse. When he reached the top, he dragged the unresponsive body to the surface and looked at the face.

Relief came over him, followed quickly by fear. It was Sabrina. But not the one he knew. This Sabrina was lifeless and pale. He had her in his arms again, but she didn't appear to be breathing. He felt for a pulse and was relieved to feel a very faint one, but faint was better than none, right?

Please, please let her be okay, God.

"Sabrina. Oh, don't die on me. Come on."

He swam to the cliff and slung her over his shoulder. He knew he must be hurting her immensely, but he didn't have time to be gentle now. He scaled the cliff, feeling the rocks rip open his palms as he went higher and higher.

When he finally reached the top, he laid her on the ground to examine her. Again he put a finger on her throat to feel for a pulse. The faint thrum he'd heard seemed to have disappeared. He let out a roar of anguish, and administered mouth-to-mouth resuscitation. Maybe she just needed help breathing. Please let it be that. He could handle anything else, just not losing her.

After what seemed like forever, her body shuddered and she spewed out an obscene amount of water. He rolled her to her side to allow it all to exit and rubbed her back. When she finished coughing, he returned her to lying on her back. She stared up at him as her whole body shook from the cold. He hesitated, unsure of what to do. He didn't want to risk moving her and injuring her even *worse*.

She took a shuddering breath and seemed to stop breathing.

"Sabrina, breathe," he commanded.

"It...hurts...too...much," she managed to whisper. "Is she dead?"

"W-What should I do? Can I move you? Bring you to the hospital?"

"No...too late. Don't move me. Please, is she dead?"

It seemed important to her to hear the words, to know he was safe. With blurred vision, he nodded and lied. "Yes, she's dead. Sabrina," he whispered. Tears rolled down his cheeks unheeded, and he tightened his grip on her shoulders. "I can't...I can't just let you die. I love you."

Her lips moved as she tried to smile.

"I...love you, too. Just...stay with me."

Chapter Twenty-Three

*R*unning footsteps approached behind them, and Isaac spun, presumably ready to defend Sabrina at all costs. When he saw it was Elijah and not Louisa, he turned back to his love. His brother knelt by their side and checked for a pulse as Isaac stared at Sabrina like a man lost.

"She's alive, but barely," Elijah murmured. "Louisa's dead. I watched her die."

Isaac gave a quick nod and focused on his brother for a moment. "She can't live. She's been through too much. She wants me to let her—let her *die*."

Elijah hesitated. "We should carry her to a hospital. We can at least try."

Isaac nodded and wiped the tears off his face. He pulled her into his arms, but stopped when she cried out in pain.

"No…it…hurts."

Isaac put her back down, looking at Elijah with panic on his face. They stared at each other wordlessly. Isaac turned to Sabrina. "I'm s-s-so sorry, love," he whispered brokenly. Returning his gaze to Elijah's, he spoke in hushed tones. "We can't move her. I don't know what to do."

"You've got to let her go. She's not going to make it, Isaac." Pain was evident in Elijah's voice, but his eyes did not waver from Isaac's even as he blinked back the tears. He couldn't break down when his brother needed him most. He'd been a horrible brother over the years, but now he'd be strong.

No matter how much it hurt.

Isaac yelled with raw anger and thunder boomed around them. Even Elijah cringed at the sheer volume of the bang.

"I have to do something," he swore.

As he spoke, Elijah saw his face light up. He instantly tensed. He knew the look in Isaac's eyes. As children, he'd always seen it appear right before Isaac told him a plan sure to get their small butts paddled.

"Isaac, what?"

"I'll bite her, Elijah. It'll change her, and we can run away."

"No, absolutely not," he objected. "She wouldn't want you to risk yourself to save her. She wouldn't allow it."

"In case you haven't noticed, she's not in the condition to *allow* anything." Isaac gestured angrily to her motionless body.

Elijah glared and shook his head. "No," he repeated. Isaac growled at him, and Elijah smiled bitterly. "I won't allow you to do this."

"I'd like to see you try to stop me, brother."

Isaac knelt by Sabrina's side. He looked over his shoulder to ensure Elijah hadn't stepped closer. Elijah remained still, studying Isaac from under hooded eyes. He could continue to gawk all he bloody wanted, as long as he didn't interfere.

Once he was confident Elijah meant no harm to him, or Sabrina, he stroked Sabrina's face. Her eyes opened, and she stared at him vacantly. She was barely even here—he needed to move fast. Or he'd lose her.

"Sabrina, honey. I'm going to have to bite you. It'll hurt. A lot. I'm sorry, but this is the only way," Isaac said, as soothingly as he knew how.

Her eyes widened in horror as she licked her parched lips, attempting to speak. He leaned closer to hear her words, which were barely a whisper.

"Not...you. Elijah...please." She stared over his head at his brother, and Isaac fought the anger and pain that swelled up inside him. He knew why she said it. She was trying to protect him, to save him even now. But still, it hurt. And she must have seen it in his eyes, the doubts plaguing him even now.

"I…love…you. But no…please." Once again she looked over his head at Elijah, and he heard his brother curse. Isaac watched as she turned her eyes back to him. "I'm sorry."

He shook his head in confusion, wondering why she apologized.

"I'm sorry, too," he heard Elijah murmur from behind him.

As soon as he heard Elijah speak, he *knew*. She hadn't been asking Elijah to change her. She had been asking Elijah to help her stop Isaac from doing so at all. She was going to let herself *die*.

But he was too late in his discovery, and the last thing he saw was Sabrina's stricken face, and the tears running down her cheek.

The pain exploded in his head, and he collapsed to the ground.

Sabrina focused on Isaac as the tears ran down her face. She was dying. She knew it. But at least she'd taken Louisa down as well. Okay, well *she* hadn't, but the bitch was dead. That was all that mattered to her. Not whether she herself had killed her, but that she'd gotten the bitch down, one way or another.

Still, she hated betraying Isaac in her last moments, but she couldn't—*wouldn't*—allow him to ruin his life for her. Thankfully, Elijah had understood what she had wanted, even if Isaac himself had been oblivious.

"Take him…away. Leave me here." She breathed, closing her eyes, and waited for death to take her. She was growing weaker by the moment and knew her time was coming. Every breath was a struggle; every movement was harder than the last. When she heard Elijah move beside her, she opened her eyes for one last look at Isaac before Elijah removed him from her side.

Instead of picking up Isaac, Elijah bent over her. She looked at him in confusion, and her eyes widened in realization of what he was going to do.

"No, h-h-h-he'll kill you."

Elijah looked at her in sorrow. "I don't think so."

Sabrina felt fury and fear overcome her, but was left wallowing in helplessness as he leaned over her motionless body. Oh, how she longed to fight him off, to punch his nose and kick him, all while she screamed.

But she couldn't. The last of her strength had left her, and she could not even utter more than a paltry whimper of protest.

Desperately searching for a way to stop him, she whispered one final word.

"Amelia...."

Elijah tensed. "I'd have done this for her, if I had the power. Now I have the means to save you, and by God I *will* use it. I won't watch you die again."

Elijah bent over Sabrina and cringed. He hadn't had human blood in a year, at least not fresh from a warm body. He'd raided blood banks on a regular basis, but it was like comparing a hot meal fresh from the oven to a meal that had sat out for two hours on the table.

He was worried he wouldn't be able to stop once he started feeding, but strictly reined in his doubts. He had to do this; he had to save her. Isaac would understand. He would see he had done what he felt needed to be done. Elijah couldn't allow Isaac to do what was against his laws and get himself killed in the process. Not when he had it in his power to save her as well, minus dire consequences, any more than he could sit and watch Sabrina die.

Not bloody likely.

Elijah leaned over Sabrina and cleared her wet hair away from her throat. He could see her pulse beating, faint and slow. She was barely alive, so time was certainly of an essence. Elijah leaned into her neck to kiss her while taking one final, fortifying breath.

He could do this.

Elijah bared his teeth and bit into her tender skin. She jerked in response and gasped beneath him. He knew he hurt her, but still he couldn't contain his moan of delight. He lapped up her blood greedily. He'd never tasted anything so sweet in his life, and he devoured every drop he could manage. It wasn't until she went limp beneath him and fell silent that he remembered who she was, and why he was doing this.

He gasped and jerked away, and in a panic searched her pale face for signs of life.

Was she drained, and dead? If so, he'd wait here for Isaac to awaken, and let him kill him as well. He would not, *could* not, go on.

Sabrina moaned, and he looked at her in renewed hope. He guiltily pushed down the animal instinct telling him to finish the rest of his meal. Instead, he bit his own wrist, drawing blood, and pressed his wrist to her mouth. The blood trickled in, and her eyes flew open in response. She arched her back in protest and tried to move her head away from his blood, but he held her firm. She whimpered, and tears rolled down her cheeks. When color came back to her cheeks, he allowed her to have her way, and he pulled his wrist back. His blood was smeared on her face, and he fought the surge of possessiveness that came over him.

Mine.

"It hurts." She gasped. "So bad."

Elijah bent over her and smoothed her hair back from her face. "I'm sorry, Sabrina. So sorry."

Isaac stirred next to him and Elijah tensed. He was going to get hell from his brother, and Isaac might well kill him.

But he wouldn't kill Sabrina, right?

Elijah shuddered and pulled her into his arms. If he was going to have to run from Isaac, he was *not* leaving her behind. He knew Isaac loved her, had even been prepared to transform her himself, but things always changed in this world. He could have not gone through with his plan, could have remembered his duties and allowed Sabrina to die on this cliff. Elijah acknowledged he'd taken the choice away from Isaac and he feared the consequences. Not for himself, but for Sabrina.

Elijah looked down into her pain-wracked face and love swelled over him. He couldn't risk her life, and he couldn't trust Isaac. He didn't know how his brother would react to the "new" Sabrina, and she was too weak and vulnerable to withstand attack. Enforcers often hunted down new changelings avidly, for they were easy prey.

Without further thought, Elijah lifted her and sprinted away from Isaac. He needed to keep Sabrina safe, at all costs.

Even from the man she loved.

Chapter Twenty-Four

*I*saac moaned, disoriented, as he sat up and cradled his head in his hands. Why was he lying outside in the cold night in the first place? In a horrifying sequence of pictures, he saw it all. Sabrina lying in the clearing, pinned down by the tree his storm had knocked down, Sabrina getting thrown into the water, Sabrina dying by the cliff's edge. He'd wanted to save her, to bite her. But they hadn't allowed him; they'd knocked him out instead.

And let her die.

He growled and jumped up, looking around madly. Had Sabrina died when he'd been unconscious? Or had she allowed Elijah to bite her, after having denied Isaac the chance to do so?

No, the *right* to do so. She belonged to him, and he to her. Yet she refused the one course of action that had been open to him. He tried not to allow it to hurt him, but it was like trying to stop the rain from falling or the wind from blowing. It wasn't possible. He heard the ground crunching beneath footsteps behind him, and he swung around in excitement. Were they still here? Had they not left him, after all?

He saw a woman and man walking out of the darkness of the trees, and tensed in apprehension. It couldn't be Sabrina. She wouldn't be able to walk. He cursed when he was able to recognize the pair approaching him.

"Sheila, Connor. What brings you here?"

Sheila looked at her companion, and Connor nodded. Sheila spoke eagerly. "We could sense a new vampire was nearby, and so we followed the scent. It led to this spot, and we saw you. Are you okay?"

He stiffened and felt rage come over him. So Elijah had changed her. Had she allowed him—nay, *welcomed* him? Thunder boomed overhead, and he cursed.

"I'm fine. There was a fight, and Sabrina was badly injured. I was here, with her, and Elijah struck me. I just woke up. I suppose he changed her while I was unconscious, and ran from me. Louisa was the culprit, and she's dead." All the time he was explaining, his mind was on Sabrina and Elijah. Where were they? Did Elijah actually think Isaac would harm Sabrina? The woman he loved?

Sheila chuckled, and he looked at her inquiringly. "You find something in my story amusing, Sheila?" He let his anger show.

"No, in your thoughts!" she exclaimed as she gestured at his head.

Shit, he'd forgotten to guard his thoughts, had completely forgotten her power was to read minds. Was he insane? He quickly remedied the problem and guarded his thoughts from nosy ears. Sheila would like nothing more than to get revenge against him for past wrongs. He knew it as well as she did. "Get out of your king's head, *Sheila*. I didn't give you permission to fish around in my thoughts."

Despite her bravado, she paled in the face of his ire. "I know what you think, Isaac, and this has nothing to do with revenge. But I do know what I see, and I see you were going to change her yourself, and the only reason you didn't do so is because Elijah stopped you.

"I know also how much you love her, and so I wonder if the lines are still drawn strictly. You have always said if there was a newborn vampire, we must hunt it down and kill it before it gains strength. 'A dead vampire is the only good vampire', as you said.

"So, Isaac, does this still hold true if the newborn is your girlfriend? Or are we simply to turn our heads and pretend these rules do not apply to you, our esteemed Ruler?"

He'd never hit a woman before, but there was first time for everything, damn it. Isaac growled, and would have leapt on her in anger if Connor hadn't stepped forward.

He forced a calming breath and ran his fingers through his hair. He loved Sabrina, but he also knew if he left and ran off with Sabrina, the Enforcers would battle for control. There would be a dissension in the ranks as they all fought to take his place. He wasn't a vain man by any means, but he knew he'd kept the men, and the few women, under his control over the years. They all looked to him for punishment, rules, and guidance. To fail them all now would mean to fail all mankind. His Enforcers would be too busy fighting each other to save mere mortals from death.

But along the same vein, he'd be able to escape all the easier if that were the case. He and Sabrina could slip under the radar, lost within the battles that would be waged. Finding the treasonous Enforcer would take second place to finding a leader, by far. They'd be able to slip away unnoticed, find a secluded spot, and let the world go to hell. He cursed and punched a nearby tree. Choose love, and curse all mankind? Or choose duty, and curse himself?

It wasn't a choice any man wanted to make. It wasn't a choice any man should *have* to make.

Sheila's gloating eyes followed his every movement and again he resisted the urge to punch her in her face. He instead forced his gaze to Connor's admittedly more sympathetic scrutiny. Though he may feel empathy for Isaac's plight, he was also one of the first who would hunt down Isaac and Sabrina if they were to run.

Shit.

"I'll take care of this situation. Don't ask me how, because I don't know yet. But one way or another, it will be taken care of. I ask you to allow me some time to decide."

Connor nodded hesitantly and refused to meet his eyes. "How long do you need?"

"Give me one day. One day, and if I don't return, you may begin choosing a new leader. If I return, we will *never* speak of this again." Isaac scowled at the pair.

Sheila smiled, and Connor nodded.

"How will we know you really took care of it?" Sheila had the audacity to question. He couldn't believe she was so eager to bring him down. So excited at the prospect of him having to kill Sabrina. Or, perhaps, more excited at the idea of being able to kill her king.

Yeah, it was probably that which prompted her sudden bravado.

"Because I will have *said* so!" Isaac shouted at the top of his lungs. He'd had enough of this shit. "Do *not* make the mistake of forgetting who I am, Sheila."

Thunder boomed as he took a step toward her. Sheila paled and backed away in the face of his anger. He studied her, not removing his eyes from hers. She looked terrified.

Good.

"I understand," Connor said simply. "But if you don't return—"

"I also understand your position. I'm in agreement with your terms. Now I ask you—no, *command* you—to leave me alone."

Sheila and Connor left his sight, and Isaac allowed his tight shoulders to sag. Suddenly, the weight of the world seemed to rest on his right shoulder.

It was excruciating.

Isaac stood on the edge of the cliff and scowled into the turbulent ocean. The wind whipped through his hair, and for once it was not perfectly in place. The clouds thundered overhead, dark and dismal. The waves crashed on the shore far below, and it was clear that the very nature of the ocean, wind, and skies were all in tune to his foul mood. His teeth clenched, and his fists tightened.

He threw his head back, his arms straight out to his side, and let out a yell of despair so loud it dominated the matching boom of thunder that crashed at the same moment. He dropped to his knees, momentarily spent.

The winds died down, and a curious calm overtook his face. The waves slowed, and the clouds lightened. He stood and walked into the dark forest with a determined, steady gait.

His decision was made.

ဆ

Elijah didn't cease his mad sprint until he reached his small hut nestled deep in the forest. Sabrina moaned louder now, and he cradled her closer to him. He'd done this to her; it was his fault. But she would feel better eventually. She wasn't dead.

She moaned as he laid her on the bed and opened her eyes. She looked around in panic, not recognizing her surroundings. She gasped and tried to speak.

"Isaac?"

Elijah flinched. "Not here." Panic filled her eyes, and he squeezed her hand. "I'm here, Sabrina. I'll take care of you. You'll be okay. Soon, you'll pass out, and when you wake up all the pain will be gone. But I'll be here through it all. I promise."

A tear rolled down her cheek, and she whispered one word.

"Isaac…."

Her eyes closed against his pleading gaze, and rejection coursed over his body. He'd bitten her, made her his, and still she cried out for Isaac. Part of him had thought—no, *hoped*—she'd be drawn to him. As she should but apparently she was immune to him even in this new world.

Why did he have to love her so much?

And how did you tell the woman you loved, the woman who you could not live without, that she couldn't see the man she loved because he might very well kill her?

He lowered his head to the bed beside her and groaned.

Life sucks.

Chapter Twenty-Five

Sabrina lay upon the bed. Her whole body felt like it was frozen in ice. She longed to writhe, scream, and shout. But yet, the worst she could manage was a pitiful whimper. She didn't bother to open her eyes any longer. She'd only see Elijah hovering over her, worry and pain in his eyes. He hadn't left her side yet, seemed scared to leave her—as if she would vanish into thin air if he weren't standing guard over her.

When she'd written her books, she'd always described the changing from a human to a vampire as fire. Fire burning its way through the body as it killed all living pieces inside a human. Oh, how she *longed* for fire. She shook from the cold enveloping her, and her teeth chattered, breaking the silence of the hut.

She knew she was supposed to be unconscious by now, had heard Elijah muttering it to himself. Apparently her hearing was already affected by the change. Everything was becoming so much clearer. Squirrels ran on the roof above, and deer grazed outside. She wondered how far away they were from her and Elijah, before deciding she didn't care. Elijah pulled her out of her reverie when he leaned over her, and placed his hand over her heart. He frowned in concentration and his eyes darkened. He clearly wasn't happy to feel that her heart still beat. It didn't even seem to be weakening, or slowing. If anything, it seemed stronger than ever before.

Which, apparently, wasn't a good thing.

Elijah jumped up and stalked to the other side of the room to pace. Even if she hadn't known he was worried from his earlier muttering, she would have known by the telltale pacing. He ran his fingers through his hair and sighed. She smiled, and then grimaced at the pain the small movement caused. Sign number two: running his fingers through his hair. Both he and Isaac did that when they were upset.

Isaac.

Where was he? Had he let her go, knowing they could not be together any longer since Elijah had bitten her? Did he despise her now, knowing she was his enemy?

A hated vampire.

Her heart lurched, though not from the venom coursing through her veins. It was caused by the thought of an eternity of endless days without him by her side. She wished she'd died instead. It would have been a quicker, more merciful death.

Instead she'd be forced to live forever, knowing somewhere out in the world, he lived, too. Every time she looked into Elijah's eyes, or saw his beautiful face, another part of her would wither away to nothingness. Unless Isaac hunted her down and put her out of her misery.

Was it sick she was excited that she'd at least get to see him *one* last time?

ȣ

Isaac had been wandering through the forest for hours. Elijah had been extremely cautious in covering up his tracks. He didn't want to be followed, that much was obvious. He cursed and kicked a boulder. It groaned in protest before rolling across the forest floor. He'd passed this damn spot at least three times.

Had Elijah run in circles throughout the forest, trying to confuse anyone who would attempt to follow him? It certainly wouldn't surprise him. Elijah was extremely talented when it came to disappearing. He'd known he'd be unable to follow Elijah, and so had tried to concentrate on a newborn vampire's scent. He would know it anywhere, but yet he failed.

It was infuriating.

By now her heart would be dead…while her body morphed into that of a monster. He growled low in his throat and punched a tree. He needed to get to her before the others did; he needed to be the one to find her. If only he could pick up her damned scent. He'd always been able to track new vampires. They were easy to sense, and even easier to kill. But this one time when it mattered most to him, he couldn't find her.

He flared his nostrils and lifted his head before he hissed and whirled around. Elijah stood behind him. He threw himself at his brother—the anger swirling inside him taking over his senses. All the hours of worrying, all the hours of agony, came spewing out of him as soon as he laid eyes on his brother's grim face. Elijah glided backward from the force of his blow, and they collided into a nearby tree. Elijah hissed at him and punched him in the nose. Isaac flew back and landed on the ground, holding his nose as blood gushed out of it.

Jesus Christ, how many times in one night is my nose going to get broken?

"Shit," he muttered.

"Sorry, but we haven't got time for games." Elijah spoke between clenched teeth.

Isaac glared. "Where is she?"

Elijah tensed visibly at his question. "She's safe. I don't know whether I should tell you her location or not. Tell me, is she in danger from you?" He arched an eyebrow and awaited a reply.

Isaac snarled at his brother's question, fighting the fury that washed over him. It was a logical question. In any other situation, he'd have respected his brother's loyalty to Sabrina's safety.

But, damn it, he wasn't supposed to hide her from *him.*

"She is in danger, but not from me," he swore. "I need to get her. To hide her."

"So after everything she told you, after she pleaded with you not to change her, not to risk yourself, you're going to go to her anyway?"

Isaac growled and leapt to his feet. His nose had already started to heal, and it didn't throb nearly so badly anymore. "She's coming with me. Forgive my sarcasm, but she's hardly in the shape to argue, now is she?"

"She's still awake."

Isaac froze and whispered, "What?"

"She's not dead. She's not even unconscious. She just lays there, unmoving and silent. She moans every once in a while, or calls your name, but that's it."

"*Oh my God.*"

"What? Did I do something wrong?" Elijah exclaimed when Isaac stood rooted to the spot, as if in a trance. "*What does it mean?*"

"Oh...my...God. Nothing. It was all for nothing," he murmured as amazement, shock, and finally...relief coursed over his body. He laughed so hard he could no longer stand.

"What has gotten into you, Isaac? Snap out of it, you ass!" Elijah exclaimed. He stalked to his brother's side and cocked back his fist, prepared to break his brother's perfect nose again.

"Don't even think about it," Isaac hissed, dead serious as he shoved Elijah using all his strength. "It was all for nothing," he said, wonder in his voice. "All this time, all this agony, and she's one of *us.*"

"What do you...?" Clarity showed in Elijah's eyes as he paled. "She's an Enforcer?"

"Yes. Yes, now everything makes sense. Why I couldn't sense her as a new vampire. Why I couldn't catch her trail at all. I was hunting the wrong creature."

"She's one of you." Elijah's eyes were shadowed, and his face pale. Pale, even, for a vampire.

Isaac forced his gaze back to his brother and felt a wave of pity wash over him. He knew without *too* much jealousy Elijah had hoped this would be his one chance at Sabrina. Had hoped she'd be forced to choose him. That hope had just been destroyed.

He walked to his brother's side and laid a soothing hand upon his shoulder. He met Elijah's eyes, so like his own. "She's one of us. She is, and will always remain, mine. I'm sorry for your loss, and for any pain you might feel. But you have to realize...it's over. This fight is over. She's not Amelia. I'm sorry, Elijah. I'm sorry for your loss of Amelia. I know now you loved her more than I ever could have. But Sabrina is different—she is *my* Amelia. Do you understand?"

Elijah nodded, and a tear ran down his cheek at his brother's words. He gasped in shock as Isaac drew him into his arms and hugged him. "I'm sorry, Elijah," he repeated.

"Well, are you ready to go tell her the good news? I'm sure she'll be thrilled," Elijah said.

"Yes, absolutely yes," Isaac chirped. His smile, he was sure, reached straight down to his soul. He couldn't help it. He was the luckiest man on Earth.

"Follow me." Elijah led the way silently, and his shoulders dropped in resignation.

For once, Isaac didn't argue.

ℬ

Sabrina lay awake, thoughts of Isaac running through her head. She couldn't get him off her mind. Even as pain wracked through her body, she thought only of him.

Where was he? What was he thinking? Feeling?

In the thirty minutes since Elijah had left, she'd discovered she could move her hands. She wasn't certain what this meant, since she was supposed to die, and heal afterwards.

She strained her ears when she heard footsteps approach the hut, and calculated the direction from which they approached. From the east, and there were two sets of them, so it couldn't be Elijah. And, unfortunately, no mere mortal ran so fast. Her heart quickened, and she tensed upon the bed. She couldn't even jump up to defend herself. She tightened her fists, her only line of defense against intruders.

The door swung inward, and her eyes focused upon the occupants who moved into the small room. She sighed in relief as her eyes focused first on Elijah, and quickly skimmed to the shadow standing behind him. She gasped and whispered, "Isaac."

Isaac rushed to her side, rudely pushing past Elijah in the process. Elijah glared at Isaac's back and left the hut. The door closed behind him as he left; she knew he had no desire to watch this reunion. Isaac knelt at her hips and cupped her face inside his hands. He kissed her, and happiness exuded from his eyes.

"Sabrina, what are you doing to me, lass?"

Sabrina forced a wan smile to her face and responded, "I'm sorry, Isaac. I never wished for us to be enemies. I—" She was prepared to tell him to leave, to save himself, but was cut off by his finger pressing against her mouth.

He grabbed her hand in his and stared into her eyes warmly. "I love you, Sabrina. We would never be, and could never be, enemies. I know now what love *really* is. I thought I had loved before, but I was wrong. You are my first, and, only love. You'd never be my enemy," he vowed.

"I love you, too, Isaac." She squeezed his hand, and he looked down in surprise at her hand, beaming at her.

"I'm going to get you out of here, to somewhere safe," he said. "There is much to do."

"I can't let you do that, Isaac. You spoke earlier of love. Of being ready to do anything for the love of your life. Well, I feel the same. I will give you up, for your safety. I don't do it lightly, but I must insist. I won't leave with you. Not because I don't love you, but because I love you too much." She was amazed she had managed to finish her speech without crying.

"Oh, Sabrina, I love when you're all fired up. Truly, I do. But in this case, you're getting all worked up for nothing."

"Excuse me, I don't think so—" she argued. If he thought he could just carry her out of here and ignore her wishes, he'd soon see how wrong he was. Even if she *could* only move her hands. She could do a lot with hands. Punch, scrape, and gouge out eyes....

"Yes, you are. You see, you're one of us." Sitting by her side, he allowed her to absorb his meaning. When she gaped at him, her mouth ajar, he nodded at her unasked question. "Yes, you're among the chosen...the elite...."

"The Enforcers," she whispered in awe. "Oh my God, you've got to be kidding me. God couldn't be so kind."

"No, I wouldn't kid about this, my love. You're one of my kind— you belong with me, in every way now," he assured her, squeezing her hand. She returned his squeeze, all the happiness bubbling inside her. He winced as she gripped him, laughing as he protested, "Ouch, watch it there...."

"Oh, sorry," she murmured. She looked at their joined hands in surprise. *She* had hurt *him*?

He kissed her nose and stared into her eyes before declaring, "I would've run away with you, regardless of your species."

"I would have told me no, regardless of your desires," she quipped.

They stared at each other, neither backing down in their stance. Finally, they both broke out in laughter.

"What about Elijah?" she questioned.

"What about him?" He raised an eyebrow and shrugged.

"Will he still be our enemy? Do I have to *kill* him?"

"He's our enemy, yes. But we can avoid each other. I've been doing it for over one hundred years."

"But, we can't. He's family."

"Look, we can worry about this another time. Really, Sabrina, you're killing my ego here," he teased. "I just told you that you can live with me forever, and you worry about Elijah?"

She blushed. "I'm sorry. I know you still love him. I hate to see you upset."

"We have an eternity to figure out my feelings. All you need to know now is I love you." He beamed at her, love shining in his eyes.

"And I love you, Isaac. Forever," she vowed, amazed to know she had forever to spend by his side, loving him. Suddenly, forever took on a new meaning, and she smiled as he kissed her nose once more.

"Forever," he promised.

On the other hand, perhaps forever was not long enough....

~ABOUT THE AUTHOR~

Photograph by Deb Moran

Best-selling author of all things romance. Diane believes strongly in a happily-ever-after for everyone. She especially loves tortured heroes and heroines, as can be seen in her stories. She is repped by the fabulous Lauren Hammond of ADA Management.

Diane Alberts lives in Northeast Pennsylvania with her husband, four kids, a bird named Nemo, and two clown fish named Blue and Jewel. She lives in the mountains-but wishes it were the beach. She has been writing since she was in elementary school, but only recently fulfilled her dreams of being published in 2011.

Visit Diane online at:
www.dianealberts.com

Kill Me Tomorrow
A 1Night Stand Story

Jasmine Baruch is a jinn—a supernatural being who fights demons with fire. While that's difficult enough, she's got bigger problems. She's a virgin, and in the jinn culture, that is sheer blasphemy. Jinn are supposed to be passionate, promiscuous creatures—everything she isn't. Due to marry the next day, she takes matters into her own hands by using 1Night Stand. But, like the rest of her life, nothing is easy. The man chosen for her, though incredibly gorgeous, is a demi-sanguine; a half-human, half-demon—her enemy.

Gavin Werbato is looking for an easy night of sex. Nothing more, nothing less. Instead, he gets a gorgeous jinn convinced it is her duty to kill him. He can certainly think of better things to do with her soft hands than murder. He need only convince her of that...

Can the fire sparked when these beings collide be controlled, or will it consume their world as they know it?

Absolution
An Honor Guard Series Story

Eva can't believe Joseph dares to show his face to her after he'd cheated on her with a stripper—in her bed. She'd kicked him out, and has no desire to let him back in, despite his claims of being assigned to protect her from the Cartel. Her life very well may be in danger, but she fears more for the safety of her heart.

Joseph made one foolish mistake a year ago, and has been paying for it ever since. She might not want to allow him into her life again, but he doesn't care if she despises the very thought of him. His duty is to keep Eva alive, even if it might end up being the death of him. Because he never stopped loving her.

Can they put their painful history aside, and work together against her enemy?

Or will the past prove too strong to be forgiven?

Broken

A 1Night Stand Story

Staff Sergeant Matt Warwick returns from war with two broken legs—and a shattered future. Abandoned by his fiancée, he withdraws into a protective shell to hide from the pity filled glances thrown his way. His squad worries he's fallen into depression, and arranges a 1NightStand through the renowned Madame Eve. Matt agrees, but fears he will not be able to satisfy his date, for who would want a crippled man in their bed?

Tiffany Forsen escaped a brutal relationship, and seeks to jump-start her life with a fling. Bars aren't her scene, so when she hears of the fabulous 1NightStand service, she contacts Madame Eve immediately. All she wants is a night of fun with the hot guy in her picture-but winds up with much more. Can she convince him that when she sees him, she doesn't see a crippled man…but a hero?

Or will his defenses keep her at arm's length?

www.decadentpublishing.com